JOHN THORNTON

UNDER CONTROL

Can love really conquer all?

© John Thornton 2025

Published by Songbird Press
Paperback ISBN: 978-1-0682279-0-5

All rights reserved.
No part of this book may be reproduced in any form or by any electronic or mechanical means, including in information storage and retrieval systems, without permission in writing from the author.

The author has asserted their right under the Copyright, Designs and Patents Act 1988 to be identified as the author of this work.

This book is a work of fiction. Names, characters, places and incidents are either products of the author's imagination or are used fictitiously. Any resemblance to actual persons, living or dead, events, or locales is entirely coincidental.

JOHN THORNTON

UNDER CONTROL

SONGBIRD
PRESS

Life is what happens to you while you're busy making other plans.

Anon

1

'Do you want more jelly, Doctor Westwood?'
I glance at the blood pressure monitor beeping irritably, red numerals flashing their warning in the subdued light of the endoscopy room. Ninety over fifty-five, low but acceptable under these dire circumstances.

'Yes, thanks, Mary.'

She starts to disconnect the empty intravenous bag and replace it with more gelofusin.

'And turn that racket off, will you?'

She presses a button on the monitor and the superfluous beeping ceases. Easier to think without that intrusive noise. Hard enough to stay focused at the moment.

I return my attention to the screen displaying the view down the endoscope. Fresh blood seethes and intermittently wells up, like an active volcano, trying to escape the narrow confines of the patient's oesophagus. I plunge the endoscope in and press firmly on its suction channel. The screen turns crimson as I attempt to remove sufficient blood to identify and treat the source of the haemorrhage. After a minute or so, I pull back the endoscope. The redness clears but the view seems unchanged from when I began the aspiration. She must be bleeding rapidly.

The patient on the trolley beside me, Mrs Briggs, is seventy-four and isn't likely to withstand much more of this. She is sedated, probably blissfully unaware and won't remember the part she has played in this drama. If she survives? Blood coats her lips, like lurid lipstick, emphasising the pallor of her skin. A lock of her grey, bedraggled hair falls across her closed eyes. Laila, the nurse at the head of the trolley, gently tucks it away, before introducing her suction tube into the patient's mouth.

'There!' Mary, the endoscopy sister, cries.

'Yes, I saw it.' An enlarged blue vein, like an earthworm, just below the inner lining of the oesophagus is spurting rhythmically. Oesophageal varices. Not a surprise. I have come prepared and have fitted a device which will release tiny elastic bands by twisting a control wheel on the handle of the endoscope.

My right hand hovers over the wheel, poised for another glimpse of my target. I aspirate briefly. Yes! I turn the tip of the endoscope onto the squirting vessel, suck it a little way into the suction channel of the scope, twist the wheel to fire a band then release the suction. A bobble of vein is now visible, at its centre the dark red bleeding point, the defect in the vein's wall obstructed by the constricting band below it. I apply bands to the other large varices which appear potentially dangerous.

'Let's turn up the lights then.'

A nurse bustles through the door carrying bags of blood for transfusion. 'Shall we start it?' asks Mary, her voice betraying her concern.

I look at the monitor. Mrs Brigg's blood pressure has dropped to seventy-eight over fifty. 'Yes, run the first unit as fast as it will go.' Mary and Laila check carefully that the patient's details match those on the bag before replacing the gelofusin with it, then wheel her trolley out into the recovery area.

I move to the desk at the corner of the room and begin to record the procedure on one of the units' computers, alone for the first time since the session began five hours ago. I finish my report, check it and hit the print button. As the machine hums and whirrs, I am obliged to pause and contemplate the unprepossessing windowless room, two of its apple-green walls crammed with cupboards packed with equipment, much of the other two covered by posters and guidelines. The decrepit printer clatters to a halt.

I realise I am smiling as I sign a copy of the endoscopy report above my name and title: Dr Miles Westwood MB ChB (Hons), MD, MRCP, Consultant Physician and Gastroenterologist. Not for the first time, I contemplate whether all the letters after my name are a bit over the top. Maybe I should drop the MB, ChB: the basic medical qualification is implicit from the title of doctor, but then I'd have to omit the (Hons) and I am reluctant to do that. As one of only four per cent in my year who had been awarded honours, I am proud of my achievement. I glance at the printed date, 8th June, 2000. Adam will be six on Monday.

The report needs to be filed in the patient's notes, now with her in recovery. Time to see how she is doing. Mrs Briggs is the only patient left there, still sedated, eyes closed. A nurse by her bed is busy writing on a chart. The transfusion is dripping speedily and the monitor, no longer flashing, shows her blood pressure to have improved to one hundred over seventy-two. I need to hand over her care and speak to her husband, waiting anxiously, then I'm done here.

I turn away. A young woman with a concerned expression is looking at me. A stethoscope slung round the back of her neck proclaims her status as a doctor.

'Hello, Doctor Westwood. I'm Lucy, Doctor Steven's house officer.' A little uncertainly she continues, 'We're on take and have just admitted a man, sixty-two, shocked and vomiting blood. Doctor Stevens wondered if you would endoscope him for us?' She looks up at me entreatingly.

I sigh. 'Sure, but get him up here quickly, otherwise the nurses might lynch me.'

A pretty smile. 'I'll go and do it right away. Thank you.'

****

The windscreen wipers are like a steady drumbeat, marking time on my slow, spasmodic journey. Ahead, a dense array of blurry, red lights. A siren blares in the distance. A jam. Not my favourite sort. Eric Clapton's band is jamming on my background music. How many meanings does the word have? I think of five but there are probably more.

My brain is past its best today. I am conscious of a tic below my left eye, a tiny protest by my body and mind that happens occasionally when I push them hard. It hasn't been an easy week so far and being 'on take' last Saturday and Sunday meant that I had started it already tired. The emergency work is interesting and rewarding, but is even more intense and prolonged than my routine duties. Still, I console myself, the muscular twitch will resolve after a meal, a beer and an hour's relaxation.

****

'You're late.'

The aggressive, accusatory tone is unmistakable. I glance at the kitchen clock: twenty past nine but in reality, nine ten. Clare deliberately sets it ten minutes fast to discourage tardiness. Even though we all now know of her subterfuge, she refuses to adjust it to the correct time, claiming it is still beneficial in promoting our punctuality. Perhaps she's right? Difficult psychology.

Clare undoes the apron she is wearing and tosses it aside carelessly onto a stool. Not a good sign in someone so obsessively tidy. She stands facing me, taut, like a sprinter on the blocks. A flippant, though truthful, reply from me – "just had to help save a couple of lives" - isn't going to cut it. An apology would definitely be safer.

'I'm sorry. My endoscopy list ran over.'

She lifts her chin further and with exaggerated sarcasm spits out, 'And when does your endoscopy list not run over?'

Good question. 'There's a blue moon predicted soon.'

She stares at me in disgust. For most of the ten years we've been married she would smile or even laugh at my poor attempts at humour, but lately all my efforts to charm her are rebuffed. How sad to see the near-perfect features of her face, framed by her long dark hair, drawn into this ugly mask. Perhaps I should try another subject, one of mutual interest?

'Are the boys in bed?'

'Of course,' she snaps.

'Did you read them a story?'

'Yes, but they don't like MY stories. They want dragons and monsters.'

'Clare, they're boys. Dragons are cool right now and they're on the side of the good guys.' I wish they were.

'But Luke's only four. He still isn't clear whether they

really exist. I don't want him having nightmares.'

'Is he?'

Her eyes flick away. 'And don't go sticking your head round their door, it's taken me long enough to get them settled,' shaking her head for emphasis. 'If you want to read to them, you should get home earlier, then I wouldn't have to do everything.'

'Right, I'm off to bed. Getting another migraine. Dinner's in the microwave.'

She walks past me towards the kitchen door before pausing and turning. 'Oh yes. I'm taking them to see granny and granddad tomorrow, for the weekend, so we won't be here when you get home.' It doesn't appear that I'm invited. Admittedly I have private patients booked to see me on Saturday morning but I could drive down afterwards. It isn't that far to Bournemouth, but I'm not going to protest.

'Okay. The sea air will do the boys good.'

Dare I? I take a deep breath and plunge in. 'Another time, when you get back, we need to talk more about it.'

She takes a pace towards me. 'It? It?'

'You know,' I say in exasperation. 'The girl who died of meningitis.'

'She was a person, Emma Richards, not an 'it'.' Her bottom lip quivers. 'And I've told you, she died because I didn't make the diagnosis.'

'You don't know that. Not for sure. She might have died anyway.'

'Then why am I facing an investigation?'

'Nowadays people want somebody to blame. Look, the girl, Emma, what was she? Twenty months? You know that the diagnosis of meningitis in babies and toddlers is very hard, difficult to distinguish in its early stages from all the other infective illnesses they get.'

'I should've given her antibiotics. I nearly did, but you know the pressure G.P.s are under not to prescribe them. I'm sick of reading about it in the papers.' Her eyes drop and her body sags a little. Almost a whisper, 'She had a rash. When she got to hospital, they found a rash.' The tell-tale sign of meningitis.

'It might not have been there when you saw her. It all happens so fast. You looked, didn't you?'

'Only at her face and abdomen, not her back and legs. I should've done. We're just so busy. I should've done and now she's dead.'

I regard her sympathetically, wanting to take her in my arms but feeling it wouldn't be welcome. 'Clare, we all make mistakes.'

Her eyes fill with anger, her nostrils flare. 'even you are against me. You think I made a mistake.'

'I didn't mean it like that.'

'How did you mean it? And when was the last time you made a mistake and your patient died, eh?' I break eye contact, trying to think of such a case. Then I realise I should be more astute and deflect the question. Before I can decide on an answer, she sneers, 'You see, my clever physician husband, you can't.'

She spins around and stalks out. At least she doesn't slam the kitchen door, probably in consideration of our two sleeping sons.

2

Almost a year since I began private practice and it still feels exotic, though not indulgent. Without it, Clare and I couldn't service such a large mortgage and have assumed the escalating burden of school fees. Her reservations about queue jumping quickly withered under the burden of financial reality.

A ping from my mobile. The message reads: "Forgot card for Adam. Please get one. C." What has happened to "love, C" or the little "x"? I text back: "OK".

The last patient doesn't seem to be coming. I may as well go and buy Adam's birthday card now. I switch off my mobile. Why not? I'm not on call and this way I'm free of the insatiable demands of the NHS.

It isn't far into the centre of town and I will struggle to park on a Saturday afternoon, more sensible to walk. And the weather is glorious, too hot to be wearing my suit jacket and a tie. I bundle them into my car with my briefcase, partially roll up my shirtsleeves and set off. It is enjoyable striding out after my sedentary morning but this isn't going to be enough exercise. I resolve to go for a run on my return home. It will help to clear my troubled mind.

The High Street is bustling. I slow my pace, not just out of necessity to avoid the throng of happy shoppers, their bags and children's buggies. It is relaxing to re-join normal life. The card shop is near the bottom of the street.

It is her perfume I notice first. Expensive, a whiff reminiscent of frangipani and my one Caribbean holiday. I look out of the corner of my eye. She is tall, her face hidden by long blonde hair. A bare arm saunters across the cards in front of me, selecting one before quickly rejecting it.

'Oh, why is this so hard?'

Is that addressed to me or just an expression of frustration? I glance sideways again. She is now facing me, so it must be a question. Turning to my left to look at her, I'm unprepared for her beauty: stunned and lost for words. Lightly tanned, minimal make up, she is wearing a simple but well-cut, cornflower-blue sundress over a slim, near-perfect figure. No jewellery. I can't see her left hand. What is she? About thirty? Her eyes, almost matching the colour of her dress, appraise me. Her irises have tiny speckles, as if the light of stars is shining through a clear day-time sky. She must be aware of her effect on men and seems amused by my silence. I realise my mouth is open a little and shut it quickly.

'I don't know why I'm bothering,' she continues in a self-deprecating tone. 'My nephew can't read. He's only two.' She drops her eyes demurely, as if accepting her self-proclaimed foolishness. I gather my thoughts. This is something I can deal with. I pick a card from the shelves showing a large green steam train and press the button. The card emits: 'Choo choo, choo choo.' She begins giggling. Just then no sound could have been more enticing to me and I laugh along with her. When was the last time I laughed?

As she begins to compose herself, she manages to utter, 'I don't think my sister will be too pleased if he keeps doing that all day,' before pressing the button again and giggling some more. She takes the card from me.

'Who are you buying for?'

'My son, Adam.' I can see that she is absorbing the implications of this information. Turning back briefly towards the shelves, I select a card and show it to her. 'I thought I'd give him this one.' She nods in approval. We go to pay.

Outside the shop and still together, she inclines her head towards the bottom of the High Street, her hair shimmering in the sunshine. 'I'm thinking of walking this way.'

'So was I,' I lie.

We fall into step with one another and before long are walking along the riverbank. Now that the initial impact of her appearance has subsided, I feel more at ease with her. The laughter has helped.

'I'm Miles,' I offer.

'Freya.'

'Freya, that's pretty.'

'My mother is Swedish. Freya was the Scandinavian goddess of love. Some of the girls at school used to tease me about it.' She blushes. It is captivating. I don't think too many men would be mocking her claim to that status now.

Then she asserts, 'You've been working.'

I smile in amusement. 'How do you know?'

She waves a hand at me. 'Suit trousers, black Oxford shoes, not Saturday casual wear.' Observant and clever, as well as beautiful. Not for the first time, I reflect on how unfair it is that some people, myself included, hold most of the winning tickets in life's genetic lottery.

'So, what do you do?'

'I'm a doctor, a consultant gastroenterologist. I've just been doing some private practice.'

'That must be fascinating. Do you love it?'

'Most of the time, though I could do with a bit less work.'

She laughs. 'Tell me about it. Statesbank make sure I give them my pound of flesh.' She flashes me a rueful smile. 'Sorry, not the best expression to use to a doctor. I worked for them in New York for four years before moving here a year ago.'

'You're a banker then?'

'No. I'm a commercial lawyer. Pretty boring compared to you, I bet.'

The town is behind us now. Surrounded by a patchwork of fields, we continue to stroll along the path and like the river our conversation meanders on. The sun is hot on my back, a bead of sweat runs down my spine. A dragonfly, iridescent blue, hovers in front of us before darting away. A sense of peace envelops me. Round a bend, a pub appears, green and white striped umbrellas over the garden tables. The sound of happy voices is carried upstream towards us. She squeezes my left arm briefly, though it feels as if the heat of her touch lingers.

'I'm thirsty. Let's get a drink.'

'Good idea.'

We take possession of a river-side table as another couple depart. Couple? I try to suppress that concept, though cannot ignore that by tacit agreement neither of us has enquired further about our families. Now that we are seated, it is easier to scrutinise her left hand. No ring, but at the base of her fourth finger is a circle of paler skin. The waitress arrives with our order. For a countless time, I marvel at the pleasure of the first gulps of cold beer on a hot day. This is bliss. I deserve it.

Freya stares at me, smirking.

'What's so funny?' I chuckle. Her amusement is infectious.

'You'

'Me?'

'Yes you. In the card shop, you were so tense, wound up tight. And now ...'

'And now, I'm not.'

She holds my gaze. 'Your job must be stressful, tell me about it.'

So, I do. She listens attentively, never interrupting, nodding encouragement if the flow of my monologue falters. It is cathartic. When my words trickle to a close, she pronounces her judgement, 'You're very lucky you know, having such a worthwhile career.'

'I know, I know. I wouldn't want to change what I do.'

She is smiling at me coquettishly. The sun behind her is now lower in the sky, reflecting off her golden hair, creating the illusion of a halo. She twirls a lock of it around a finger. I am entranced. 'I'm off to the ladies. Back in a minute.'

It seems that even goddesses have bodily needs, I reflect wryly. I watch her as she walks across the garden. She is tall. Are blondes taller on average than other Caucasian women with dark hair? I ponder idly. Leggy blondes.

Where is she? She's been a long time. We ought to be getting back before it goes dark. She skips, like a schoolgirl, across the grass towards me. 'Come on.' She gestures with her head towards the pub and gives one of my arms a gentle tug. 'You have to see this view.' She leads the way, glancing over her shoulder to check I'm following. 'Upstairs. You can't see it from this floor.' At the end of a first-floor corridor is a large window. From this vantage point, above the bushes surrounding the building, the patchwork landscape stretches into the far distance. There is no doubt, it is idyllic.

'Look there.' She encourages me animatedly, pointing

and applying gentle pressure to my back with her right hand to turn me in the correct direction. 'Do you see it?'

'Yes, I can.' It isn't difficult. On the only hill amidst the gently undulating countryside, stands a round, stone tower. It is in ruins but perhaps more wondrous for that. 'To think that long ago, the lord that built that tower probably owned all this land, all that he could see.'

She turns towards me. 'Happiness is the art of the possible.' Her hand, still resting on my back, slides down and takes mine. She leads me a few paces across the corridor to a door, before conjuring a swipe card from a pocket in her dress and opening it. A gentle pull on my arm and we are inside. She quickly closes the door, puts the lock across it. Her hand keeps me in her grip. Head tilted a little to the side, her grin is playful, teasing. She moves closer still. Her free hand comes up and gently caresses my face, before entwining her fingers in the hair at the back of my head. She lifts her chin a little and lips slightly parted, guides my head towards her. Our tongues explore, fencing. Soon, her back arches, like a bow, towards me. Her groin presses firmly against mine. I am lost.

****

Where am I? A moment of alarm as I wake. I open my eyes fully and look around. Soft early morning light filters into the room. Clothes lie crumpled on the floor, a red thong nestled on top of my trousers. I can feel the warmth of her body. One of her legs is across mine, a hand resting on my chest. Her eyes are closed, golden hair strewn across the pillow.

She stirs. Her hand presses against my chest. Possessively? But I am not hers, I am taken. And what about her? No ring. Recently divorced or at least separated? Less to lose. I couldn't bear to relinquish my family, any of them. I love my wife. Such a cliché but undoubtedly true. My devoted wife of ten years, my best friend, the mother of our two sons. How have I done this? And at a time when she needs me more than ever. Terror assails me. What if Clare came home last night, instead of tonight? My phone is off. What must she have thought? What should I say? I shudder, a mixture of fear and shame. Perhaps the movement disturbs Freya. Her eyelids flicker open.

'Hello,' she murmurs, a verbal caress. She stretches, a slow, luxuriant movement. Feline.

'Freya.'

'Uhmm.' Almost a purr.

'Freya. I can't do this.'

Her head shoots off the pillow, so discordant with her earlier languor. She looks down at my face, my expression, determining if it is consistent with my words. Her eyes narrow, lips tighten. Then her hand slides down across my abdomen and discovers my morning erection. She moves her encircling hand up and down.

'He thinks you can.' With her other hand, she flings aside the sheet covering our bodies and straddles me. 'And so do I.' She sinks down onto me. 'It's two against one.' Her hips begin to move up and down. I close my eyes and surrender to the power of democracy.

****

I wake yet again. She is still on top of me, asleep. Gently, I ease her off. Her eyes open a little. 'That was good,' she murmurs.

'Yes, it was. It was wonderful, unforgettable.' I sigh. 'But Freya, I really can't do this.' Glistening eyes open wide now, her look wrenches at me. I quickly climb out of bed. Safer. 'I can't,' my tone harsher than I intended, a disguise. 'I have a wife and two children. I love them.' An affirmation and a plea for understanding. 'I can't see you again.'

I dress quickly, though struggle to find my second sock, hidden under the bedspread. A last look, a tear is trickling down her cheek. Closing the door quietly, I hurry down the stairs to the lobby.

'Good morning, Mr Wright.' A breezy, welcoming tone. There is no one else here. He is talking to me. A small, middle-aged man with thinning black hair, dark jacket, white shirt and nondescript tie - no concession to Sunday morning. I go over to the reception desk.

'Good morning. Can I have the bill, please?' Do I have enough cash to pay? Using a card would create a record that Clare may discover and there would be the embarrassment now of the name on it not corresponding with the alias Freya seemingly has chosen for me. I also realise that I don't know the room number but he doesn't ask. He taps on his computer keyboard and instead enquires, 'Did you sleep well?'

'Fine, thanks.'

He looks up at me. 'Ah, it appears your partner has settled it already.' Freya must have done that when she booked the room during her ostensible visit to "the ladies". I daren't return upstairs and offer to pay.

'She'll be checking out a little later.'

'Of course. Not a problem'. Is there a hint of a knowing smile? I make my escape and don't look back.

3

I sit back in my swivel chair and sigh. The end of my Saturday morning private clinic and Freya hasn't appeared. I'd been tortured by the possibility that she would make an appointment to see me as a private patient under a false name, no matter how many times I told myself it was fanciful. It would have given her half an hour without interruption to confront me, try to persuade me to continue our relationship. This whole week has been a torment, never knowing if she would show up or call.

Last Sunday, I had trudged back to my car, through drizzle and under a leaden sky - such a contrast to the day before, but in keeping with my mood. Once home, I had forced myself to concentrate. There must be no clues to my escapade for Clare to discover. My muddy shoes needed to dry and be cleaned. I had taken them off at the front door. The mud stains on my trousers could not easily be accounted for. I'd bundled them in a bag which I put in the boot of my car and taken them to a dry cleaner near the hospital - not the one Clare normally uses. The receipt for the drinks in my trouser pocket I'd burnt. The smell of Freya's perfume lingered on my shirt. That had to go to the cleaner too. I'd showered, washed my hair then scrutinised my naked body, including my back. No scratch marks.

My concocted alibi had not been tested. Clare had been tired when she and our sons arrived home on the Sunday evening and had quickly called it a day. I was left to put Adam and Luke to bed, a simple joy I'd been deprived of for the last couple of evenings. More dragons and monsters were required.

Work had been a boon, too intense to permit much contemplation of last weekend. It had been the nights that were the worst. Three a.m., sufficiently rested for sleep to be elusive, too early to get up. I had ruminated on events, preparing for eventualities, analysing my emotions. Clare has been too withdrawn to detect any change in my mood or behaviour my guilt may have engendered.

Now, perhaps, my life can move on.

Hungry, better to eat here before going home. I leave my consulting room. None of my consultant colleagues are in the staff dining room. Only the local weekly paper is available for me to read over lunch. I scan the newspaper. An article on the front page catches my eye. A car accident last Sunday morning. The photo shows a badly damaged sports car rammed into the side of a people carrier. A twenty-nine-year-old woman taken to hospital with head injuries. Freya? It could be Freya.

Food abandoned, I drive quickly but carefully to my NHS hospital, keeping my mind on the road, not wanting to repeat Freya's possible mistake. If it is her? Once I'm parked, my attention turns to determining her location. If she is still here? Oh no, what if she's died? How am I going to account for wanting to see her? I could pretend I've been asked to do a consultation but it's awkward not knowing her surname. Head injuries are usually taken to the neurosurgery ward. I'll start there.

But if she is there, what will I say to her? What if she has visitors? Her husband or at least, her ex-husband could be present. These dilemmas cascade through my brain. I need to keep calm. I manage during medical emergencies. Take some deep breaths. Classic advice and it seems to work. Thinking more clearly now. Some of my fears are unlikely. Visiting time is not until three pm, an hour and a half away. I have to do this. Confidence is key. I'm a consultant at this hospital and certainly look the part today in an expensive suit.

I stride onto the ward. A young nurse assistant is sitting at the nursing station, looking bored and apparently considering which chocolate to choose from one of the two boxes open in front of her. Hasn't she work to do? She watches me approach.

'Hi. I've been asked to see a patient who was admitted with a head injury last Sunday. Freya ….. Oh, what's the surname?' I ask in feigned frustration.

'Johnson.'

'Yes, that's it.'

She passes me a set of notes and indicates with a toss of her head some side rooms further down the ward. 'B3'

She doesn't offer to accompany me and I move away to avoid becoming ensnared by any questions before examining the notes. I glean: Mrs Freya Johnson, date of birth 12th September 1970. Admitted 11th June 2000, 11.20am. Road traffic accident. Right extra-dural haematoma evacuated later that day. Fractured right ulna. This is serious. She could have died, probably would have done if the blood compressing her brain had not been drained so promptly. What will I find? A "vegetable"? Please no.

My heart is pounding rapidly, responding to a surge of adrenaline. My palms are sweaty, fists clenched, primitive responses to a threat. I'm not in danger. But is that true? I could lose my family if Clare finds out. In disgust, I suppress that thought. How can I be thinking of myself after all that Freya must have endured? I raise my right hand, hesitate, then knock twice.

'Hello. Come in.' My spirits soar. I push the door open and there she is, standing by the window, holding a glass of water and dressed simply in loose black trousers and a cream round-neck sweater. No nightdress, a good sign. Her right forearm is in a plaster cast. She has a dressing on the right side of her head, from which some of her golden hair will have been shorn. She regards me with a quizzical, slightly vacant look. 'Hello. Are you a doctor?'

I shouldn't be this amazed. Some degree of traumatic amnesia is almost inevitable after the sort of head injury she has suffered. 'Yes, I'm Doctor Westwood. You're Mrs Jackson?'

She pauses before answering. 'No, Mrs Johnson. I think. I'm having trouble remembering things at the moment.'

'Sophie Jackson?'

'No, I'm Freya. Definitely Freya.'

'Oh, I'm sorry. The nurse must have misheard me and directed me to the wrong room.'

'Don't worry. I'm glad of any distraction right now. I can't concentrate to read or watch TV.' She waves her good arm towards her head wound.

'What happened to you?' I fish.

'A car crash.' She shrugs. 'So I'm told. I've no idea where I was going. My husband was abroad at the time, so he can't tell me.'

So, she is still married and living with her husband. Did she take her wedding ring off just before approaching me in the card shop? I see that she is wearing one now. Wryly, I realise how premeditated my seduction was. I shake my head unconsciously. She misinterprets this as a gesture of sympathy.

'Oh, it could have been worse. They've told me I could have died without emergency surgery. I'm lucky to have been close to a good hospital.' She lifts the plaster cast on her right arm and grins. 'And I'm left-handed.'

I'm impressed by her positive attitude. 'That's good. Are you going home soon?'

'Monday, I think. Somebody is going to come and look after me during the day, make sure I don't do anything stupid. Just 'til I get better.' She gives the little self-deprecating smile I've seen before.

'I hope that's very soon.' And I do. Of course I do. But part of me, the less admirable part, hopes she doesn't remember the afternoon and night we spent together.

'Well, I'd better go and find the patient I'm meant to be seeing. Bye. All the best.'

'Bye, doctor.'

THIRTEEN YEARS LATER

4

'Twenty, nineteen.' Adam calls the score with authority. It is correct. No dispute and in any case, he is no longer someone you would argue with too readily. At eighteen, he's now as tall as me and more heavily built. Gleaming with sweat under the late afternoon sun, he serves for the match. The well-played return is heading for our sandy volleyball court. I fling myself full length to keep the ball in play. Luke spikes it down. We have won.

Adam and Luke high five, before sharing congratulations with our fourth player. I am back on my feet, probably looking a little ridiculous as the front of me is covered in sand from head to toe. Adam bounds over and slaps me firmly on the shoulder in celebration. Luke asks, 'Are you alright, Dad?'

I blow some sand from my mouth. 'Yes, I'm fine.'

Luke, my little boy, now sixteen and six foot three. Gone is the gawky early adolescent, limbs growing faster than his brain could adjust to. Strange to think of your brain not knowing your own body's size or being tongue-tied by the novel surge of testosterone. He pats me on the shoulder, more gently than Adam.

I cannot fail to notice the changing nature of our relationship. He is now solicitous of his middle-aged father. Middle-aged. I don't like that term. At forty-eight, I have passed my physical prime but I am still slim and fit. I run, swim at weekends and assuming Adam is not occupying it, work out in our home gym. And I still have all my hair, even if some of it is grey at the sides.

'Come on Luke! Race you to the sea,' Adam challenges. 'Ready, steady, go.'

Luke pulls ahead, fashionably overlong shorts flapping round his knees. No surprise, he is remarkably fast. But in his direct line is a large, elaborate sandcastle, Union Jack paper flag planted proudly on its summit, in itself a surmountable obstacle. With his long legs, Luke could easily leap over it without breaking stride but the castle's owner, a young boy, is still attempting to improve his masterpiece. He could move unexpectedly and be hit by one of Luke's powerful legs. My moment of concern passes as Luke diverts his run. Adam splashes first into the sea, triumphant. I smile fondly and wonder, yet again, at the differences in personality between them despite their similar upbringing.

They are swimming out. I hope they don't go too far but I need not worry. They slow and turn to swim parallel to the shore. I smile in amused understanding. They are going to cruise the length of the beach, checking out the girls. The joys of youth.

Well, this not so youthful body of mine could do with a wash. I start walking in a leisurely manner towards the sea, savouring the day. Two girls, late teens, are playing with wooden bats and a ball in front of me, their lithe bodies generously displayed by their skimpy bikinis. I slow my pace further to admire them a little longer.

When does looking become staring or even leering? I wouldn't want to be accused of leering. Yet the older I get, the greater the disparity in age, the more likely it is to be judged that way. Not fair or at least, not a view based on biological reality. Evidence indicates that the peak age of physical attractiveness of a woman to a man is age eighteen, even when men are asked to judge by faces alone. Not information one would want to volunteer in female company. It was bound to generate a barrage of scorn. "So, you think we're all past our sell by date, do you?" Or even, "Perhaps you like them younger still, Doctor Westwood?" No, sometimes it is better to keep quiet.

Yet considered dispassionately, it is entirely predictable once you know that the peak age of female fertility is also eighteen. Thus, men who mated with women of that age, before the days of contraception, were more likely to pass on their genes than men who mated with older women, giving those genes that encoded a preference for younger women an evolutionary advantage.

And often, people only think about such matters in a modern context, failing to realise that such behaviour has developed over many millennia. After all, it wasn't that long, in historical terms, since many adult women were dead before the age at which a British middle- class woman has her first child these days. So, can I be forgiven for looking at those girls? "It was my genes, guv. Honest, I couldn't help myself." Perhaps not a viable defence?

I smile and wade into the sea. It is cold but pleasantly so

after my exertions. I swim out with a leisurely breaststroke. Now there's a word: breaststroke. How had that survived in our current fastidiously correct society? How about cheststroke? Less provocative. And for that matter, why is the fastest swimming technique called crawl? A suitable alternative doesn't immediately spring to mind. I turn on my back and begin to float, bobbing up and down in the gentle swell, the sun hot on my face, a taste of salt on my tongue.

I sigh. I might look at women but apart from Freya, I have never strayed, despite the many opportunities and temptations presented to me over the years. I wonder how she is. Hope she made a good recovery.

For months after our fling, I had felt guilt, mainly at betraying Clare, but, perhaps irrationally, at somehow being at least partly responsible for Freya's accident. And the probably paranoid fear that if Freya fully regained her memory, she would try to contact me and renew our relationship. As a doctor, I wouldn't be hard to find. Maybe she had remembered but decided to respect my decision and not imperil my marriage. I will never know but if she had, I am eternally grateful.

I'd resisted the terrible temptation to tell Clare about my night with Freya, to confess and beg for a forgiveness that might not be forthcoming. In time, the urge to seek absolution faded, diluted by the passage of the months and years.

Once the meningitis case had been resolved, Clare had returned to being her usual cheerful self. We met at medical school and had known each other for six years and were a couple for three years before we were married. I realise that I have now been with her for more than half my life and almost all of my adult one. We've recently celebrated twenty years of marriage, our 'China' anniversary, Clare informed me.

Ridiculous. Who thought that one up? When she told me, my first thought association was of dropping a teacup on the floor and it shattering. But our marriage is not fragile. Apart from those torrid months when Clare endured that investigation, it had thrived. I can have no complaints as to how well she has cared for me and our two sons, successfully juggling the demands of part-time general practice with bringing up the boys.

I turn upright and regard the beach. My gaze focuses on Clare, chatting to her mother, Joan. Since Joan's husband died of a stroke last year, we have tried to spend more weekends here to ease her bereavement. Not that it is a hardship to be in Bournemouth on a summer weekend and the family house is large and comfortable. Too large, now that Joan is alone. But she won't move. It's imbued with too many memories. Fifty-one years they were married, a real achievement. Perhaps Clare and I could make it to fifty years of marriage as well?

Right now, could I be happier? I have my health, a worthwhile fascinating job, no money worries thanks to my thriving private practice, two fine sons and a marvellous wife. I've worked hard to achieve this, or rather Clare and I have worked hard to achieve this. Now, most people would probably see me as a lucky man. For some maybe an object of envy, questioning whether it is fair for me to have so much?

I shiver. It is time for me to swim back to shore.

5

Jenner Ward: twenty-eight beds, arranged as four single-sex bays of six and four individual rooms, shared with another consultant gastroenterologist, Andrew Roberts. My team are waiting for me, clustered round a notes trolley. Rakesh, the house officer or F1 as they are now unappealingly designated, is small, intense and apparently ill at ease in the company of his immediate superior, Angela. She is tall and large – not fat, more Amazonian. I feel a twinge of sympathy for him. Raj, a fourth-year registrar, has the assurance of his years of experience. I just wish he wasn't quite so deferential. Is this because it makes me feel old?

And Jane, a physician assistant, a newly conceived and created post. She has very limited medical training. Since she joined us nearly a year ago, she has become a valued member of the team, now knows how I work and my idiosyncrasies, is able to prompt a new house officer to order investigations I am likely to request. A few years older than me, short, a little overweight and usually wearing a happy face.

We greet each other and then I enquire, 'How was the

test, Angela?' She sat the first part of the membership of the Royal College of Physicians exam earlier this week. Gaining this qualification is essential to her career progression to consultant physician. This is her second attempt.

'Better than last time.' She holds up her left hand with her first and second fingers crossed.

I look around to see if there is a nurse who might accompany us but there are none evident. So few British people want to be nurses nowadays that the hospital has to send delegations abroad, sometimes halfway round the world to the Philippines, trying to recruit them. What will happen when this resource is exhausted? Are there nurses on Mars?

'Any chance of a nurse?' Angela grins, perhaps at my eternal optimism. I shrug. 'Let's go.' Rakesh begins to push the notes trolley into the first bay. One of its wheels begins to squeak. One day I'll remember to bring some lubricant for it.

The sign over the first bed indicates its occupant is Hilda Taylor and has my name below hers, but the bed and the chair beside it are empty. Just then the door to the bathroom nearby opens. A walking frame emerges, pursued by an elderly woman, head bent forward, checking that the frame and her feet do not betray her. Behind her comes a pair of outstretched arms, ready to catch her if she falls backwards. They are attached to a nurse I have not seen before. Long fair hair tied back, a curvaceous figure emphasised by a uniform a little too tight.

Mrs Taylor carefully manoeuvres herself into her chair, sinking down with a sigh of relief. Duty done, the nurse turns towards us and pushes a stray lock of hair away from her eyes. 'Hi. Doctor Westwood?' I nod and smile. 'I'm Julie, a new staff nurse. Would you like me to join your ward round?'

'Yes, please.' Perhaps we don't need the Martians just yet?

Just over two hours later, results discussed, treatments up-dated, prognoses both optimistic and dire pronounced, and with a few fortunate patients declared fit for discharge, we have finished on Jenner Ward. Time to begin our "safari": the trek round the hospital to see our out-lying patients and multiple referrals. Angela has assumed the role of tour guide. Clutching a list of the remaining patients to see, she leads the way. She doesn't need to carry an umbrella to remain in view.

'Can I go home?'

How many hundreds of times have I been asked that question? Mrs Sinclair is our last patient on the round today. She musters a gap-toothed smile, her remaining teeth the colour of old ivory.

'Look, my twins have gone.' She pulls up her nightdress to expose her abdomen for me to consider. 'Well, maybe one of them. What do you think?'

Mrs Sinclair is sixty-two, well past child-bearing age. Her so-called twins had been ascites, free fluid in her abdominal cavity, secondary to her alcoholic cirrhosis. More a sign of death than new life.

We regard each other, she in hope, me assessing her physical state. Her cheeks are a mass of broken capillaries. They will not change but the large naevus on her forehead, like a Hindu bindi, is distinctly less florid than before, as is the redness of her palms. Both are indications that the dilatation of her blood vessels caused by her liver disease is settling. Certainly, her abdomen is less swollen. I pick up her weight chart. She has lost twelve kilograms in response to diuretic treatment since her admission just over two weeks ago, almost all fluid. She hasn't that much true body mass, her arms and legs are wasted, matchstick limbs protruding from a swollen torso.

- UNDER CONTROL -

This is her third admission. The first time she had presented with bleeding oesophageal varices, but I had treated and now eradicated those by endoscopic banding. We had kept her alive so she could continue to drink.

'Let's see what your blood tests show.' Jane hands me Mrs Sinclair's serial data chart. Her liver function tests have improved a little since admission but remain seriously impaired.

'Are they better?'

I look up from the chart towards her. 'A bit.'

'So, can I go home?'

Does she not understand, as many patients do not, that time is relative? Not in the sense that Einstein proposed but that her death would render time irrelevant to her. Better to spend a few more days in hospital as an investment in a longer life. Or does she just want a drink? Not the sort currently being offered by the tea lady as she clatters by with her trolley laden with an urn, cups and saucers.

Ah, I'm a doctor not a jailer. I try and probably fail to sound stern, 'Yes, but you know what you need to do.'

She looks sheepish. 'I should do. You've told me often enough.'

I could easily reply, "So why don't you?" But there is no point. She is a flawed human being. Is that tautological? None of us are perfect. And she has other problems to contend with. Her hands are gnarled by rheumatoid arthritis, but evidently the deformity is not so great as to prevent her putting alcohol to her lips.

'Doctor Westwood, please can I have a word with you in private?'

An unusual but not an unreasonable request. I gesture for my team to go back to the nursing station and pull the curtains round - an illusion of privacy. She sits up in bed. I move the bedside chair so I can sit and face her. If we are going to be having an intimate conversation, I don't want to be looming over her. I incline my head, waiting for her to begin.

She makes fleeting eye contact then starts tentatively. 'I know I need to stop drinking. I have tried. Done the counselling, Alcoholics Anonymous, even flirted with religion. Hasn't helped. And you've tried with your pills, the antidepressants, the acamprosate and that new one, nal...'

'Naltrexone.'

'Yes, that's it. The problem is that I like drinking. Can't do it in moderation, one leads to another. It's my life now.' She quickly holds up her right arm, red palm towards me, to prevent me interjecting. 'Yes, and I know what you're going to say: alcohol will be the death of me. You've told me. I understand.' She pauses and looks at me beseechingly. 'I can't stop. I can't.'

She shakes her head and tears begin to roll down the filigree of dilated blood vessels disfiguring her cheeks. 'But I want you to understand that you've not failed. It's me, only me, who has.' A small sob escapes her. 'And I'm grateful, Doctor Westwood, for all you and the other doctors and nurses have done for me, for your care and kindness, and for the extra time you've given me.'

I don't know what I can usefully say or indeed if I am too choked by emotion to speak at all. I nod to indicate my understanding and sit with her in silence a little longer. Then I try once again, more in hope than expectation. 'Is there anyone you could go and stay with for a while?'

Her rheumy eyes flit to a framed photograph on her bedside cabinet. A middle-aged man and a young girl. She looks at me forlornly. 'No, there's nobody.'

Not a surprise. Alcoholism is a story of progressive loss.

Loss of driving licence, loss of job, loss of self-respect, loss of family and ultimately, loss of life.

'I'd better go. My team are waiting. I'll send you an outpatient appointment. Please come. And if you miss it, you can always ring my secretary. I'll tell her to give you an urgent one, whenever. All the best.' I leave her bedside curtains pulled while she regains her composure.

I re-join my team. We set off down a long hospital corridor for lunch in the Postgraduate Centre. Jane breaks the silence. 'She's a lovely person. Such a shame.'

'Umm' is all I offer in return.

She tries again. 'Why do you think she keeps drinking?'

I give her a rueful look. 'She says she likes doing it. But I don't know, Jane. I really don't know.' We continue our procession down the corridor. I reflect sombrely that we can save so many people from disease these days but saving them from themselves is much harder.

6

'The blue or the black?' Wearing a low-cut black bra and matching flimsy panties, Clare stands before me in our bedroom, holding up two dresses for my inspection.

'I thought you'd decided on the red one?'

'I changed my mind.' I cast an overt look over our bed, now adorned by a variety of rejected outfits. 'Again,' she adds, followed by a cheeky grin.

'You'll look beautiful whatever you wear.' I move nearer her. She backs away.

'Don't you dare!'

'We've time.'

'No, we've not!'

Her tone brooks no argument. I take a pace back and give a brief laugh to show I'm not offended. Satisfied I'm no longer a danger, she asks, 'Which one?'

'The blue, it goes with your eyes.'

A fleeting smile. Discarding the black dress, she steps then wriggles into the blue one before turning her back on me and lifting her long dark hair. 'Zip me up.' I do as I am bid.

She turns to face me, grins and pecks me on the cheek. 'Later.'

'Promises, promises.'

I go to check on the preparations. Most of the furniture downstairs has been moved to the edges of the rooms. Fragile ornaments have been relocated to places of safety. Adam and Luke have draped a 'Happy Birthday' banner in the hall. The caterers are bustling away in the kitchen. The guests aren't due for half an hour yet. Under control.

The party is now in full swing. The house is packed with people, well in excess of the fifty I'd asked the caterers to provide for. Once the idea had taken root in her brain, Clare was insistent she wanted a "proper" party, not a sedate middle-class dinner gathering, and that required a "critical mass". This, it appears, she has attained by inviting almost all our friends and many of her acquaintances. Adam and Luke have leavened the age mix with some guests of their own.

The food has long since disappeared. There is still alcohol to be had but now the event seems to be running primarily on good cheer. The hubbub of multiple conversations is all-pervading and uplifting. Clare, high heels discarded, is dancing enthusiastically to Abba's Dancing Queen. Even Adam has been obliged to participate by his girlfriend, the lack of rhythmicity of his movements probably accounting for his reluctance. Or is it the other way round?

Edging my way through the crowd towards Luke, who is watching with amusement the antics of the dancers, I pat him on his back. 'Well done with the music.'

He smiles and shrugs. 'Not hard, Dad. I just downloaded the list Mum gave me.' He laughs. 'Never heard of most of the songs. Really old school.'

Old school it may be but it is good to see Clare letting her hair down. Until recently, the atmosphere in the house had been tense as Adam revised for A levels and Luke for GCSE's. Both of them are now awaiting their results.

It is now after two am and the last guests have just departed. Clare and I are in the kitchen. We survey the debris. I put an arm round her waist and give it a gentle squeeze.

'Good party?'

'Great party.'

She turns to face me. 'Hey, you. Later is now.' And in case her cryptic comment is lost on my tired brain, one of her hands strokes my bottom.

'Okay. I'll just lock up.'

A few minutes later, despite her bedside lamp being on, I find her fast asleep. Softly, I kiss her forehead, before undressing, turning off the light and slipping quietly into bed beside her.

****

Slivers of sunlight intrude past the edges of our bedroom curtains. Motes of dust dance languidly in the brightness, too dazzling to look at. I close my eyes again. There is no need to get up yet. It's Sunday and my mind is still a little muzzy from the alcohol I drank last night.

I begin to feel uneasy. What's the matter? I am annoyed that my foggy brain, normally so sharp, is not offering me a quick answer. Maybe it's just my imagination. It's quiet. Nothing is wrong. I start to relax again.

Then it hits me. It is too quiet. I cannot hear Clare's breathing.

I turn in our bed to face her. She is completely still. Her pallor is alarming and there is a slightly waxy appearance to her skin that my job has rendered me familiar with. I reach out to touch her, then pause, my hand a few centimetres from her face, not wanting to feel what I expect. I summon the courage. Her face is cold, too cold. My training takes over. I try to palpate a carotid artery pulse and then, in desperation, attempt to feel the other one. Her eyes are open, pupils widely dilated. I switch on my bed-side light and bring it towards her face. Her pupils remain fixed. She has gone.

I know death, but in a hospital bed, not mine.

This cannot be. I must be dreaming. But what little part of my logical mind is still functioning, despite my horror, tells me that I am not. I pull her awkwardly towards me, lay her cold face on my bare chest and begin to stroke her hair rhythmically.

I am keeping her a little longer.

7

'Luke, the cars are here,' I shout. No reply. Adam is standing next to me in the hall, pale but looking resolute, ready to go. We exchange a look of understanding. One of us needs to fetch him.

'I'll go. Tell them we'll just be a few minutes.' My legs seem heavier than usual as I walk up the stairs, before knocking on his bedroom door. He doesn't answer so I enter uninvited. He is standing with his back to me, staring out of a window. At least, he has his suit on.

'Luke, the cars are here. We need to leave.' He turns towards me, eyes red and moist, his expression desolate. One of our newly purchased, black ties is draped over his open-neck white shirt. I hug him then grip his left shoulder firmly. 'Luke, if you didn't cry because your mother has died, you wouldn't be normal. But now we have to do this for her, give her a good send off.'

'I know.' He sniffs and wipes his tears with a handkerchief. I have two spare ones in one of my pockets; tissues might not prove equal to the task today. Standing in front of a bathroom mirror, he puts on his tie and combs his hair.

Guilt assails me as we go outside. Clare's coffin is in the hearse, of course. Horrible to think of her in there. I shouldn't have sent Adam out to face that sight alone, but I didn't consider it at the time.

I need to be at my best today, to help them through this and to perform. I've self-medicated appropriately: immodium to quell the turmoil in my bowels, propanolol to suppress my elevated adrenaline level and prevent excessive emotion impairing my mental function.

We hadn't been churchgoers. I was not going to have a stranger, albeit a well-meaning vicar, uttering anodyne platitudes about her and pontificating on the resurrection and the life. None of us believe in that. Nor did Clare. I am giving the eulogy. It's my duty.

We sit in the car following the hearse in stony silence, not trusting ourselves to speak and perhaps crack our fragile composure. Joan is with us. She seems to have shrivelled and is holding so tightly on to Luke's hand that her knuckles are white. The journey to the crematorium passes in a blur.

Clare and I had never seriously discussed whether we wanted to be buried or cremated. We felt ourselves too young for such considerations, though our medical experiences should have belied this. But when we were newly qualified doctors, we regularly signed cremation certificates and in those impecunious days, were pleased to be paid for doing so. "Ash cash." The gallows humour was a coping mechanism. I had remembered Clare once declaring that when we went, we ought to do the decent thing and be cremated too. Maybe it was only partly in jest. I never knew and perhaps she didn't either.

The arrangements had been delayed while a coroner's post-mortem was conducted to determine the cause of her death. A massive bleed into her brain. It had obviously been quick. Hopefully, she had never woken. And the post-mortem had also discovered two berry aneurysms, a consequence of congenital areas of weakness in her cerebral blood vessels. Presumably, another one had burst to cause the bleeding that killed her. If, as more often happens, she had bled around and not into her brain itself, she might have stood a chance.

But as a physician I could not escape the conclusion, one I would not be sharing, that the rupture of the vessel had been precipitated by a rise in her blood pressure due to her alcohol intake that night. Not that it had been that high. Nothing like the Mrs Sinclairs of this world, probably no more than quite a few people drank from time to time, but more than her usual modest consumption. "Eat, drink and be merry, for tomorrow you die". How appallingly prescient for Clare.

There is already a crowd waiting to greet our arrival. I nod to them, acknowledging their expressions of sympathy as I lead our sad little group inside. I can talk to the mourners later but, for now, I have to stay focused.

We squeeze into the front row of pews, Joan on the inside, then Luke, Adam and lastly me, next to the aisle. I won't get past the boys' long legs if I sit further in. Clare's coffin, bedecked in flowers, rests in front of us. We hold hands and wait in silence, lost in our thoughts.

The vicar appears and, as requested, gives only a brief welcome before calling me to speak. My throat feels tight as I rise to my feet. But I can do this. I have to do this. I stand next to the coffin. The smell of the flowers, particularly the lilies, is strong and heady. Momentarily, I feel faint but I dismiss it. My body will not betray me, not today.

I turn to face the mourners. The place is packed, every seat taken, with more standing. Seeing it so full only heightens my sense of loss and I need a few extra moments to recover. An actor's dramatic pause before speaking? I wish.

'Thank you all for coming today to pay your respects to Clare. I hadn't expected so many, but then I suppose I hadn't been expecting to do this at all, at least not for a few decades yet. Of course, I know how perilous our lives are but probably, like the rest of you, it's more comfortable to pretend these disasters happen to other people.' This is not about me. Talk about Clare and stick to your speech, I chide myself.

'Seeing you all here is a testament to the selfless life Clare led, an indication of how many lives she touched and bettered. Clare believed that being a doctor is a great privilege, an opportunity to help many people and even occasionally save their lives. She thought that there was no better job for her. Being a doctor, was an extension of her altruistic personality, her caring essence.'

I take a deep breath and survey the gathering. They are still, watching me intently in the unnatural silence. 'And now, she is no longer here.' Joan emits a sob, quickly stifled. Luke puts his arm around her shoulder. 'But we should give thanks that Clare had a full and rewarding life. A happy childhood with her parents, Joan and Frank. She was the wonderful product of their devoted care.' Joan looks up at me and gives a wan smile in appreciation.

'I believe you judge a person's worth not only by what that person has done but also by what he or she leaves behind. I'm not just talking about producing our two fine sons, that was the easy bit - at least for me.' I am rewarded with a brief susurration of amusement, a partial release of some of their tension.

'No, I'm talking of the hard part. The caring for them, the love she lavished upon them, the love that enabled them to grow into the fine young men they are today, and the love that they are now able to bestow on others and, in time, on their own children. And, who knows, maybe via their children to their grandchildren. That is the greatest part of Clare's legacy: love, enduring love.'

****

Clouds scud overhead, propelled by a stiff sea breeze. The four of us troop solemnly to a sheltered part of Joan's walled garden. I carry the urn containing Clare's ashes. Adam and Luke have dug the hole. A small cherry blossom is laid flat beside it, along with a stake and watering can. I am not sure how much Adam buys into my idea of Clare's ashes nourishing and becoming part of the tree. Luke appears more sympathetic to the idea. Joan, for all I know, may think it's mumbo-jumbo. But all of them recognize the value of having a symbol and a place where they can remember her.

I've brought four sets of thin rubber gloves for us to wear. Luke, in particular, may not want the residue of his mother sticking to his hands or under his fingernails. We kneel down on the grass next to the hole, Joan with some difficulty. Not to pray but better to stop a gust of the capricious wind stealing her remains from us. 'My creaky knees,' she offers apologetically. I manage to stop myself uttering the facile observation, "it will come to us all". It hasn't for Clare.

I take the top off the urn and offer it to Joan. She scoops a handful of ash and carefully sprinkles it in the hole. Luke, Adam, and I then do the same. I tip what little remains along with the rest, before helping Joan to her feet and put an arm around her shoulder. Seagulls squawk overhead, seeming to mock our little ceremony.

Adam cuts the cover off the root ball and he and Luke

plant the tree in its new home. Mid-September, a good time to plant a tree. Clare returning to the home she was brought up in, returning to her roots.

Planting and watering complete, we regard the symbol of my dead wife, supported by a stake, rather limp and uninspiring just now. It will appear sturdier next spring, I tell myself. They all look at me as if I should say something profound, but I feel so empty.

'Grow big and strong and beautiful' is the best I can manage right now. We trudge back up the garden to Joan's house.

8

Adam is looking out the window, watching the flat countryside roll by as we travel north along the M11 in my BMW. Three A stars and a place to study law at Caius College, Cambridge. Nearly there now.

'Excited?'

Out of the corner of my eye, I see him turn towards me.

'Yes.'

'And nervous?'

'Only a bit.' He returns to his reverie.

We pull up outside the Stephen Hawking Building. I'm impressed by the standard of accommodation, a considerable upgrade on the spartan hall of residence I began my university life in. It doesn't take long to collect the key to his room and unload his few belongings.

'You're lucky to get into this hall.'

'Good planning, Dad.'

Difficult to dispute that, even if I wanted to. I've seen on Google Maps that he's now situated only a few minutes' walk from his college, the faculty of law and, not least, the university rugby club.

We walk back outside towards my car. I've not been to Cambridge before and would like to look around, but I think I should let him explore his new environment alone, not cramp his style. I can see the sights on a future visit.

I put my hands on his shoulders, hold him at arm's length and look directly at his face. I want this moment etched in my memory. Unsurprisingly, he begins to appear embarrassed.

'I know, Dad. Work hard.'

I smile. 'That's not what I was going to say. It was: "enjoy yourself".'

Two attractive girls are walking by, briefly pausing their animated conversation to give Adam admiring glances. His eyes flit towards them then he winks at me. 'Shouldn't be too hard.' I laugh and begin to turn towards my car.

'Dad, look after Luke….and yourself.'

I raise my right hand a little in acknowledgment. It's easier than speaking right now.

I drive away. There's no need to rush back and Luke is playing away in a school tennis match. I decide to take a more rural route home.

The traffic is minimal on this sunny Saturday afternoon. I make steady progress through a succession of picturesque villages before stopping at a lay-by. Standing in lambent light under a majestic oak tree, I watch a combine harvester efficiently scythe through a field of golden wheat and discharge its bounty into large containers pulled by two accompanying tractors.

I sigh deeply. We've done well, Clare. Forgive me, my love, but today I am happy.

9

I'm tired and hungry. It's six forty-five on a Wednesday evening and the day has been particularly demanding. Still, I didn't want to refuse to see this private patient today, he sounds to be in need of urgent treatment. But where is he? I venture out of the consulting room and call his name: 'Mark Johnson'. Just then, a man hurries in from outside and lifts an arm in acknowledgement. We move towards each other and shake hands.

He is clearly jaundiced. I've seen his date of birth on the embryonic case notes my private secretary has created. He is a couple of years older than me but looks more. Less hair, a little overweight, and being the colour of amber doesn't help.

I introduce myself, 'Miles Westwood.'

'Hi. Thanks for seeing me so quickly. Sorry I'm a bit late; my flight was delayed.' An American accent. He brushes some snowflakes off the shoulders of his navy-blue overcoat.

'Not a problem. I thought it might have been the snow.'

He smiles, displaying abnormally white teeth, probably had them treated in the States. Now they only serve to accentuate his skin discolouration. 'The snow isn't so bad here. It's much worse in New York.'

I lead him into the consulting room. He takes off his coat, revealing a well-cut, if somewhat crumpled, dark grey suit. I settle into my seat. He perches on the edge of his.

'You must be wondering why I've flown from New York to see you?'

'Well, I didn't think my reputation had spread that far,' I offer with what I hope he perceives as a wry smile. Sometimes some gentle humour helps the patient to relax, but it has to be finely judged.

He smiles back at me. 'Maybe not, but I phoned a friend you treated here and he told me you were the man to see.'

'Thank you.'

'I've been in England fourteen years now, with the bank. My family is here. I wanted to get sorted out at home.'

'Okay. So, tell me how you are.'

He eases himself back in his chair and begins. 'I was away on business last week and started to feel tired and nauseated. My bowel motions went pale. I wondered if I'd picked up a bug. Then a few days ago, I noticed the jaundice. At first, I thought I was just keeping my tan well. We went to Antigua for Christmas.' He looks at me expectantly.

'Do you have any pain?'

'No, nothing.' Not the answer I want to hear.

'Are you or have you been taking any medication recently?'

'No,' he shakes his head for emphasis. Wrong answer again.

'Are you itchy?'

'Yes, all over. Is that something to do with it?'

'Yes, it is.' His symptoms are classically those of obstructive jaundice. The absence of pain makes it less likely this is due to gallstones and is more in favour of a malignant cause.

In the past, he has not had any serious illness. He doesn't smoke and drinks alcohol moderately. On examination, there are no signs of chronic liver disease. His abdomen feels normal.

'What do you think?'

I'm not willing to give him a straight answer to that question just yet. Better to order some investigations. This is one of those occasions when I hope my clinical diagnosis is wrong. 'You need an ultrasound scan, like pregnant mothers have, and some blood tests. Then we'll have a better idea of what's going on. You could have the scan here tomorrow morning. It would be best done with you fasting, so no breakfast, please, just a few sips of water. I could see you this time tomorrow to discuss the results.'

He considers this information for a few moments then nods his head. 'That's great. See you six thirty tomorrow.'

We rise from our chairs and he gives me a firm handshake. Once he's left, I sit back down again and sigh. Giving him the bad news tomorrow isn't something to look forward to.

****

This time he's in the waiting room when I arrive. Casually dressed today and seemingly by himself.

I'd asked my private secretary to phone him this morning, before his scan, ostensibly to confirm this evening's appointment but in reality, to encourage him to bring his wife with him. Less worrying than my suggesting that last night. A little easier to hear bad news if you're not alone, as well as not having to tell his wife himself or apologise for not asking pertinent questions while he was still too shocked to think clearly.

'Evening, Doctor Westwood. Would you mind waiting a

moment before you see me? My wife dropped me at the door and is trying to find a parking space.'

'Of course.'

'I didn't want to be late again. Ah, here she is.'

I look towards the entrance. A tall blonde woman in a stylish black coat is walking towards us. It is Freya. No doubt. Looking older, of course, but still slim and beautiful. I realise I'm holding my breath and staring. He's probably used to men staring at his wife.

She stops in front of us. 'Doctor Westwood, my wife, Freya.' She offers me a token, tense smile. I cannot detect any indication that she recognizes me. I look at him, have to keep looking at him if I am to think clearly, and it's crucial; he deserves my full attention.

'We're in the same room as yesterday.' I lead them in. There's little point asking him how he is. I did that yesterday. It would only be procrastination and all they want to hear is the test results. 'Your liver function blood tests show that your bilirubin, the substance that causes the jaundice, is more than ten times what it should be. Some of the other liver blood tests show what we term an obstructive pattern, suggestive of there being a blockage to the liver.'

I start to show them a printed diagram of the appropriate anatomy, using my biro as a pointer. (See page 48 - ERCP anatomy). This here is your liver. A big organ, it has plenty of work to do helping to process the food you eat and remove toxins from the blood.' I raise my gaze to him. 'It's the build-up of some of those toxins that is making you feel ill and causing the itching.'

I pause, perhaps unnecessarily, to let them absorb and consider this. 'The liver makes bile which aids the digestion of fat. It flows down what we call a biliary tree.' I indicate with my biro. 'Here are the branches in the liver draining into the tree trunk, the common bile duct, which takes the bile into the duodenum. That's the part of the small bowel just past the stomach. Your liver makes bile continuously but of course you eat intermittently, so you store the bile in a reservoir off the side of your common bile duct, your gallbladder.'

'Finally, your pancreas'. I point at the organ on the diagram. 'It makes the digestive enzymes. Importantly, the duct that takes them into the duodenum uses the same exit as the common bile duct.'

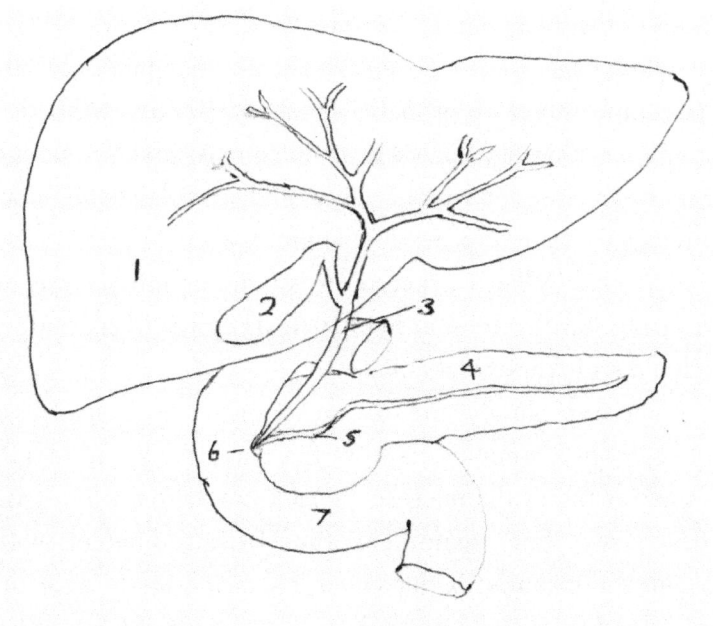

1. Liver
2. Gallbladder
3. Common bile duct
4. Pancreas
5. Pancreatic duct
6. Papilla
7. Duodenum

Complicated, but they're both intelligent and, with the

aid of the diagram, it's fairly clear.

And once I tell them the terrible news, they won't be able to take in too much more. I sit back to show them that the lecture is over and pick up the scan report.

Mr. Johnson pre-empts me speaking further.

'Do I have gallstones then? That's what my friend had and you took one out of his bile duct with an endoscope.'

I wish I could give him an unqualified yes. 'The scan shows that you do have gallstones.' He looks relieved. 'But they are in your gallbladder and the scan hasn't shown any in the bile duct. Ultrasound doesn't always manage to image stones in the ducts but...' Another "but"

and a bigger one. 'The scan shows your bile ducts are dilated and therefore probably blocked.' I pause. 'And that the cause of that blockage is probably a mass in the pancreas, near where the pancreatic duct and common bile duct converge to drain into the duodenum.'

'A mass. What's a mass?' A querulous interjection by Freya. It's hard to look at her, particularly with her wearing such a distraught expression.

'The scan can only indicate an abnormal area. Ideally, we need a biopsy, some tissue from the mass, for a pathologist to look at under the microscope to know better what it is.' I nearly say "but" again. This time I use a different word though the meaning is the same. 'However, along with the liver blood tests, I did another one, a tumour marker called Ca 199. It's very high.'

'What does that mean?' Freya again.

'It means that this mass is almost certainly a cancer of the pancreas.' As is usual in these circumstances, they are stunned into silence by the gravity of my words. I have learnt that I need to wait while they try - and possibly fail - to assimilate this information and its implications.

Eventually, he asks quietly, 'Can it be removed?' A look of longing on his face but I am about to extinguish any realistic hope. How much harder to cope with the diagnosis of cancer without hope to cling to, however improbable? This is one of the few times when I wish I had a different job.

'The scan also indicates that the cancer has spread to your liver, so it wouldn't help you if we operated on your pancreas ... I'm sorry.'

Another silence, this time broken by Freya. Her eyes are moist. Her bottom lip trembles as she speaks. 'Can it be cured another way then?' She probably knows the answer to this question but needs to hear it from me.

'No, unfortunately not. When your husband is less jaundiced, he could have some chemotherapy, but it would be to extend his life, not be curative.' I choose not to inform them that the chemotherapy is not particularly effective. There is only so much tragic news that I think it is reasonable to impart at one time.

'So, what do we do now?' asks Freya plaintively.

This part is easier. 'I'll arrange another scan, a CT scan. It will give us more accurate images. And I'll present your husband's case at a multi-disciplinary meeting, a gathering of consultants from appropriate specialities where we decide on the best management to recommend to each patient.'

'Don't you know?' Freya again. A bit "below the belt" that one.

No irritation escapes into my voice as I reply, 'Yes, I do. And the meeting is not until next Wednesday and, as the appropriate management is clear, I don't think we should wait 'til then before treating your husband.

He needs an endoscopic procedure called an ERCP. I

could do that next Monday morning.' I focus on him. 'What I'll do is put a stent, a tubular structure, up your bile duct to bridge the narrowed area and relieve your jaundice. You'll feel much better then.' What I should have said is: "I'll try to insert a stent". Success isn't guaranteed even though I've been performing ERCP for seventeen years, but I don't want Freya challenging my competence again. 'And I may be able to obtain some tissue samples to spare you the need for a biopsy.'

'Is it safe?' Freya asks.

I was about to tell them. 'There are risks. The main one is irritating the pancreas causing an inflammation, called acute pancreatitis. That happens in 1-2% of patients and a few patients who develop this complication die from it. There is also a small risk of bleeding or perforation of the duodenum as I'll probably need to make a small internal cut to get the stent in. But you have to see those risks in perspective. An ERCP is a lot safer than surgery.' I turn to fully face him again. 'You'll be heavily sedated, so you'll know little or nothing about it.'

He stirs from his recent passivity. 'Okay. That's good enough for me. Let's do it.'

10

The unmistakable odour of vomit pervades the staircase. It is coming from the boys' bathroom. No one in there. I tap gently on Luke's door then peek in. He is lying on his side in bed, a good position if he is sick again. He stirs reassuringly. The room reeks of alcohol. One doesn't need an experienced nose like mine to detect it. I close the door quietly.

The likely culprit identified, no need to check on Adam, home for the weekend. Now that he is at university, he has become more jealous of his privacy and he may not be alone.

Both of them had gone out to a party last night and not returned before I went to bed. I'd been concerned that even though they were taking taxis, the roads were treacherous with the new snow. If it lasts a few days more, we will have our first white Christmas for years. Maybe it's an indication of my getting old: fretting too much.

I check my watch, a Patek Philippe. It was my father's. Perversely, it survived the car crash, though my parents didn't. The driver of the other car also died. The postmortem had shown his blood alcohol to be well over the legal limit.

This event and the harm that I regularly see excessive alcohol consumption cause, sometimes leads people to assume I disapprove of drinking entirely.

But it is a matter of balance, letting intellect and knowledge rule over your emotions, something my more zealous colleagues seem to find difficult. They would have you believe alcohol is an unmitigated poison, ignoring that our simian ancestors adapted to consuming it millions of years ago when they ate over-ripe fruit in which the sugar was fermenting. Putting aside the social benefits of sensible drinking, moderate drinkers live longer than teetotallers. The zealots prefer to ignore this inconvenient fact. It is possible alcohol saves more lives than it kills. But not in my family.

Well, no time to change out of my suit and clear up the mess. I'd be late for my Saturday private clinic. In any case, Luke should deal with it himself. Clare probably would have done it for him.

Late afternoon, home again. Walking past their bathroom, I'm pleased to smell bleach. I knock on Luke's door and enter. He's sitting at his desk, looking the worse for wear, Facebook on his laptop screen.

'Hi, Dad.'

'Hi. How's the hangover?'

He gives me a rueful grin. 'I'm coping, did what you told Adam before now, drank plenty of water, some apple juice and took two paracetamol.'

The transmission of wisdom. The fluids counteract the dehydrating property of alcohol and fructose in the apple juice facilitates the alcohol's metabolism. Even if they don't help much, at least the sufferer feels he or she is doing something useful. I had learnt not to underestimate the placebo effect. What I'd not advised Adam, and was not about to inform

Luke, is that the most effective remedy is a limited amount of more alcohol. "The hair of the dog" does work, at least to some extent.

I put my hand on one of his shoulders and give it a gentle squeeze. 'Are you okay otherwise?' He's been down, understandably, since Clare's death, not helped by Adam disappearing soon after to Cambridge.

'You mean about Mum?'

'Yeah.'

'Not too bad. Getting there.'

Probably a fair assessment of his progress. How am I doing for that matter? Am I getting there, wherever that is? The paperwork hadn't been too emotive but I haven't cleared Clare's clothes out of her wardrobe yet, still like to look at them, imagine I can catch the lingering smell of her or at least her perfume. Haven't reset the kitchen clock to the correct time.

And I'm not going to remove some of the family photographs that adorn our - rather my - bedroom walls. The two of us at our wedding twenty years ago, young and radiating happiness into the camera lens, another of the pair of us at a ball, Clare resplendent in a new red dress. And perhaps my favourite, the most recent one, the four of us together at a family party, smiling, united, a successful team.

Am I caring for Luke properly under these changed circumstances? The pair of us rattling around a house that now, at times, seems too big. Certainly, we are not eating as well. I'm making an effort to come home earlier in the evenings and spend more time with him but is it enough? Is a family without a woman still a family? Are we just two men getting by?

Luke sighs. 'Dad, last night I was at the party and there was this girl from school there, Imogen, that I really like. I'd started to think she liked me too but she was all over another guy. Older, never seen him before.'

'So, you drowned your sorrows.'

'Guess I did.'

'Next time, a better move might be home in on another girl, even if you're not that interested and let Imogen or whoever see you doing it. You're more attractive to a woman if other women find you attractive.'

He studies me for a moment, perhaps wondering how his middle-aged and previously long-married father knows these things. 'Cool, I'll remember that.' He hesitates, 'But Dad, the girl you use to make yourself more attractive, isn't she going to be upset when she realises what's going on?'

'She may not realise and you might find you like her more than you'd first thought.' He doesn't appear convinced. 'Whatever you do, if you get drunk, you can't do anything effectively. Can't even look after yourself properly.'

'Yeah, after what happened with Adam, I should know about that.'

I say nothing and wait for him to continue. I must look puzzled.

'You don't know?'

I shake my head.

'Look, I shouldn't have said anything. He's alright Dad, really. But I don't want to tell you. Will you ask him yourself?'

'Okay.'

****

I can smell cooking. It must be Adam; Luke hasn't acquired any culinary skills yet. I put down the newspaper and go into the kitchen. It is in remarkable disarray as Adam, his broad back towards me, prepares his meal.

'Hi, what are you making?'

He glances over his shoulder. 'Oh, hi Dad. My speciality, chicken and rice. Do you want some?'

'No, thanks. You do your chicken too hot for me.'

'If you'd told me earlier, I'd have made some less spicy for you.'

'No problem. I had a meal at the hospital.'

'Well, there'll be plenty if you change your mind.' He grins. 'I don't think Luke is up for eating just yet.'

'Sure. I was talking to him this morning. He, umm, he let slip that you'd had a bit of trouble recently.'

He turns to face me fully, not looking pleased, and turns off his cooking. 'I didn't want him to tell you. Don't want you worried, particularly at the moment.'

'Thank you, but now I'll be more worried if you don't tell me what happened.'

'I know.' He sounds annoyed. Was what I just said too patronising? He's hardly an idiot. He takes a deep breath before embarking on his story. 'I was at a party with Matt at the rugby club here a week ago and saw this girl I fancied. She was with another girl who wasn't bad either. I thought we should make a move on them. But he'd gone outside for a smoke. A cigarette, Dad, not a joint, in case you're wondering.'

I wasn't, but, nevertheless, am glad of the reassurance. I know Adam doesn't smoke tobacco; don't think he does drugs. From his tone, it doesn't sound as if he approves of them, hasn't taken them up in his first term at university then.

'I went outside to fetch Matt. There were some guys shouting at him, getting arsy, ready for a fight.'

'How many?'

'Six.'

Not good odds then. 'What did you do?'

'I dashed across to him and shouted at them, "What's your problem?" Matt gave me the answer; told me they were the guys who did Josh. Do you know about Josh?'

I do. Clare had told me. Earlier in the year, Josh and Matt had been set on one evening. Matt got away but Josh had been badly beaten up. Had his head kicked in. Needed a metal plate in his skull and time in intensive care. An urban horror story.

'Yes, I know. What did you do?' I repeat.

'I pulled Matt back against the wall of the clubhouse and told them "Touch him and I'll fucking kill you".'

I take a long deep breath. 'What happened?'

'They kept taunting us for a while, probably seemed longer than it was, then they left.'

The terrifying potential of their situation appals me and unthinkingly I say, 'Were you pissed?'

Adam stares at me intently, as if trying to see into my soul. I feel uneasy. After a few seconds, he says, 'No, Dad. He's my friend. I couldn't leave him.'

I lower my head in shame that I had suggested he would have to be drunk to do what he did.

'Sorry.'

I say no more. No more needs to be said. I turn and leave the kitchen.

11

So here we are, the endoscopic team with their assorted paraphernalia in the imaging department. The large room is window-less, soul-less and dominated by the equipment in its centre. We are waiting for him to be brought to us. I sit on a stool. My stomach grumbles, ready for its lunch. It will have to wait, a hurried sandwich later, if I'm lucky. I've done four ERCPs on NHS patients this morning, all successfully. I hope I can do as well for him.

One of the medical students currently attached to my team, Nada, walks in. A small bespectacled young woman with short, jet-black, curly hair. She has a quiet, polite manner, reluctant to ask questions but nevertheless I suspect she is very bright.

She smiles shyly. 'Good morning, Doctor Westwood. Please can I watch you do ERCP?'

'Of course, Nada. Have you seen any before?' She hasn't so I show her the special endoscope we use for this procedure.

He arrives on a trolley. Mary, stouter and hair now completely grey, is still the endoscopy sister. She performs the usual checks, though I know for certain he is the correct patient and I have already completed the consent form with him earlier this morning.

Even in the two days since I'd seen him previously, his jaundice has worsened. He's become almost fluorescent, like a streetlamp. Mary finishes attaching his monitoring equipment and I move across to the fixed table he is now lying on. The curved arm of the X-ray image intensifier arcs above his waist, its screen and another one that will show a magnified view down the endoscope are across the table facing me.

Placing a hand on his shoulder, I give him my most reassuring expression. 'Ready?'

He looks determined, his decision made. 'Sure.'

As I sedate him, I reflect briefly, as I have done many times before, that it can't be easy to surrender control and trust one's life in such an intimate way to another person.

Time to begin. I insert the endoscope into his mouth, through his oesophagus and stomach into his duodenum. 'That's our target, Nada, that small nipple-like structure, the papilla.' The thought flashes through my mind that she is so shy, she might be embarrassed by my likening it to a nipple but it is the only accurate description.

Unfortunately, there is no welcoming orifice. One has to delve between its tiny folds to discover the way into either the common bile duct or pancreatic duct. The anatomy is variable to add to the challenge and my task today is not going to be made easier by the fact that his papilla is swollen and distorted by the pressure of the tumour behind it.

Mary hands me my preferred cannula which I pass down through the slim channel of the endoscope until its tip protrudes into the duodenum.

'So, Nada, first we have to insert the tip of the cannula

and angle it in approximately the correct direction. Then we use the guide wire inside it to help us find the way into the common bile duct. We then squirt some contrast fluid up the duct and use the X-ray machine to see better what's going on.'

I begin: subtly and repeatedly adjusting the cannula's position, while Mary advances and retracts the guide wire time and again. This is a team procedure.

After a few minutes, we have not succeeded. I decide to inject some contrast fluid in what I suspect is the optimal direction. A faint trickle of contrast ascends the bile duct. If fluid struggles to pass through, then it's going to be hard to pass anything solid past the stricture.

'I think we're going to need a slippy wire, Mary.' I exchange the guide wire in the cannula and we try again. After a further prolonged effort, I feel a slight give and the wire slides in the correct direction.

But not as far as I would like.

I am now able to advance the cannula over the wire and inject some more contrast past the obstruction and outline the duct. As expected, it is dilated, but its lumen tapers at both ends, like a sausage. There is a tight narrowing not only at the obstruction we have just crossed but also above - a double stricture.

I explain to Nada, 'The other end of the common bile duct, where it joins the liver - the top of the biliary tree trunk, if you like -, is constricted, almost certainly compressed by swollen lymph glands infiltrated by cancer cells.'

Mary and I set to work again trying to pass the slippy guide wire through the second stricture. It proves a more formidable obstacle than the previous one and after many attempts I call a halt. 'We'll try with a balloon catheter, then, Mary.'

Nada takes the opportunity to ask quietly, 'What happens

if you can't get the wire in far enough?' I turn my focus away from the two screens and towards her.

'Then I won't be able to insert the stent, his jaundice will get worse and he'll die very soon. A radiologist could try passing a guide wire in the opposite direction, through the liver, but it's riskier and there's no guarantee he or she would have any more luck than us. Unless we can improve his liver function, he won't be able to tolerate chemotherapy.'

'Surgery?'

'A last resort, possibly. But I think the surgeon would also struggle with the bile duct blocked at both ends and he's high risk for an anaesthetic, being so jaundiced.'

She looks at me, more openly than before. 'So, no pressure then?'

From many other students, that would have seemed a flippant remark but Nada somehow manages to convey real empathy with it. I find myself smiling, and in the process, relaxing a little.

'No pressure then,' I agree.

We try again with the balloon catheter. After some time, we still haven't succeeded. Last try, I think. No luck. It's not going to be my last try though. It's a silly mental game I occasionally play to keep my spirits up. The last try is usually the most successful one. A few more "last tries" and finally the wire eases past the second stricture up into a bile duct within the liver. Now we are winning.

I take some tissue samples, dilate the two strictures, and slide a stent over the guide wire. Dark brown bile, escaping its imprisonment, gushes into the duodenum, proving the efficacy of our efforts.

I look down at Mark Johnson. He's never stirred. Just as well. I don't think I could have managed with a moving target.

Mary smiles at me. 'I think you're getting better at these, Doctor Westwood.'

'No, it's just your expert help that makes it seem that way.' She grins.

'Thank you all.' The other members of the team have been almost silent and invisible to me during the difficult procedure. Now they are chatting happily. I remove my heavy lead radiation-protection coat, a literal weight off my shoulders, and leave X-ray.

Nada scampers after me. 'Doctor Westwood, thank you. That was fascinating and... inspirational.' She looks embarrassed but I'm flattered.

'So, when you're in a difficult situation in future, Nada, you'll remember: no pressure then.'

She laughs. 'I will. I will.' She walks away with a jaunty step.

The clock on the wall shows one thirty-five. If I grab a sandwich now, I can eat it while I type my report into the computer and just make it to Outpatients on time. I hope the clinic isn't too over-booked today.

****

It was a vain hope and I finish Outpatients late, as usual. Still, now all I have to do before I escape home is see Mr. Johnson. I knock on his room door. A female voice calls, 'Come in'. Freya, predictably, is here, sitting in the chair next to his bed. They both look at me intently, awaiting the verdict.

'It went well. I've inserted a stent and it's draining your liver satisfactorily.' Some of the tension eases from their faces. I wait a few moments before asking, 'How are you feeling?'

'Yes, a bit better, I think.' Already, he is beginning to

look better. His jaundice has taken on a more matt hue.

'That's good. Have you had something to eat yet?'

'A little.'

'Any pain in your abdomen?'

'No, it's pretty good.' Probably no pancreatitis then, despite all my fiddling around. I check his charts: pulse and blood pressure satisfactory, no temperature.

'Okay,' I pronounce, 'you can go home then. You'll need a week or two for the jaundice to fade and to gradually feel better. I'll refer you to one of my oncology colleagues, Doctor Kendall. He's very good and specialises in these sorts of problems.'

'Fair enough. Will I see you again?'

'Well, I'm here if you need me. Just call my secretary. But for now, I'll leave you in Doctor Kendall's capable care.'

He offers me his hand to shake. 'Thank you. Great job.' Freya just looks at me morosely. She is all too aware that this battle may be won but the war, ultimately, will be lost.

12

'There's our new chief executive,' Jane says, as we walk down a long corridor at the end of a Friday morning ward round. I am quietly amused at her excitement, as if she's spied minor royalty.

'Yes, I know. He came and spoke at the Consultants' Committee meeting last Wednesday evening.'

'He's not very impressive, is he?'

Middle-aged, short and flabby, there is no doubt that physically he is not a man who would inspire you to follow him into battle, though, on second thoughts, Napoleon managed well enough. He is talking animatedly to the long-standing head of human resources, Mrs Owen, a tall thin woman in her fifties, walking beside him with more than her usual stoop. They make an ill-assorted pair and pass us by without a glance.

Once they are out of earshot, I reply to Jane, 'Maybe not but what really matters is the quality of the decisions he makes.'

'Well, I don't think you're going to like this decision,' she says, struggling to suppress a smirk.

'Go on,' intrigued, as she knew I would be.

'He's going to change the names of all the wards. The medical wards are going to be called after flowers and the surgical wards after trees.'

'What's Jenner Ward going to be then?'

'Rose Ward. What do you think of that?'

I exhale deeply. My first thought is that it would be inappropriate to share my views on this with Jane. The chief executive had spoken to the assembled consultants at our meeting only two days ago and never mentioned overhauling the ward names. He must have realised he would only encounter objections. After twenty-five years of working in the NHS, I understand that most new managers feel the need to change things, to stamp their mark on the system and justify their existence, regardless of how well that system might be performing already. This, along with the frequent re-organisations inflicted by politicians, ensure the NHS is perpetually in turmoil. But even so, why start a new job by potentially antagonising such important members of your team?

An unsettling thought crosses my mind. I remember a couple of years ago, a fellow gastroenterologist at a nearby hospital propounding his view that NHS managers increasingly view doctors as just another category of staff, a more troublesome one than most, who need to be taught their subordinate place. If our new chief executive is of that opinion, then how better to announce it than by abolishing ward names that celebrate the achievements of eminent doctors? It doesn't auger well.

There is nothing to be done about it though. A ward by any other name is still a ward. Though I expect Jane would understand this allusion to Shakespeare, it is too poor a comment to voice. Instead, I say, 'Well, it could have been worse.'

'How so?'

'It could have been re-named chrysanthemum.'

She laughs. 'That's true. More effort, and I'd have to learn how to spell it.'

My mobile vibrates in my pocket. Unusual. Most communications arrive through my bleep. My home number is displayed on the phone. Luke should be at school but Adam has just returned from Cambridge for a long weekend. I accept the call. 'Hi.'

Adam's anguished voice responds. 'Dad, sorry to disturb you at work but I've got a pain in my chest. It's really bad.'

I stop walking and the rest of the team grind to a halt. An icy feeling of dread pervades me but my brain is sharp, perhaps the latter a consequence of my medical experience. 'One moment, Adam.'

I turn to my registrar. She looks at me in concern, distress must be written on my face. 'Stacey, would you mind seeing the last couple of patients, please?'

'Of course.' The ward round trundles on without me.

'Right, when did this pain start?' Not the best question, I reflect.

'About an hour and a half ago, I hoped it would just go but it's got worse. It's like someone is sitting on my chest.'

Sounds cardiac. But why should my seemingly very fit son have a heart problem? 'Is your breathing okay?'

'Yes, it's just the pain.'

'If you take a deep breath, does it hurt more? Try it.'

I hear him inhale and exhale deeply. 'No, the same.' Probably not pleuritic pain then.

'Okay.' Of course, it's not okay, but I have reached the inevitable decision. 'I'm going to ring for an ambulance for you. Better I do it. Lie down and wait. It shouldn't be long.'

'I'm already lying down.'

'Good. Don't go rushing around packing a bag. I'll tell them to expect you here.'

'Alright, Dad. See you soon then.' Mock cheerfulness. He must be scared, particularly all alone there.

I ring 999 and manage to remain polite but firm while persuading the woman I am speaking to that it is an emergency and a paramedic ambulance straight away is necessary. I look at the medical rota downloaded to my phone. The cardiology registrar on call today is Doctor Sachs. I know her. We've done some medical emergency takes together. She's able and fairly senior. I call her bleep from a hospital phone on the corridor wall.

'Doctor Sachs.'

'Hi, Rebecca. It's Doctor Westwood.'

'Hi. You're not the consultant taking emergencies today, are you?'

'No, I'm not but I'd be very grateful for your help.'

'Sure. What would you like?'

'It's my eldest son, Adam. He's nineteen, very sensible, not a wimp. He's just rung me to say he's developed severe chest pain this morning. It sounds cardiac. I hope I'm wrong. I've just ordered an ambulance for him so he should be arriving in A&E soon. Please would you see him urgently?'

'Of course. He's top of my priorities now. I'll tell A&E. to expect him and to let me know the moment he arrives. Sorry he's not well.'

'Thank you.' I expected nothing less but still feel overwhelmingly grateful.

What to do next? I call home on my mobile.

'Dad.'

'How are you?' I'm relieved to hear his voice and try to

stop mine betraying too much concern.

'The same. I've opened the front door.' Very sensible. He's probably considered the possibility of him losing consciousness. I hadn't thought of that.

'Well done. Look, the ambulance should be on its way and they are expecting you here. There's a very good registrar, Doctor Sachs, going to see you the moment you get here. It's better if I'm not around. I'd just get in the way. You'll be in good hands. I'll be along to see you a bit later.

'Okay, Dad. You know best. I can hear the ambulance now. Better go.'

I can also hear the sirens through the phone before he disconnects. A strange word, "siren". I hope he isn't being lured to his doom. Melodramatic nonsense, but it vindicates my decision that it's better I'm out of the way while he is cared for more dispassionately.

13

I sit in my office, flicking through e-mails, deleting the unnecessary majority and keeping the remainder until I can give them my proper attention. Stacey has agreed to do my afternoon endoscopy list. Luckily, it's all uncomplicated gastroscopies. She's competent at those. I've left it long enough. I'll go and see how he is, what's happening.

My office phone rings. 'Miles Westwood,' I answer.

'Miles, it's Julian.' I recognize the cultured tones of one of the cardiology consultants. 'I've just seen Adam. It's clearly a cardiac problem. The blood tests show his troponin is over 50.'

'What! I've never seen one that high. That's…that's over 500 times the upper limit of normal.'

'Yes, probably too high to be a myocardial infarct. More likely to be myocarditis.'

'Look,' he pauses to allow me to consider this, 'that's what I think but I'd like to be absolutely sure his coronary arteries are patent so I'm arranging to do an angiogram on him soon.'

'Miles?'

'Yes, sorry, I'm still here. You must do what you think is best. I'm grateful, Julian.'

'Okay. We're just moving him to the cath. lab. now but it will be a little while before we start. I thought you might want to see and wait with him.'

'Yes. Yes, I do. I'll be right there. Thank you.'

It's not far from my office but it's foreign, a place in the hospital I've never ventured to before. I turn a corner and there he is, in a small area outside the cardiac catheter laboratory. Temporarily all alone, in a hospital gown, lying on a trolley, connected to a pulse and oxygen saturation monitor, blood pressure cuff on his arm, cannula inserted in his left hand. His eyes are closed. He looks pale. The monitor reveals a rapid heart rate but I am encouraged to see his blood pressure is satisfactory.

I move next to his trolley and put a hand on one of his. 'Hi.' He turns his head slightly towards me and gives an almost imperceptible nod. Closed in on himself, just enduring. 'Do you understand that they think you have myocarditis. That's an infection of the heart, probably by a virus. But they want to be sure that there's no blockage of the blood vessels by doing a special x-ray, an angiogram.'

'Yes,' almost a grunt.

'Adam, I've been thinking. There's something I really need to ask you.'

A flicker of interest crosses his face.

'Sometimes cocaine can cause spasm of the coronary arteries and lead to a heart attack. Did you take any in Cambridge last night before you came home?'

He opens his eyes wider and fixes me with that unsettling gaze he possesses. 'I don't do drugs, Dad,' he states firmly.

'Sorry. It was important I asked.' He closes his eyes and lies there, very still.

'Is the pain bad?' But I don't really need to enquire, it's evident from the drawn look on his pallid face. Just a brief nod again in reply. He must have been given analgesia. I pick up his drug chart from the end of the trolley.

'They gave you diamorphine two point five milligrams intravenously.'

'What's that?'

'Heroin.'

He snorts. 'Over-rated.'

'I think you need a bigger dose. Back in a minute.' So, I go to try to procure more heroin for my son.

****

My gut feels like it's tying itself in painful knots and my head pounds. Sitting alone on a chair in the joyless space outside the catheter room, I wait for Adam to return. Why do they call it a laboratory? Hardly encouraging for patients with its connotations of experimentation. Even without such a provocation, a few patients seek reassurance they are not "guineapigs".

I'm not worried about the angiogram itself; it's his prognosis that's my concern. Some previously fit young people die of myocarditis. I don't know the statistics and can't face Googling the disease on my phone just now.

He has to recover. After Clare, it wouldn't be ... fair. I shake my head. Was it tempting fate when I reviewed my good fortune lying in the sea at Bournemouth only seven months ago? Nonsense. But if I did believe in some supernatural entity, what Faustian pact would I make to have Adam safe and well again? Lost in thought and seemingly staring at the blank wall opposite me, I register someone speaking my name and turn to face the source of the sound.

'Miles,' he repeats. I am surprised to see Alan Smith, a microbiologist. He seems, like me, to be an incongruous visitor to this cardiology enclave. 'Are you okay?' There is real concern in both his tone and facial expression. It must be obvious to him that I am not and before I can even reply, he has taken a seat near me.

I relinquish my introspection. 'It's my son, Adam. He's in there having a coronary angiogram.'

'Really?' He looks shocked 'How old is he?'

'Nineteen.'

He ponders this for a few moments. 'Do they think he's got a congenital abnormality of his coronary arteries?'

'No, probably myocarditis.'

'Oh.' It can be very expressive, that little word "oh".

We sit in silence for a short while before I feel impelled to talk. 'You know, Alan, it's strange being on the other side of the fence. I find myself doing the same as any other patient or their relative, wondering why, where he got it from, though I realise we'll probably never know.'

He smiles sympathetically. I open up. 'I was just thinking about a passage in the Bible. I'm not religious but there's this story in the Old Testament, maybe you know it, about King David. His son, Absolom, is killed in battle and David cries out, "Oh Absolom, Absolom my son, would that I had died for thee".' I realise I may sound foolish but I don't feel it.

He shakes his head gently before looking at me with compassion. 'I understand, Miles. I do. But try not to think like that. I know it must be hard after what happened to your wife. I'm sorry for your loss. But Adam will get excellent care here and the chances are good that he'll make a full recovery.'

I nod to acknowledge his effort at reassuring me. We sit in silence for some minutes.

Eventually he proffers, 'I think these viruses and bacteria have even more to answer for than we realise. In my opinion, they are probably responsible for many important diseases whose cause is unknown, ones that even many doctors don't conceive as being due to a chronic infection.'

I lift my drooping head and reply, 'I agree. After the way the Helicobacter pylori story has evolved, you'd find many gastroenterologists more receptive to that idea than most.' He is clearly pleased by my response.

'Do you know much about Chlamydia pneumoniae?'

'A little. A common cause of chest infections, often mild, but then the bacterium can persist within the cells of blood vessels and bronchi.'

'Yes, that's right.' He is more animated now. 'About half the population are infected by adulthood and three quarters by sixty-five. Not only can it take up residence in blood vessels but it is particularly found in the atheromatous plaques themselves. And as you would expect, it induces an inflammatory response that could well be the initiating factor for myocardial infarctions and some strokes.'

I consider this for a few moments. 'Makes sense to me. It's accepted that another species of Chlamydia can narrow and block women's Fallopian tubes and cause infertility, so it hardly seems a great intellectual leap to conceive that Chlamydia pneumoniae can do the same to coronary and cerebral blood vessels.'

'Exactly.' He is nodding vigorously. 'If the bacteria weren't there to initiate the process, then it might not matter how high a person's cholesterol is.'

I raise my eyebrows and almost smile. 'You think the cardiologists are too hung up on an incorrect, or at least an incomplete, theory? Like gastroenterologists were entrenched in believing gastric acid caused ulcers before the importance of Helicobacter pylori was appreciated.'

'Yes. It's a good analogy.'

'Hmm. Well, I certainly observed some senior gastroenterologists fight tooth and nail against Helicobacter. Not surprising when you consider it was over-turning their entire life's research work.'

'You can judge the greatness of a man by the time he is able to delay progress.'

I laugh. 'I haven't heard that one. But what about the younger cardiologists, perhaps with more receptive minds?'

'But are their minds really more receptive?' Alan suggests. 'And? as atheroma is now responsible for the majority of cardiology's workload, what junior cardiologist wants to consider and research a concept that would destroy his or her future. It's heresy and we all know what happens to heretics.' And can you imagine their consultants' reactions when they learnt they no longer needed to do all those lucrative private angiograms and angioplasties?' He smiles. 'They wouldn't be able to pay their mortgages.'

Then he stops suddenly, though it seems to me that his diatribe is unfinished. Perhaps he is having second thoughts about denigrating cardiologists when Adam is under their care. I think he is examining my reaction as to whether he has over-stepped the mark. I want to show him he has not.

'I can see that it would be a huge advance if we could treat the cause of atheroma with antibiotics, stop myocardial infarctions, angina, aneurysms and some strokes. Not to mention preventing vascular dementia which often, it seems to me, gets labelled as the more fashionable Alzheimer's disease. There'd be a real increase in average life expectancy, a considerable demographic change.'

He smiles, then resumes, 'To be fair to the cardiologists, trials of antibiotic treatment in myocardial infarction haven't been that encouraging. But that doesn't mean the idea is wrong,' he is quick to add. 'Some of the Chlamydia exist in a resting phase, like hibernation, in the vessel wall and are unresponsive to antibiotics when they are not actively dividing, and that's even assuming the antibiotics can get at them in sufficient concentration while they're surrounded by all that cholesterol.'

'So, what's the answer do you think?'

'Well, I certainly think there needs to be more research on something so potentially important. In the long run though, the answer has to be vaccination against the organism. You're on Jenner Ward; you shouldn't need any persuading of that.'

'Not much longer.'

'Oh, are they reorganising you to another ward?'

'No. The new chief exec. is re-naming all the wards after flowers and trees.'

'The little devil. When did you hear this?'

'Just now, from my physician assistant.'

'It says something when she knows before you.'

Just then, the catheter room door opens and Julian emerges. Tall, slim, and wearing green scrubs, he pauses a moment, perhaps to consider whether he is breaching confidentiality by speaking in front of Alan, before advancing towards me. My anxiety re-surfaces. I stand up.

'His coronaries are fine.' He announces. 'Clean as a whistle.'

'How is he now?'

'He's asleep since we gave him that extra diamorphine. We've vacated a bed on the coronary care unit so we can keep a better eye on him. He's on his way there now.'

'Thank you, very much appreciated." I shake his hand, perhaps squeezing a little too hard. He walks back into the catheter room. It is taking me a few moments to absorb this information.

Alan claps me lightly on the back. 'Good news'.

'Yes. Yes, it is.' He smiles benignly and leaves me standing there. I set off to coronary care. Even if Adam is asleep, I need to see him and be there when he wakes up.

****

I knock on Luke's bedroom door.

'Come in'

He's sitting at his paper and book-strewn desk under the window, looking tired. His laptop for once is not displaying Facebook; instead, the screen shows a series of chemical equations.

'Hi, how's it going?'

'Not bad. Got to have this chemistry in for tomorrow.' He grimaces.

'Can you do it okay?' I can still remember enough A level chemistry to assist him, if necessary.

'Yes. It's just the amount of work we're given.'

I offer him a sympathetic look. 'I'm off to see Adam now. If you've this much to do, there's no need for you to come.'

'Do you think he'll mind?'

'No. You saw him yesterday. He'll probably be discharged tomorrow and be home for a least a week then.'

Luke looks relieved, perhaps both as a consequence of Adam's improvement and also his being allowed more time to complete his homework. He stands. I'm still not used to him being taller than me. Then his shoulders sag a little and he asks entreatingly, 'Dad, it's a bit scary isn't it? First Mum then Adam?'

'I understand. But Adam is getting better and nothing is going to happen to you or me.' I hug him tightly. I've told him what he needs to hear. Statistically, it's a fair prediction but, of course, there's no way to know for sure.

14

Saturday, early afternoon, my private outpatient clinic is finished but now I must go and see Mark Johnson. I think of my mother saying: "saving the best to the last". Hardly appropriate in this instance. He has not responded well to chemotherapy and is terminally ill. There were no beds free in the local hospice. Not unusual, difficult for it to control its bed occupancy given the unpredictable length of stay of its occupants. So, at his request, I have admitted him here.

I knock on the door of his room and enter even though there is no response. He may not have heard or be asleep. But I find him awake, lying in his bed and alone.

'How are you?' But it's unnecessary to ask. He looks awful - yellow, wasted and weary. His jaundice has partially recurred. The ultrasound scan that I ordered on admission indicates that the stent is still patent. Sometimes stents block, but not usually this quickly. It's only two months since I inserted it. There are no signs of infection, so the jaundice is, as the scan shows, a consequence of more of his liver being replaced by metastatic cancer. Only the chemotherapy can potentially deal with that and it hasn't.

'Not great,' he replies with obvious under-statement.

'Have you any pain?'

'No, no pain.' That is often the situation in these sorts of cases. The impaired liver function causes a raised blood level of opioid peptides, the body's natural counterparts to morphine and heroin. This accumulation is probably analgesic and sedative. 'That's a kindness, isn't it?' he adds.

I wonder who he thinks is being kind to him. 'That's good.' I sit down on the chair next to his bed to show him I'm not in a hurry to leave.

'I've not got long, have I?'

It must take courage to ask a question like that, even when your body is screaming the answer at you. This is not a time to obfuscate. He deserves a frank response. 'No, you've not.'

He makes a sound somewhere between a sigh and a moan.

'I'm sorry. I wish I could have done more.'

'Not your fault. You've done your best.'

'Thank you.'

His expression is bleak as he turns to stare out of the window. The sky is clear blue. On a grassy slope opposite, daffodils are flowering in all their golden splendour, a herald of spring with its promise of new life. It must be particularly difficult to accept death on a day like this. He turns his gaze back towards me.

'I worked hard, struggled to get where I am - where I was - in the bank. I had it all mapped out in my head, then bam! This happens, no warning.'

I shake my head a little, not in disagreement but at the mystery of it all. 'Man plans, God laughs,' I say.

He smiles wryly. 'I don't believe in God. Ought to, I suppose. My parents were Catholic, but I could never get into religion. No After Life for me. Perhaps, just as well, I'm not sure where I'd be going.'

Unbidden, cruel thoughts flash through my brain: do they need bankers in heaven? And: don't rich men have to pass through the eye of a needle?

'No,' he continues, 'as far as I'm concerned, when you're dead, you're gone. Nothing left. Well, maybe your kids. I've got a great one, a daughter. My genes will go on without me.'

I just listen. After a pause, he resumes, 'I could have done it differently. Should have spent more time with her and Freya, not as much at the bank, neglected them while I pursued my career. Now I can never make up for that.'

'We all sometimes wish we had done things differently.'

'You too?'

'Yes, of course. Me too. But it seems to me that you've done your best, you've provided well for your family, better than most men. And you clearly love them.'

He closes his eyes. At the time, I think it's because he's exhausted but later realise, it was to reflect on his life better. I can hear the ticking of his alarm clock, amplified by its position on top of his bed-side table. After a while, it seems as though he has fallen asleep. I am about to stand up and leave when he speaks. His eyes remain closed. I have to lean forward to hear.

'I had an affair. Fourteen years ago, thereabouts. Seems a…'

Lifetime? Too painful to use those words?

'An age ago now. Stupid. Even at the time I realised it wasn't anything special. But the girl was young and very willing and Freya and I were going through a hard time. Then Freya had a car crash. Could have died. It made me realise I didn't want to risk losing her. I broke off the affair. I've been faithful ever since. Freya never knew.'

He gives a brief, sardonic laugh. 'I've never told anyone before. It feels good. I understand now why my mother used to look happy sometimes after Confession, though it's difficult for me to think she had anything worth confessing.'

'Maybe we all do,' I say, and wish I hadn't.

'You're like a priest, aren't you? I can tell you things and it stays confidential, right?'

'Yes. I'll keep your secret'.

He musters a hint of a smile. 'Thanks for listening. And for looking after me.' He offers me his hand and nods as I squeeze it gently.

What does it mean, that small nod – recognition, respect, a bond created by a fight shared, an acceptance of his situation, a goodbye? I don't trust myself to say more and leave. I close his door softly and stand in the corridor outside his room, dabbing my eyes with my handkerchief and blowing my nose. Round the corner comes a staff nurse, pushing a drug trolley.

'Are you alright, Doctor Westwood?'

'Fine, Sarah,' I lie, before escaping to the car park. I raise my head towards the sun, enjoying the warmth on my face. Such a simple pleasure.

The sound of a powerful engine announces the arrival of a black Mercedes SL sports car. It drives in too fast and pulls into a parking space in front of me. Freya clambers out from the low seat. Her skirt rides up her thighs as she does so, triggering memories of our night together which I promptly suppress. I'm obliged to speak to her. She walks towards me and I greet her, 'I'm glad we met.' I mean now, but do I also mean then?

'Yes, I wanted to catch you.' She can only mean now, can't she?

I gesture towards the hospital entrance. 'Shall we go inside and talk?'

We walk back to his ward. The visitors' room is unoccupied. On the way, I look for a nurse to join us, anticipating the upsetting conversation Freya and I are going to have. I can only see Sarah, still on her drug round. A printed notice is hung on her back: "Please do not disturb the nurse during the drug round." A sensible exhortation to minimise dispensing errors but not helpful to me right now.

We sit opposite each other in the soulless room. People vary so much as to what they want to discuss under these circumstances, so I wait for her to begin. She is straight to the point.

'How long has he got?'

'Not long, a day or two maybe.'

Distressed, she looks away. A patchy flush begins to spread up her neck. She waves her left hand at nothing, a sign of her anguish. The sun flashes off her large diamond engagement ring and weaves its reflection on a wall. 'I would have looked after him, you know. Right to the end. But he wouldn't let me. Said he didn't want me to have too many memories of how he is now, had to remember him how he was before he got sick'.

'I understand.' And I do. I really do. What man wants a fit, healthy wife to see him so disgustingly degraded by disease? Better to go like Clare.

She fixes me with her gaze. 'But what I don't understand is how he got this. He was so well before.'

'I can't answer that. I'm sorry. We just don't know the cause of pancreatic cancer.'

She glares at me. I am taken aback. 'But why, why don't you know? Doctors are meant to be very intelligent, aren't they? And here you are in your shiny hospital, full of high technology. Why don't you know?'

Her voice is thick with bitterness. I am used to relatives becoming aggressive, venting their pain and grief on me. Doctors are so much more tangible than fate or any god, but her vituperation is exceptional and, with our strange relationship, more wounding. She is sobbing now, head bent. I want to touch and comfort her, but I'm her husband's doctor, not her lover.

The door opens a little and Sarah pokes her head round the door, no doubt alerted by Freya's sobs. Rarely have I been so glad to see the "cavalry". She comes over and puts a comforting arm round Freya's shoulder. She gives me a sympathetic glance and gestures with her free hand for me to leave. Relieved, I heed her unspoken advice.

Yet again, I've left Freya crying.

15

Why do I feel so down? It's not like me. I need to be logical, though, ironically, I sometimes tell patients that feelings defy logic. Objectively and most importantly, Adam is much better. His latest scan demonstrates his heart is working well and he's not been troubled by any arrhythmias, so he's been able to return to Cambridge. He's banned from the gym, running, and his beloved rugby, but these are only temporary restrictions.

Luke is proving to be more resilient than I anticipated. The more sensitive of my two sons, he has not dwelt on his initial fears about Adam's illness and seems to be moving on after his mother's death. I am continuing to spend more time with him. We often exercise in our home gym together, though I refuse to partake of the protein shakes he considers to be an essential adjunct to the work-out. His latest variety is bright blue, reminiscent of anti-freeze. He has taught me FIFA football on the PlayStation. I'm even beginning to win occasionally. Whereas before I might have felt I was frittering away my time, now I rationalise that I am fulfilling my parental obligations.

And how am I coping without Clare? I think I've managed as well as can be expected, as the oft-used medical expression goes. I still wake some mornings - or worse, in the middle of the night - having forgotten briefly she is not there before the cold reality intrudes. The photographs of her still adorn one of my bedroom walls. Other memories of her are often triggered by simply being in the house we lived in for much of our married lives. But you can't talk to memories and there is no escape from the conclusion that I am lonely.

There is more. I have a new revulsion at being at the mercy of disease.

Before Clare's death and Adam's myocarditis, I had felt to be in control of my life, but now the capriciousness of life and death appals me. Of course, in my job, I knew that intellectually and I'd coped fairly well with my parents' sudden demise. Perhaps that's easier, the natural order of things, parents going before their adult children. But it's only when illness affected my immediate family personally, that I really felt it.

Even work is no longer as satisfying. So often it now seems to be a rear-guard action, a delay of the inevitable, a fight for an individual victim of a disease rather than against the disease itself.

I must admit to having been hurt by Freya's scorn. It had seemed so unreasonable at the time, but was it entirely unjustified? Why wasn't the cause of pancreatic cancer, and for that matter, of more diseases known? What was stopping us? Money for research was important but inadequate finance wasn't the sole answer. Novel techniques and technology were advantageous but, fundamentally, the answers often lie in new ideas. Sometimes, not even new ideas, but ideas that had been ignored or discarded by the medical establishment, for whatever reason.

I am trying, Freya. At least, I'm trying. In the weeks since our fraught conversation, I had thought repeatedly about the usual type of pancreatic cancer: adenocarcinoma, struggling for a flash of insight into its cause, but it feels like swimming through seaweed.

Isn't it outrageously arrogant to even consider that I can just work it all out? But throughout history, people have done just that. Most famously Einstein, discovering secrets of the universe armed with no more than a pencil and paper. I'm certainly no Einstein but then the task I am attempting is much simpler. I've had original ideas before that have stood the test of time. And if there is the slightest chance of success, shouldn't I try? It's too easy to leave it for others.

Perhaps my mood is not so inexplicable, how could anyone feel cheerful while contemplating such a dreadful illness? Pancreatic adenocarcinoma causes around nine thousand deaths per year in Britain and around three hundred and thirty thousand fatalities per annum globally. Almost always a death sentence, the very large majority die within five years of diagnosis and many much sooner.

With most other cancers there is more hope.

Nor does the response of the various cancer organisations and pressure groups inspire any optimism in me. Their usual litany of demands for earlier diagnosis and faster treatment seem like a reflex response. There is little doubt that such measures are helpful in colon cancer and some other malignancies, but how can they not see that these are not going to make much difference in this condition?

They know that cancer is not one disease but many, so why do they maintain that one solution fits all? Most patients have no symptoms from their pancreatic tumour until the disease is incurable, nothing to encourage them to consult a doctor. Unless you have one of the rarer, less aggressive cancers, shortening the diagnostic and treatment intervals by a few weeks, when the patient's situation is almost always irremediable by surgery at the time of presentation, is not going to make a realistic difference. You might as well try to correct flooding by putting the rain back into the clouds.

Enough. I've sat here alone for too long with my bleak ruminations. Exercise and fresh air will do me good. I change into my running clothes and set off.

The scent of the bluebells as I run through the woods is heady and clean. One did not need to cling to the view of physicians in the Middle Ages that bad air is the cause of disease to believe that this fresh smell is easing my morbid thoughts. I run steadily and comfortably, generating endorphins, the opiates of the athlete.

I am in no rush to return home, revelling in the delights of spring and its eternal message of resurgent life. On and on I go, further than usual, until I emerge beside the river. To my astonishment, the pub where Freya and I were together lies ahead. I have not been there since and this does not seem the right moment to pay it even a fleeting visit again. Time to turn for home.

****

Despite my prolonged run, sleep will not come. Yet again I am obsessively analysing the risk factors for pancreatic carcinoma in my head. Smoking doubles the risk. And obesity. But then, being overweight is known to promote a variety of cancers, so it may be a non-specific effect. The cancer is more frequent in diabetics, but most cases of the commonest sort of diabetes, type two, are partly a consequence of obesity, so again there may not be a direct causal link.

And why does the cancer almost always develop near the exit of the pancreatic duct, where it joins the bile duct? That should tell me something.

What about gallstones, the commonest disease of the biliary system. Stones are more prevalent in patients with pancreatic cancer, but how does that work?

****

I wake without knowing why. My semi-rural home is silent and the room in total darkness. My body clock informs me it is the middle of the night. Nevertheless, I am not drowsy. My mind is crystal clear and unencumbered by the barrage of daytime stimuli.

And here it is. An answer, or rather a highly plausible hypothesis. It seems so simple and yet, those ideas are often the best.

How could I have not thought of it sooner? For that matter, how could others not have thought of it before? There are so many other highly intelligent doctors out there, some undoubtedly cleverer than me, but I have learned that I think a little differently to most, have an ability to see a problem afresh, not constrained by the "tramlines" of current dogma.

I test my hypothesis mentally against what is thought to be known about the disease. It certainly ticks many of the boxes and, as I consider it further, perhaps it provides a unifying explanation for some of the other diseases of the pancreatic and biliary systems. The pieces of my intellectual jigsaw are slotting into place.

This is too exciting for me to sleep again tonight.

16

I wake in my armchair. The ten o'clock news that I had attempted to watch is long since finished. I must stir myself and go to bed. My grand ideas have been put on hold by reality, the exigencies of striving to provide satisfactory care in an ever-declining National Health Service.

On this morning's ward round, there was only Jane, my physician assistant, to accompany me. Thanks to the European Working Time Directive and the vagaries of their rota, there were no junior doctors. It doesn't have to be so. Many of them would be willing to derogate in order to gain greater experience but the Trust is unwilling to pay them for the extra time.

However, the directive could not prevent junior doctors, who had already worked their maximum hours that week in their own hospital, acting as locums in another one, their services often acquired via an expensive locum agency. It's economically inefficient and the lack of continuity of care caused by this farcical arrangement is potentially harmful to the patients, since care and discharge are delayed.

Unfortunately, the costs of the latter are more difficult to quantify than the juniors' salaries.

I had managed to finish my ward round just in time for an afternoon in Outpatients, even more over-booked than usual. Returning to my office, I found my picture of Clare and the boys on the floor, a casualty of an avalanche of notes from one of the piles on my desk, the desk that I had cleared the evening before.

But I will not be ground down. I am going to test my ideas. Tomorrow is another day.

****

'Go straight through, Doctor Westwood. He's expecting you,' the secretary bids me breezily.

Nevertheless, I knock before entering his open door. He takes off his reading glasses, jumps up to greet me and shake my hand. He is nearly as tall as me, of similar age and in good shape.

'Miles. Good to see you. Have a seat.' He gestures towards a rather battered, hard-backed chair opposite his desk.

'Sorry about yesterday. My ward round ran over.'

He shrugs. 'I understand. You didn't need to make an appointment, you know.'

'Thanks, but I wanted to come when it was convenient for you to talk to me.'

'Of course. But first, how's Adam?' He's remembered my son's name. His concern is obviously genuine and the welcome so warm, I think we could work well together.

'Much better, thanks. And I'm very grateful for your being with me while he was having his angiogram.'

He sits there smiling. His hair is grey, at odds with the youthfulness of his face. Is his grey hair premature or does having a happy personality retard ageing? Such speculation is for another time, he is waiting expectantly for me to continue.

'You'll remember you distracted me by discussing that bacteria and viruses may be the cause of some common diseases that we don't think of as being infective.'

'Yes.'

'Well, I wonder if I could interest you in helping me do some research along those lines?'

'Go on.' He nods encouragingly.

'I want to investigate whether gallstones are caused by a bacterial infection. You see, at the moment, the prevailing theory of gallstone formation is a metabolic one. In Western societies, most gallstones are formed from cholesterol, which the liver excretes into bile. But cholesterol is a fat and is insoluble in water, so the liver also secretes bile salts which work like washing-up liquid, surrounding the cholesterol molecules and allowing them to disperse in the aqueous bile.'

'Okay. I'm with it.'

'However, if there is an imbalance: the liver excreting too much cholesterol or not making sufficient bile salts or a combination of both, then the bile becomes overloaded, so-called supersaturated, with cholesterol. Crystals can then precipitate out and over time grow into gallstones.'

'I'm waiting for a "but".'

I have to smile. 'But there are many people with supersaturated bile who don't have stones.'

'In other words, the supersaturated bile is a prerequisite for stone formation but not the whole story.'

'Spot on.' I'm impressed.

'And this is where you think the bacteria fit in?'

'Yes. I think that somehow they disturb the bonding of the bile salts to the cholesterol and initiate the stone formation in people with supersaturated bile.'

'Fair enough, but bile is usually considered to be sterile. Are you suggesting we'll need to identify a low-grade infection that wouldn't normally be detected?'

'Yes, I am, and to do that I think we need to discover a new bacterium.'

He sits back in his seat and ponders this for a few moments. 'Sounds challenging. Do you have any ideas about how to find this new bug?'

'I do but I need you to help me turn the ideas into reality.' I look at him hopefully. 'I think the bacterium should be a Helicobacter. So just as Helicobacter pylori can colonise the mucus layer on the lining of the stomach, it seems to me that there may well be another species of Helicobacter which may infect the mucus of the biliary tree.'

'That makes sense. So, if that is the case, there may be few or no bugs in the bile itself.' He pauses a moment. 'Presumably, we could look for them in removed gallbladders?'

'I agree. I thought that was the way to start. Ethical committee approval would be a formality so we could begin almost straight away.' I stop, realising I'm getting a little carried away. 'That is, if you're interested?'

He taps the biro he is holding on his desk a few times while he contemplates my proposal before declaring, 'Sure. It's an intriguing concept and gallstones are certainly an important disease, so I can't see why not.'

'Thank you.' I'm relieved.

'A few practical questions though.'

'Fire away.'

'Money?'

'There's a gastroenterology trust fund which I control. It's money given to the department by grateful patients and one of its designated uses is research. My colleague, Andrew Roberts, won't object. With a bit of effort, I could raise more. There's certainly enough to get us started.'

'Okay, and do you have any thoughts on finding this putative bug?'

'Well, I would defer to your expertise but I realise that Helicobacter pylori is difficult to visualise even with special stains.'

'Hmm. Even so, I think we should start by trying to find your Helicobacter by staining methods. They may not be very sensitive as a test and miss some cases where the bacterium is present, but if we can discover it in just a few specimens then we have proof of concept.'

'As for staff, some of the laboratory technicians work part-time and I can think of a couple of good ones who may like to do more hours. I can't see why we shouldn't help you.'

'Alan, that's fantastic. I'm really grateful.'

'Just one more question.'

'Sure.'

'If we find this bacterium, what are we going to call it?'

'I was thinking maybe Helicobacter bili.'

He is grinning. I don't know why. 'A boy then. Okay, we will do our best to deliver you bili.'

17

'Where's the board gone?'

I am on Rose Ward. Perhaps the new name might be more acceptable to me if the ward could be made to smell of roses, but this morning there is an unpleasant odour wafting towards the nursing station where my ward round is about to start. The white board I am referring to usually hangs here and identifies which patient is in which bed and which consultant is responsible for them.

Guy, my new F1, until a moment ago had appeared relaxed as well as tanned after his holiday. Now, he looks beseechingly at Jane, perhaps not wanting to be the bearer of bad news. Is there any other sort here?

Jane, irrepressible as usual, steps into the breach. 'The new chief nurse has had them taken down on all the wards. She says it contravenes patient confidentiality. Oh yes, and now only the patient's first name is allowed to be written above their beds. We can't put their surname or consultant.' There's a glint in her eye. She realises that I am not going to be pleased by this information.

I pause and take a deep breath, think before saying something I might regret. 'So, how do we know who's who and if they're ours?'

'Well, all our patients' notes are hopefully in our trolley. We just have to find the patients they correspond to.'

'And how, Jane, do you suggest we do that?'

'We could ask them their names.'

'But some of them are confused. They don't know their names or answer "yes" to any name you suggest.'

'We could ask a nurse.'

I swivel my head to scan the ward. 'Can you see any nurses to ask?'

'I suppose we will have to ask the patients their names and check their identifying wrist bands as well.' She is grinning now; fine creases have formed at the corners of her brown eyes. A sense of humour is a helpful survival attribute here.

As I am unable to recommend anything better, we make a start. However, as we enter the first six-bedded bay, a problem immediately becomes apparent.

'I see. The first patient is called Peter, then we have Peter, then Sam, then Pete, then Lionel and last but not least, Peter."

Jane cannot control herself any longer and explodes into laughter. Not appropriate in view and earshot of seriously ill patients but it would be unkind to rebuke her under the circumstances. I half wish I could share her mirth but this is so obviously a medical disaster waiting to happen. I'll need to speak diplomatically to the new chief nurse and try to change her mind, even if I make myself unpopular in the process.

****

Now that we've made a start on the research, I feel a sense

of anti-climax. I've done what's necessary to have the gallbladders that are removed in the operating theatres sent promptly to the microbiology laboratory and have put up some posters encouraging donations to the Gastroenterology Trust Fund. It's up to Alan and our two newly recruited, part-time technicians now to try and find Helicobacter bili.

If it's not present or something like it, where does that leave all my grand ideas? It ought to be there. In the distant past, Helicobacter pylori could have migrated through the mucus layer the short distance from the stomach to where the bile and pancreatic ducts exit into the duodenum or been carried there in intestinal fluid and over time, adapted and evolved into a different species colonising the bile ducts.

Increasingly, I feel guilty not to have shared all my ideas with Alan from the outset, not just the one about gallstones. He was so willing and open with me. There is time, though, to rectify my omission. And he might have thought my plans over-ambitious. A gradual approach may be better. And I've a reason to be cautious.

I sit in my office after a busy day. When are they not? As usual, case notes and letters have appeared while my day was spent on the wards, in Outpatients and Endoscopy. They are scattered across my desk haphazardly. I have asked more than once for my current shared secretary to arrange them in neat piles, it's less depressing to return to, but my entreaties fall on deaf ears. Does she secretly blame me for generating so much work?

There is still some light coming through the window. I am glad to see the back of winter, going to work and coming home in the dark, rarely seeing any sunlight, except at weekends. At least there's a window in the cramped office I share with Andrew Roberts. Not all my colleagues are so fortunate.

It hasn't much else to recommend it. The paint is peeling off the walls and ceiling in ever greater quantities, falling like pale green snow on my computer and the paperwork littering my desk. The office hasn't been decorated since before my arrival here over thirteen years ago.

Perversely, most of the other offices in the corridor have been. They are now all shiny, spick and span. Some even have new furniture. When I enquired as to why we had been omitted, I was informed that the decorated offices are surgical, while Andrew's and mine, of course, is not. The surgical budget is in surplus, the medical one in deficit.

I asked management when the last time was the medical budget had not been overspent but no answer was forthcoming. Perhaps their records do not go back that far? And like a dog with a bone, though I really should know better by now, I enquired whether the management budget was in surplus. The click of a phone being disconnected was my reply.

Regardless, I know the answer. Financial restrictions don't appear to apply to our masters. Their pay rises considerably outstrip those of the other hospital staff. Since I have been here, their number has grown hugely. And the outside management consultants they employ from time to time are notoriously expensive. Why is it they give external "experts" such credence, while all but ignoring the views of the medical staff?

Rather than ruin my back, when I was appointed, I'd paid for a new office chair as the only pragmatic decision. But I am damned if I am going to pay for the office to be decorated or come in at a weekend to do it myself, one of the ones when I'm not on call. I could charge it as an expense to the Gastroenterology Trust Fund but that doesn't seem ethical, not the use the donors had envisaged.

My maudlin reverie is interrupted as I become aware of the office door opening a little. The head of a dark-haired, middle-aged man intrudes round the side.

'Hi, Doc.'

'Hi.' Does anyone use that abbreviation, doc, anymore? Bugs Bunny excepted – "what's up, Doc?" Luke used to love watching those cartoons – Looney Tunes. Looney reminds me of a notice on one of the secretaries' office walls – "You don't have to be mad to work here, but it helps."

He is still talking. I should pay attention. The door is now fully open, revealing a small man dressed in scruffy clothes, armed with a vacuum cleaner.

'You match watch?' I am puzzled momentarily but then he continues, 'Great goal Rooney score.' Ah yes. We have established during our previous evening exchanges, his limited English notwithstanding, that we are both Manchester United supporters.

'Yes, I watched. Great goal.'

He beams at me, remarkably delighted by my agreement. He appears such a cheerful soul, despite his menial job. A reproof to my despondency just now.

'You work?' he asks.

Am I working or just moping? 'Yes, I work.'

'I come back.' Still smiling, he closes my door. I hear him start to clean the room next door.

My stomach grumbles, ready for dinner. It'll have to make do with some of my small stash of chocolate and a cup of coffee for now. It's decided. I am working. I have a desk to clear of paper. The e-mails, less visible, may have to wait.

18

Sunday morning. I'm tidying the kitchen, having cooked last night. Not my forte or an activity I enjoy, partly because I resent the time involved, but I am trying to make an effort, fill the culinary void left by Clare's absence. Otherwise, Luke might subsist on take-away pizzas and kebabs, supplemented with occasional fish and chips. Perhaps I should buy him some vitamins?

I've doubled the cleaner's hours. The gardener now comes every week. I've less time to keep the garden tidy now I shop for groceries much more. But that's an unexpected pleasure, touring the supermarket, bundling what I want into a trolley, giving only cursory regard to prices. A privilege, that. But most of all, in the supermarket, I enjoy feeling a part of normal life, leaving the oppressive turmoil of the NHS behind.

I wash the salad bowl Clare and I bought on holiday in Avignon over twenty years ago. I can remember the date exactly, 14th July, 1992, Bastille Day. We had arrived at the only campsite in our Volkswagen Golf and parked a little distance from the administration hut while I went to register.

- UNDER CONTROL -

The rude man behind the reception desk was insistent, despite my entreaties, that the site was full. The smirk he offered to his colleague as I left convinced me otherwise.

Clare was incensed and decided that we had been refused entry for the crime of being English. After a tactical retreat of about twenty minutes and with me sunk down into the passenger foot-well, she had driven in without stopping. We erected our tent in one of the available spaces and Clare registered it the following morning. A fait accompli.

That evening we had stood on the famous bridge over the Rhone watching the celebratory fireworks, imaginatively released from a succession of toy boats sailing down the river. After the display ended, we had been borne along by the multitude to the old town square where a band was playing with gusto. We had danced the evening away, in between drinking red wine at a café table on the edge of the square. For us, the universal toast of the day : "Liberte, Egalite, Fraternite", had a somewhat different meaning: our overcoming French antipathy.

Ever since, Clare had always forbidden the bowl being subjected to abrasive pads or the dishwasher for fear of damage to it. Even so, the years have faded its vibrant colours to a pastel palette of red, green and yellow.

I hear the front door close. Luke has gone to play tennis. I glance over my shoulder. Adam, home this weekend, walks in. Black T-shirt tight over his well-developed shoulders and pecs, he looks slightly dishevelled, but happy and a picture of health.

'Hi.'

'Hi.' I place the bowl gently on the draining area. As I turn fully from the kitchen sink towards him, the rubber gloves I'm wearing start to drip on the floor so I remove them.

A concerned look appears on his face. 'You okay?' he asks.

'Yes...But last night?'

'Dad, I'm nineteen,' he declares in exasperation. 'I stayed at a girl's place. When I'm at uni. you don't know if I come home at night, do you?'

The logic of his reply is irrefutable. 'No. Sorry. I suppose I'm a bit sensitive, after Mum.'

He looks at me sympathetically. 'Alright, next time I'll phone or text.'

'Thanks.'

He moves towards me and hugs me. I'm taken aback by this overt display of affection. It's not Adam's style anymore. Then, along with that penetrating gaze of his, he ventures, 'Dad, you seem a bit...

'A bit what?'

'Grumpy.'

'Do you think I'm getting old then?' Why am I being so difficult with him?

'No, quite the opposite. Look, Luke and I have been talking.' They've been discussing me. Hardly surprising. Adam looks awkward but persists. 'It's ten months since Mum died. You need to start looking for someone else. That's what she would have wanted.' He grins. 'At least, go and get yourself a shag.'

I hadn't seen that coming and laugh. 'Then I wouldn't be so grumpy?'

'Probably not.' He laughs as well, the tension broken. 'Is there no one you fancy at the hospital?'

I consider this. Of course, there are attractive women around and a few have started trying to flirt with me, presumably aware of my availability. Why am I not interested? Am I afraid of becoming known as an ageing womaniser and having my dignity undermined? 'I don't know, Adam. It's difficult.'

'Well then, how about a dating website? Loads of people use them now. It's cool, really.' My eldest son is giving me advice, good advice. I should heed it.

'Okay. Tell me what you think is an appropriate website and I'll have a look.'

Disconsolate, that evening I scroll slowly down the smiling faces and personal profiles. There are just so many. I should see that as advantageous but right now it seems overwhelming. I can't fault the choice of website. Have Adam and Luke spent a considerable time selecting it? There are women here with whom I ought to be compatible.

I need to create a short list. The website will facilitate that by allowing me to record my favourites. I suppose I should do this by appearance and then have a further cull of those whose profiles are unappealing. That's logical. Though if love makes fools of us all, logic can't have much to do with it.

There is another dilemma. The younger-looking faces may be more appealing but the younger the woman, the less likely I am to be compatible with her. I want the possibility of a relationship, not just a shag. Maybe I should read the profiles first and then look more closely at appearance, would that be best?

I begin but, before long, my eyes become moist and the words begin to blur.

19

'Just one more'. That's what I'd said to Alan when he'd rung me a little earlier, asking me to call in to the microbiology lab. One last outpatient to see. A final task before I could comply with his request.

Shit! I scowl at the desk-top computer as if it is somehow responsible for the scan result and may repent under my glare. Liver and lung metastases. The location of the primary cancer not identified by the scan, but, on the basis of the blood tumour markers, likely to be in the colon.

I'd seen her for the first time last week and expedited her scan personally, not that it was going to make any difference to her prognosis. The scan had only been reported this afternoon and I was unaware of the result when Alan phoned.

Last time she'd come alone, but today her husband is with her and a child, a dummy in its mouth, thankfully asleep in its buggy. The look on her face, on both their faces, when I tell them.

Incomprehension, disbelief, horror. All their plans destroyed by my words, however kindly and optimistic I try to make them.

And the inevitable questions: Why? Why me? Why my wife? Why so young when we expected to grow old together?

Nowadays, there is the expectation that death, from illness at least, doesn't claim young lives. It is a triumph of modern medicine, but also makes the few exceptions more poignant. No consolation that you are a statistical outlier, the one marked down by fate, just one more.

Once they've gone, my eyes begin to fill. As the outpatient nurse bustles in with a pile of notes, I quickly dry them with a tissue. Not seemly for a consultant to cry, but I'm not made of stone.

****

'Hi, have a seat.' He waves expansively towards the battered chair by the side of his desk. There is an energy about him today, like a restless child. My gloom begins to abate under his radiant smile.

'I've something to show you.' Alan pauses, for dramatic effect or is he uncertain where to begin? 'We've looked for a Helicobacter, or any bacteria for that matter, in the bile from the gallbladders of the gallstone patients. We tried a variety of different techniques and various stains but we can't find any.'

I'm not perturbed by this. His demeanour clearly indicates that good news is on the way. 'It's not that surprising. Bile is a hostile environment for bacteria. Did you know that the Anglo-Saxons used ox bile as an antiseptic?'

'No, I didn't.'

'I thought physicians were omniscient?'

'Not this one.'

'Anyway, when we examined the inner surface of the gallbladders, in the mucus layer, with a couple of the special stains and under high power microscopy, we found these.' He passes me a photograph. There are a few unimpressive black dots adjoining the cells lining the inside of the gallbladder. He taps on them with a biro. 'See?'

'Yes. Are you sure they are bacteria?'

He smiles indulgently, a teacher with a slow pupil. 'I agree, it's difficult to be sure from that photograph alone but look at this one taken with an electron microscope.' He proudly passes me another image for me to inspect. 'That's one of them magnified thirty thousand times. Look, it's rod-shaped with a spiral structure, like a screw without the head. That shape probably helps it to burrow through the mucus lining the gallbladder. And see…' His biro pointer is brought back into action. 'It has these whip-like flagellae at one end to propel it.' He drops his biro back on his desk and sits back in his seat. I wrest my gaze from the electron micrograph and wait for him to pronounce his verdict. 'Its appearance is definitely that of a Helicobacter.'

'Could it be Helicobacter pylori?'

Again, the tolerant smile. Of course he's thought of that. 'As you know, pylori has an enzyme that breaks down urea in gastric juice, generating ammonia that neutralises the acid in its local environment and helps it survive in the stomach. This bacterium has no urease enzyme activity. It's different. It's bili.'

I offer him my hand across the desk. 'Well done, Alan. Well done.' I look again at the electron micrograph. Even after all these years as a doctor, it is still a source of wonder to me that such tiny creatures can kill a person.

'Rather pretty, don't you think?'

Seeing so often the destruction it may cause, I find it difficult to agree, but I don't want to spoil his ebullient mood. 'Pretty? I thought you'd decided it was a boy and now you're implying it's female?'

'A femme fatale?' he suggests.

I nod. I can agree with that.

'I'd offer you champagne but …' He doesn't need to finish. The hospital is an alcohol-free zone. 'How about a coffee instead?'

While he is away temporarily, I regard his room. Larger and more pleasant than mine. There are no patient notes burdening his desk. Instead, small piles of paper laboratory results which I presume he is checking, cluster to one side and two photographs, turned obliquely to me. A variety of plants adorn the remaining surfaces. A red and white amaryllis is flowering majestically. His basement room opens onto a courtyard with yet more plants in pots and a bench. The evening sun is climbing up the wall opposite me, leaving the courtyard in shade.

'Do you like it?' Alan has returned. 'We bombard ourselves with so much information. I sit out there sometimes to clear my head.'

'It's lovely. I wish my office was the same.'

'Okay, where do you suggest we go from here?'

'Well, we've made a start by demonstrating that patients with gallstones have Helicobacter bili in their gallbladders and we can confirm that their bile is supersaturated with cholesterol using the bile samples we've saved from them. But there are three other possible permutations: people with bili but unsaturated bile and people without bili with either supersaturated or unsaturated bile. If we could show that people in those latter three groups didn't have gallstones, it would strengthen our case considerably.'

Warming to my theme, I continue. 'With ethical committee approval, we could collect bile samples from healthy people. They'd have to swallow a tube to enable aspiration of bile from their duodenum so we could measure its cholesterol saturation. But we are left with the problem that the Helicobacter aren't present in bile itself.'

'Umm. You may be able to charm some volunteers into swallowing tubes, but not to donate their healthy gallbladders to medical research.'

"Yes, and I haven't thought of an ethical and practical way to obtain tissue samples from healthy people that we could analyse for bili.'

Alan is still smiling at me benignly, seemingly unfazed by the difficulties, I've outlined. 'So,' he says, 'we need a blood test. That has to be the answer. I'm working on culturing Helicobacter bili. Assuming I can, then we should be able to develop an antibody blood test to identify if it is present in an individual or not.'

'Do you think you could do that, Alan? If you could, our research would really take off.'

'Me alone? No. We're going to need help, and not just a technician. We need an experienced scientist working full time on this and that means money, probably more than your trust fund can stretch to. I think it's time we applied for a research grant.'

I sigh. His suggestion is all too predictable but, nevertheless, I've shied away from thinking about it.

For the first time this evening, his smile slips. 'Is that a problem?'

'Maybe. Let me explain. I've never told anyone this before, apart from Clare. Before I was appointed as a consultant here, I was researching why some of the complications of liver disease occur such as bleeding oesophageal varices, ascites, the terrible itching and so on. Often ideas come to me really easily. Most people would think that was a gift but

I have so many it can sometimes seem like a curse. But the manifestations of liver disease were hard. I read reams and reams of research papers and thought about the problem for months, until eventually I developed a coherent hypothesis. The early results I generated were very encouraging, so I tried to publish them but the prestigious journal to which I submitted my paper appeared to lose it.'

'Lose it?' Alan interrupts. 'What does that mean?'

'It means that after nearly a year of waiting and trying to get a decision, I learnt that one the two reviewers had not responded. In the end, the journal decided to reject my paper.'

'I presume you sent it to another one?'

'Yes, but in the meantime, my ideas were published by somebody I managed to discover later was the reviewer of my paper who had not responded.'

'That's scandalous. I'm really sorry.'

'It's life, Alan.'

'So, what did you do?'

'I did nothing and moved on. What I'd tried to publish was only part of a much larger idea, so I attempted to explore another aspect of it. But, to cut a long story short, I again found my ideas plagiarised before I could publish them.'

'Bloody hell! I've never heard anything that bad before.'

'Unsurprisingly, I didn't embark on any research when I arrived here. I thought I was done with it forever.'

Alan exhales audibly. 'I can see why you're nervous of applying for a grant but the prestigious research bodies must use trustworthy experts.'

'I'm not convinced your last two words sit easily together. The people who stole my ideas were both very eminent. Think about it. If we apply for a grant that's reviewed by someone who's spent most of their professional life researching a problem and they think we may have the answer, how do they wipe their brain clean of our idea? Won't they start work on it straight away? And, given that they're already established with a research team, they're probably well placed to make the potential discoveries first.'

Alan sits Buddha-like, his eyes unfocused, as he considers my sorry tale. I feel guilty to have spoiled his earlier happiness. Eventually, he murmurs, 'I've never thought of myself as naïve but what you've just told me…' His voice trails off. Then, he stands up abruptly and asks, 'What do you want to do?'

'I'll get the money we need. I'm not sure how just yet, but I promise you, I will.' He stares at me, weighing me and my words. I continue hurriedly under his disconcerting scrutiny.

'Alan, there's more to this than just gallstones, important as they may be. What I'm more passionate about investigating is cancer. I'm sorry. I should have been upfront with you about that from the start.'

'Biliary cancers? I'd guessed you were probably thinking about those. After all, the World Health Organisation has declared Helicobacter pylori as a major risk factor for stomach cancer, so Helicobacter bili may be carcinogenic in the bile ducts and gallbladder.'

'Yes, definitely. But they're fairly rare, at least in this country. What would be more important is if bili caused pancreatic cancer.'

'Wow. You'd better explain.' He sits back down.

'Okay. Earlier, you were saying that bile is a hostile environment for a bacterium and it seems to me that pancreatic juice with all those digestive enzymes must be even worse. But think, where do virtually all the pancreatic adenocarcinomas occur? In the head of the gland, near where it converges with the bile duct.'

'I'm with it,' he interjects excitedly. 'If bile refluxes into the pancreatic head, then the mucus layer in that bit of the pancreatic duct may be colonisable by Helicobacter bili.'

'Yes, yes.'

We regard each other and to my surprise, a tear begins to roll down one of his cheeks. He grabs a tissue from the box on his desk and wipes it away. I'm not the only consultant to cry then.

'Sorry.' He turns one of his photographs towards me. An attractive, dark-haired woman flanked by two teenage girls in a flower-filled garden, a picture of happiness. 'My two daughters and their mother, Alison, my first wife. She died of ovarian cancer. What she went through.' He shudders. Then, embarrassment forgotten, he says, 'Of course, I know it's a different disease but if it's cancer you want to investigate, then I'm in, Miles. All the way. I'm in.'

20

Is this stalking?
Doesn't the latest sense of the word imply a repetitive activity? But, considering its primal meaning, I am stalking. It is certainly premeditated. I cancelled my private clinic nearly two weeks ago. Adam's pep talk, which elicits fond amusement whenever I recall it and my subsequent venture on to a dating website, has been salutary. I am obliged to accept that I don't want to find any attractive, compatible woman. No, there is only one woman I desire to be with.

It has been an insidious process. At first, her derision towards me at the time of her husband's death had elicited deep resentment. I know better than her how difficult inserting the stent into his bile duct had been. In less able hands it might have failed and Mark Johnson would have died even sooner.

Subsequently, I began to have more sympathy with the frustration that had driven her scorn. And, like a poker to a fire, the negative emotions she had engendered also stirred into vivid life more positive ones, my memories of the first time we met. Initially, as in the past, I had tried to suppress them.

Having betrayed Clare with Freya, is it a repetition of that betrayal to want to be with Freya again? I do not know. But there is no escape. Freya intrudes relentlessly into my thoughts, disturbs my sleep, become an obsession I can no longer deny. I must do something.

Adam and Luke are encouraging me to find a woman to be with. They do not need to know about the past. And Clare would want me to be happy. I am not happy now and, without Freya, cannot contemplate being so.

But why should Freya be interested in me? I have evaluated this repeatedly. Apparently, she has no memory of our night together. To her recollection, she has only spoken to me under distressing circumstances. Won't I be an unwelcome reminder of experiences she wants to put behind her?

On the other hand, with the passage of time since her husband's death, perhaps her attitude towards me will have softened and become more reasonable. And I have a peace offering to set before her. Alan has identified Helicobacter bili in tissue samples I have taken recently at ERCP from patients with pancreatic cancer. It is not that much but it is a recognition that her plea was heeded, however intemperately it was delivered. It is hope. Hope that Alan and I may make progress with this dreadful disease.

Even though she does not remember it, I am encouraged in my tortured musings, to recall that she found me attractive once before. I remember the false surname she booked us in under at the pub. Will she still view me as "Mr. Wright"? I haven't changed physically that much, neither of us has. That's one reason why I don't want to approach her through a disembodied phone call or e-mail, not that I know her e-mail address.

But that day, there was more than just an atavistic physical attraction. We were easy in each other's company, in harmony before we had even touched, though whether, in my entranced state at the time and with the distortions of memory, that is a correct judgement is uncertain.

That was then. Life has changed us both mentally, if not that much physically. Now? Now is unknowable unless I see her. And is now too soon? Her emotions too raw after Mark's death? Yet if I wait, other men will begin to make advances towards her and I do not think, with my feelings as they are, that I can wait any longer.

So, I sit here in my car near the entrance of her house. Not that it is visible, only the high metal gates and a tree-lined drive. I hadn't anticipated this problem but it has dispelled any consideration of ringing her doorbell. I'm not going to talk into the intercom by the gates.

Without sight of the house, there is no clue as to whether anyone is home. I hadn't wanted to commit the subterfuge of telephoning that morning and putting the phone down if she answered. It seemed too devious and regardless, when I looked at Mark's case notes for her address, there were only his and her mobile numbers recorded, no landline. Would she answer a withheld number call? No, I must do this face to face.

I try to reassure myself that she is there. Schools are in session. She won't be on holiday without her daughter. It is too soon for her to have subjected them to the upheaval of moving home, even if she is so inclined. Another reason for me to act now. I have been here since eight thirty this Saturday morning and just have to wait for her to appear.

Fortunately, this road is on the edge of town. There are few pedestrians who may become suspicious of my persistent presence. Except for this one, who I can see in my rear-view mirror: a short, grey-haired woman returning with her dog. The last time she walked by, peering officiously at me, I pretended to be speaking on my mobile - the responsible motorist, not driving and phoning simultaneously. More than half an hour has passed since then. Is my façade still credible? I decide to simulate that I am arguing and turn my head away from her as she passes. Is this really necessary? I hardly look like a burglar casing a joint in my large, shiny BMW.

But perhaps she perceives me as a sexual predator awaiting his prey. Not too far from the truth. I laugh and my tension eases.

Come on Freya, you can't stay in all day.

As if in answer to my plea, her metal gates begin to open slowly inwards. I start my car. It is pointing towards town. She is likely to go that way. Her black Mercedes appears and sets off in the predicted direction.

I follow at a distance. She enters a large car park, thankfully not a multi-storey one. I might have lost her then. Even so, she has taken the last space. Then, a car pulls out in front of me and I hurriedly occupy the vacated position. I am fortunate again as I can see now that she is alone. Wearing tight white yoga pants which tantalisingly reveal every movement of her long legs and a pink top, she begins to walk towards the centre of town. Like I'm a pet dog on a lengthy lead, she trails me behind her as we progress to the High Street.

This pleasant procession ends as she enters a dress shop. I can hardly follow her in there. Instead, I loiter, appearing to look in shop windows. She must have been in there half an hour by now. Is she trying everything in the place?

Still, I must be patient. My plan is on track. I only need to pick the right moment and location before feigning an accidental encounter.

Here she is, now festooned with two large maroon bags emblazoned with the shop's name. I resume my pursuit, both of us weaving through the myriad pedestrians enjoying the June sunshine. For a moment, I lose sight of her and cast around anxiously before realising she has disappeared into another shop. Shoes now. Men's ones are also on sale but it doesn't seem suitable to my purpose. I pretend to contemplate the window display of a jeweller on the opposite side of the street. Not as long this time and with only one more bag, she emerges and tugs me further down the street.

A small, involuntary gasp of amazement escapes my lips as she enters the card and book shop, the one where we first met all those years ago. Ideal and a favourable augury. I quickly follow her inside. From a distance I can see that she is browsing the birthday cards. Wasn't it about this time of year we were here together last time? I remember. She has a nephew.

Here goes. I walk determinedly towards her. 'Oh, hi,' I say.

She turns to look at me. There is a moment's hesitation, which I hope is because my being here is out of context, before she favours me with a warm smile. 'Doctor Westwood. Hi.'

Despite my plans, seeing her before me like this has rendered me temporarily dumb. She does not fill the silence but continues to regard me with a pleasant expression. 'How are you?' I manage. Almost a reflex expression in my professional life.

She tilts her head slightly before murmuring hesitantly, 'Okay.' Nodding, as if on further consideration, she agrees with her assessment. She continues, 'I'm glad I bumped into you here.' She drops her eyes briefly. 'I want to apologise.'

I open my mouth to object but she raises a hand to forestall me. 'Yes, I do,' she states firmly. 'What I said to you was rude and unwarranted. I know you did your best to help Mark and he was very grateful to you. I should have been as well but it all became too much for me. Even so, I shouldn't have lashed out at you. It was cruel. I hope you'll forgive me.' She looks at me expectantly after her gushing apology.

'Of course. I understand.'

'Thank you. I know now that you've been through it too. After we last spoke, the nurse you left me with, Sarah. She was so nice. Everyone was so kind to me. She told me that you had lost your wife not long before. I'm sorry.'

I sigh. 'At least my wife died suddenly. She didn't have to endure what your husband did. And what you said to me, it made me think more about pancreatic cancer and because of that, a colleague and I have begun some research into it.'

'Really? You're not just saying that to make me feel less guilty?'

'Really. Look, shall we go and get a coffee and I'll tell you about it?'

The coffee shop is almost opposite. As we sit, she struggles to cram her bags into the space beside the table then gives them a dismissive wave. 'Retail therapy,' she offers.

'Why not?'

'Yes, why not. I'm lucky in some ways. Mark left me well provided for.' A waitress comes and takes our order. Freya resumes our conversation. 'After I saw you last, I realised that we had met before Mark became your patient.'

She's remembered!

'It was many years ago. I couldn't expect you to recall.'

What is she talking about? How could I forget?

'You must see so many patients. I'd been injured in a car crash and you came into my room by mistake, looking for someone else.'

Now I'm with it. Better play along. 'Yes, I do remember now. You'd hurt your head and had broken an arm.'

'Well done.'

'I hope there was no lasting damage?'

'No, I was lucky. I seem to be back in full working order.'

'That's great.'

The waitress sets down our coffees on the table, Freya's is a latte and mine black. She looks at my drink and suggests, 'A little austere. You're not, are you? Austere.'

'No. I'm just an ordinary man.'

She smiles. 'I think you're too modest. Tell me about your research.'

21

'Ladies and gentlemen, I hope you have enjoyed your lunch. As you know, my husband and your colleague, Mark, died of cancer of the pancreas four months ago. I have to tell you it is not the way any of us would want to go, at any age, let alone Mark's relative youth. The consultant physician, Doctor Miles Westwood, who was treating Mark, is developing some highly original and promising ideas into this horrible illness. To facilitate this research and honour Mark's memory, I have created the Mark Johnson Memorial Fund to which I hope you will contribute today.'

I sit rapt with admiration as Freya delivers her introductory speech. In a demure navy-blue dress, black shoes with low heels and her hair tied back, her appearance is a flawless meld of recent widow, businesswoman and beautiful hostess. In the four weeks since we discussed it in the coffee shop, she has organised this event. There must be around fifty people here, the majority colleagues of Mark and Freya at Statesbank, some with wives or husbands. Judging by the cars parked outside and the women's jewellery, they certainly appear suitably affluent.

And this room is magnificent, accommodating with ease the six round tables at which the guests are sat. Full length windows, draped with tied back, floor length, emerald green curtains, looking out over a wide south-facing terrace and park-like grounds allow the light to stream in. Despite Freya's sobering words, her guests are clearly enjoying themselves and will hopefully be more inclined to donate.

'So now', Freya concludes, 'Doctor Westwood is going to tell us about his research and how, if you wish, you can help.' She looks directly at me. 'Miles.' She beckons me on to the low platform at the end of the room, probably intended primarily for a band, and steps down.

I start by explaining briefly how medicine's understanding of Helicobacter pylori has been a major advance. How the bacterium is usually acquired in early childhood and then resides in the stomach for the rest of that person's life, unless eradicated by antibiotics. In some people, it may do little harm but in others it causes ulcers or stomach cancer. Having imparted that background information, it is easier to explain the potential significance of the Helicobacter bili Alan and I have discovered. I keep it brief and invite questions.

A middle-aged man in a beige suit waves his hand at me and enquires in a sceptical tone, 'Are you claiming you'll be able to cure pancreatic cancer with ordinary antibiotics?'

'No. No, I'm not. Let me explain better. It's known that the development of cancer is a multi-step process, often occurring over many years. Pancreatic cancers usually arise on a background of chronic inflammation that my colleague and I are hypothesising may be induced by Helicobacter bili. The inflammation causes the cells to divide repeatedly as part of the repair process and this is meant to stop once the damage is corrected. But eventually, in some people, a cell escapes the regulatory control.'

'Like a rogue banker,' interjects a wag on a rear table, to scattered laughter.

'No comment. Anyway, this rogue cell continues to divide and is the beginning of a cancer.'

'This regulatory control, that's your immune system, right?' asks the original questioner.

'Yes, that's correct.'

'So, if we boost our immune systems, we are less at risk, okay?'

'In theory. But there's a lot of nonsense written about this in the popular press. In practice, the best way to do that is to stay slim.' He pulls his jacket together to cover his paunch as I say this. I hope I haven't lost a donor. 'And to stay young,' I suggest, partly to lessen any offence I may have caused those members of the audience who are overweight.

The wag finds this irresistible. 'If you've got a pill for that, you can count on me contributing.' I decide it's not in my interest to respond.

'The essential point, though, is that while we may not be able to cure pancreatic cancer, we may be able to prevent it happening by getting rid of the bacterium. Prevention is better than cure. It's not as glamorous, partly because an individual never knows if he or she has been spared from developing the disease.'

I pause to let this sink in before continuing, 'Another reason why we need to develop the antibody blood test I mentioned earlier, is not just to determine if Helicobacter bili is present much more often in patients with pancreatic cancer or gallstones than healthy people, but later to start screening healthy people to see if they are harbouring the bacterium and are at risk.'

An attractive young brunette in a yellow dress blurts out

in evident alarm, 'Are you saying some of us here may have this bug inside us?'

'Yes, some of you probably do. The unpleasant reality is that we are all infested with a huge variety of bacteria, inside and out. For example, there are more bacteria in our colons than cells in our body. And viruses are even more insidious. They get into our cells, sometimes even inserting themselves into our DNA. The understanding of the harm some of them cause us is still fairly rudimentary but, in my opinion, many of us already carry the seeds of our eventual destruction within us.' This unplanned and somewhat apocalyptic pronouncement stifles further questions but seems to have created an opportune moment to present my proposal to them.

'As you've heard from Freya, we are hoping that some of you will contribute to the Mark Johnson Memorial Fund today. But I would like to offer you something in return for your possible donations. If you are prepared to contribute five thousand pounds, then, when our antibody blood test is established, we will test you and four other family members to see if you are infected with Helicobacter bili and, if you are, prescribe appropriate antibiotics for you.'

I wait as they consider and discuss my proposal. Five thousand pounds seems to me too much to request. However, Freya has persuaded me that the guests wouldn't be impressed if I asked for less and has told me that Mark's memorial fund is a registered charity, so their contributions will be tax deductible. Nobody looks unhappy and the young woman in yellow is beaming at me.

Beige suit waves to attract my attention. 'Why don't we all just take some antibiotics and get rid of the bug, if we've got it, right now?' He looks smug. Does his ego demand he knows best, is cleverer than others or perhaps he can't restrain himself from competing?

'Unfortunately, it's not as easy as that. Helicobacter pylori, the stomach bug, can only be eradicated by taking three or four drugs together. Even then, in about 15% of patients the treatment fails because their Helicobacter is resistant to one or more of the antibiotics used and we have to try again with different ones. And though Helicobacter bili is likely to be susceptible to the same antibiotics as pylori, we don't know that yet.'

He looks about to utter a follow-up question but an older woman in a lime-green jacket on the adjoining front table declares peremptorily, 'My turn, Steve.' Steve doesn't look as though he wants to argue with her.

She turns to me and asks, 'Once you've done all you hope to do, you still won't know that your Helicobacter causes pancreatic cancer. Forgive me, but I'm a lawyer. I accept that you'll have built a strong circumstantial case but not enough to convict, so to speak.'

She's right, of course. I'd hoped not to have attention drawn to this but the audience today is too sharp for that to have been a realistic expectation. 'I agree. I do have an idea how we may achieve that but I need to allow our work to progress before exploring its feasibility and discussing it.'

'You've plenty to do then,' she states in a mildly teasing tone.

'Yes, and that's why we would be grateful for your support.'

Freya has been hovering nearby and now steps back onto the platform. 'I think we should let Doctor Westwood off the hook now. Please do stay and enjoy the remainder of the day here. We'll be serving tea and cake soon on the terrace.'

Later, I stand alone on Freya's terrace amidst the discarded glasses, cups and plates scattered around me, admiring the large garden. 'Miles.' Freya hurries towards me. 'They've all gone now,' she says in a rush.

'So how did we do?'

'Guess.' She's smiling so broadly; it can't be bad news.

'I don't know. A hundred thousand?'

'More. Try again.'

'Two hundred then.' She bounces up and down a little in her excitement.

'Two hundred and twenty-five thousand. How about that?'

'That's amazing. How…?'

'Well, some were here as couples but every individual or couple agreed to donate at least £5,000. None of them wanted to look cheap. Some offered £10,000 providing you'd do ten blood samples to test their extended family. That's okay, isn't it?'

'Yes, of course.' This hasn't sunk in yet. 'Do you think some of them, on reflection, will change their mind?'

'No way. They saw me write it down on my list. They'd be too embarrassed to withdraw and frankly, I don't think any of them will want to. You really sold it to them.'

'Thanks. Even that Steve?'

'Yep. Steve can be a bit of a pain sometimes but he's okay. You handled him well. He's the sort that doesn't respect you unless you stand up to him. He's down for £10,000. And Sue, she's giving ten thousand as well.'

'Sue?'

'The one who asked you the last question.' Freya grins. 'She told me she thinks you're dishy.'

I grin back. 'Her point was good but I wasn't as impressed by her facelift.'

Freya giggles and lightly smacks me on a shoulder.

'Never say that to anyone else. She's my boss and in charge of compliance.'

So that's why Steve shut up when she told him to. 'Don't worry. I can be discreet.'

'Come on. There's something I want to show you.'

I've heard her say that before, all those years ago, and struggle to stop myself smiling at the recollection. She grasps my arm briefly and steers me towards the stone steps down to her garden. The evening is warm and calm. We walk along the long lawn between two deep borders resplendent with clumps of summer flowers. Their scent hangs heavy in the still air.

'Sue may not have been to your taste but you seemed to like Kate well enough.'

'Kate?'

'Yellow dress and cleavage. I saw her give you her card. Remember? You were talking to her long enough.'

'I couldn't get away, Freya. I was hoping you'd come and rescue me.' This is only half true. I'm not interested in Kate. Rather, I'm practising what I preached to Luke. I'd deliberately lingered over the exchange of Kate's card, giving more time for Freya to notice. I take it out of my pocket and hand it to Freya. Symbolically, she tears it in half and puts it in one of her pockets.

We walk between a scattering of trees at the end of the lawn and emerge on a long ridge. A patchwork of fields, woods and an occasional house stretches out before us towards the south coast. A truly marvellous vista, a vision of peace and tranquillity in the soft early evening light. Freya gestures towards a wooden seat. 'Mark loved it here, just to sit and unwind.'

She begins to move towards the seat but I catch her arm to stop her. It doesn't seem right for me to sit in Mark's place, despite the fact that I had sex with his wife and want to do so again.

Freya probably misunderstands my action. She gives me a brief questioning look before pulling my head towards her and kissing me. I need no further encouragement. One of my hands is stroking her silken hair, the other initially round her waist, slides down before pulling her firmly against my erection.

She leans her head back, gasping a little but smiling. Without a word, she takes me by the hand and leads me back towards the house.

****

I open my eyes. Freya, propped on one elbow, is staring down at me. 'You look very peaceful when you sleep. And you don't snore,' she adds mischievously. Her hair is tousled and her eye make up slightly smudged but this makes her even more desirable to me.

'I'm not surprised. You made sure that I was exhausted last night.'

A cloud seems to pass over her face. 'Do you think I'm awful? It's only four months since Mark died and here I am, jumping into bed with you.' She sighs and then begins to kiss me.

Our passion is curtailed by a harsh buzzing, followed by, 'Hi, Freya. It's Annabel. Sorry I'm a bit early.'

Freya presses a button on the wall by the bed. I presume she is opening the gates to the drive. 'Okay, Annabel.' She shakes her head and climbs out of bed, before draping a cerise silk robe around herself. 'A bit early!' Freya exclaims disgustedly, now that Annabel can no longer hear. 'She told me she'd bring her back at lunchtime.' She leans towards me and gives me a brief kiss, before hurrying out the door.

Reluctantly, I decide I had better get dressed. I hear the front door close as I descend the sweeping staircase into the entrance hall. Freya is talking to a girl, perhaps fourteen years old. 'Lily, this is Miles.'

Lily. One of my grandmothers was called that. A beautiful name, flowering again. And she is certainly a beautiful girl, fine regular features with her mother's blonde hair and blue eyes. 'Hi, Lily.' I attempt a charming smile but it's difficult under these awkward circumstances.

She glares at me, then tears start to flow down her cheeks. 'I know who you are. You were Daddy's doctor. You didn't make Daddy better and now you want Mummy.' She turns and runs from the hall.

Cruel, but correct.

22

I've sent flowers, the time-honoured twelve red roses. They should have arrived yesterday, certainly no later than today. But it is nearly ten pm and I've heard nothing from her. I must check with the shop tomorrow that they were delivered. Perhaps her housekeeper forgot to tell her about them? Maybe she's working really late to meet a deadline or distracted by some more important issue? More important to her, that is. Ah, this speculation is pointless. May as well try to get some sleep, see what tomorrow brings.

'Ping' goes my mobile as I arrive at work the next day. 'Thanks for the flowers, Freya', the message reads. A bit curt. I'm not sure of the best way to respond and I'm going to be late for my endoscopy list. I'll wait 'til this evening.

I settle on: 'Please can I take you out for dinner this weekend?' If I text anything more, will it look too keen and scare her away? "Treat them mean, keep them keen" flits through my mind. Is that what she's doing to me? Surely, she realises that's unnecessary, but who knows?

'Ping.' It's nearly midnight and I'd just managed to fall

asleep. I should have turned the damn thing off. I'm in thrall to it now. With trepidation, I pick up my phone and view the message: 'Can we meet for coffee, Saturday afternoon, same place on the High Street?'

My heart feels as if it's been attached to a block of concrete and thrown overboard. At least she's not dumped me by text. I'll have a chance to persuade her to continue our relationship face to face. What have I done wrong? Is it Lily's antipathy to me or something more?

I've arrived early, chosen a semi-secluded table by the window. The sun is shining in through the large plate-glass window creating a cheerful ambience. My coffee has gone cold, neglected as I wistfully watch the passers-by parade before me along the High Street. Here she is. Navy blue trousers, elegant but not figure-hugging, sensible shoes and a pale blue blouse with only the top button undone. Not a seductive ensemble, I note wryly. But she still looks stunning. She sits opposite me and offers a tentative smile.

'A latte?' I suggest. She nods, so I attract the attention of a waitress and place the order.

Freya opens her stylish brown handbag, prominently labelled: "Prada" and withdraws two sheets of paper and a bank card. She pushes them across the table towards me. 'These are the bank details, latest statement and a card for Mark's fund. You can withdraw whatever you need, as necessary. You don't need my authorisation'.

I'm pleasantly surprised. At least she trusts me. 'Thank you. This is going to make such a difference to our research.'

'I know.' There is an awkward silence that I don't know how to fill. 'Miles, I owe you an apology.'

'I can't think why.'

She shuts her eyes momentarily before replying, perhaps

summoning the determination necessary. 'Last Sunday, I was caught up in the excitement of the day, our fund-raising success. And jumping into bed with you like that… Look, it was good, no complaints, but it was indulgent. I feel I've led you on but now can't give you what I think you want from me. I need time and I have to think of Lily. Mark's death has really mixed her up.'

How can I be annoyed with her looking so sad? 'Freya, I should have shown more restraint. I plead guilty to finding you irresistible.' My attempt to inject a lighter note seems to have failed. Her face remains inscrutable. I resume, 'What I don't understand is that you told me you were taking the pill.'

'I am,' she quickly reassures me. 'I didn't lie.'

'I believe you, but that's not what I meant.'

She looks at me ruefully and sighs. 'My life hasn't been orderly for some time now. It doesn't seem fair because I'm normally so disciplined. But I've learned that, once in a while, I can be reckless, rebelling against my self-imposed constraints and I don't want any more problems. Does that make sense?'

'Yes. I understand. Freya, I can give you time. As long as you need.'

She looks out of the window. I wait painfully for her to continue. 'Annabel, the mother of Lily's best friend, has a villa in Spain, part of her divorce settlement. She's invited Lily and me to join them there. We're flying tomorrow.'

'How long for?'

'Six weeks. The bank has been good. We're going to have a complete break. I'm even leaving my phone behind. Don't want anyone contacting me and sorry, that includes you.'

I try not to let disappointment show on my face. 'Okay.' What else can I say?

'I need you to understand, I can't make you any promises.'

She plucks something from her handbag and places it on the table in front of me. When she removes her hand, I see a business card.

'What's that?'

'Kate's card. Like the one I tore up.'

I stare at her in amazement before sweeping the card away onto the floor. I stand, pick up the bank papers, and fling a ten-pound note on the table. 'Have a good holiday.'

23

Jane and I are standing by the patients' notes trolley on Rose Ward waiting to begin the ward round. One of my team is on the telephone chasing an urgent result, another is answering his bleep and the registrar is delayed in A& E. Nurses, as usual, are in short supply. 'What do you think?' asks Jane.

I think of Freya is the first answer that springs to mind. I have to keep banishing such thoughts to enable me to concentrate on work but, of course, that isn't the answer Jane is seeking. 'What about?'

'Moving wards.'

'What! I don't know anything about that.' She recoils a little in shock and at my obvious annoyance.

'Sorry. I presumed the management must have consulted you about it.'

'No, it's me that should be sorry, Jane. Not fair to shoot the messenger. But nobody told me about this, let alone discussed it with me. So where are they proposing we go?'

'Dahlia. It will be less work. It's only got twenty beds.'

That's one of the things I like about Jane, she's a "half-full" person, always looks on the bright side.

'Presumably then, there are three bays of six and two side rooms.'

'Yes, I've been and had a nosey round.'

'Only one single sex bay for …?'

'For men.'

'We'll never accommodate all the male gastroenterology inpatients in six to eight beds. We've not enough as it is, without losing the eight more we have here.' I shake my head. 'What does Marian think about this?'

'She's tearing her hair out. She was only told yesterday. Not all the nurses are moving and she's having to revise the rotas and make all the arrangements ready for Monday.'

'So, it's definitely decided then?'

'Oh, yes.'

'Which Monday?'

'This coming one.'

Three days' time. Why am I not more surprised? Our current management do not even pay lip service to working as a team with the medical and nursing staff anymore. I'll come back later and speak to Marian, the ward sister, but first I have a round to do.

****

'Good afternoon. I'm Doctor Westwood. Please may I see Mr Lytle?' I ask one his secretaries. No, not secretary, consultants have secretaries or rather a share of one. Managers have individual personal assistants who are paid more. Mr Lytle has three.

She checks his diary on her computer screen. 'He could

- JOHN THORNTON -

see you next Tuesday morning,' she says officiously.

'Sorry, but it's urgent, about moving wards this coming Monday.' I attempt an ingratiating smile, even if this does not reflect my mood.

After a brief hesitation, she appears to relent. 'I'll see what I can do. Would you take a seat outside? Please,' she adds as an after-thought. I settle into one of the two hard chairs in the corridor opposite his office, reminiscent of a naughty schoolboy awaiting the headmaster. I presume he's going to make me wait a while.

His name is on the door in gold letters: Max Lytle, Chief Executive Officer. I've never understood the need for the extra aggrandisement of "officer." If you're the boss, you must be one. How would "major general officer" sound, I ponder irreverently.

Fifteen minutes later, the personal assistant announces, 'Mr Lytle will see you now.' I walk through the anteroom, brace myself and knock on his door.

'Come.' He is seated behind a large solid wood, probably walnut, desk. Its surface is commendably tidy and shining, as if it has just been polished. He frowns briefly, most likely because, like him, I am wearing a jacket and tie. These garments are forbidden by the Trust for medical staff to wear in clinical areas of the hospital. The prohibition is ostensibly to reduce infection transmission, though I have never seen any convincing evidence to support this. I suspect that the management were secretly pleased at doctors losing such status enhancing apparel. But he can't object that I'm wearing them now, well away from patients.

His tie is an attention-attracting vibrant red, arguably a provocative assertion of rank, a red rag to a bull. His thinning brown hair is sprinkled with dandruff, like icing sugar on a sponge cake. With a brief flick of his right hand, as if batting away an irritating insect, he indicates I should take the chair opposite him.

I find my eye line is below his and notice that his desk and chair are on a pedestal, a common trick to promote dominance. He sits back in his seat, purses his lips, and without a hint of embarrassment, scrutinises me. As no words of welcome are forthcoming, I presume he is waiting for me to begin.

'Thank you for seeing me. I only learnt this morning that it's planned for the gastroenterology ward to move.' I pause, more in hope than expectation that he may express some regret about the short notice and lack of consultation. Even if I can't change his mind, perhaps I can encourage more collaboration in the future. He remains silent, so I continue.

'I want to point out to you that we will lose eight beds. Personally, I don't mind caring for overflow gastroenterology patients on other wards but the Trust has now discouraged consultants having outliers.'

He is sitting back in his seat, his fingers steepled, almost as if in prayer. A gesture displaying superiority but to me it seems ironic as I am the supplicant here. He is almost immobile, not even a nod of encouragement. Nevertheless, I have his attention so press on.

'It's generally acknowledged that patients being under appropriate specialists provides better outcomes and a higher quality of care. Also, a study performed here ....' I restrain myself from saying before you arrived a few years ago, showed that this led to a shorter length of stay. So, if the eight patients in those beds we're losing stay longer because they don't have specialist gastroenterology treatment, then there are fewer beds available for those attending A&E. Consequently, the proposed ward move for gastroenterology would be inefficient for the hospital, as well as to the detriment of patients.'

There is a fierce glint in his eyes. I wonder if I've overdone it with the final comments. The mission statement he wrote on arrival at the Trust, a copy of which is displayed ostentatiously on the wall behind him, repeatedly stresses the goal of providing excellent patient care. But that, it soon becomes clear, is not what has upset him.

He leans towards me. 'The ward move is not, as you put it, "proposed". It is decided. Decided by the management. We have wider considerations than your parochial concerns.' It is potentially a valid argument but he does not deign to share these "wider considerations" with me, or indeed why he considers optimising patient care "parochial". I try a different tack.

'I hope you realise how disruptive this is, particularly the short notice. For example, the ward sister had planned to take this weekend off, as it's her daughter's birthday party on Sunday. Now she will have to work that day to enable the move. She's very good. I don't want to lose her.' Foolish comment, my wishes don't count. 'She's an asset to the Trust,' I add.

'We all have to make sacrifices,' he declares pompously.

I'm beginning to think who I'd like to sacrifice.

'You will at least pay her for this extra work, won't you?'

He considers this for a few moments. 'She'll need to complete an EDC form.' He raises a podgy index finger, discouraging any potential interruption. 'An exceptional duties claim form. It's an innovation of mine, to enable managers to be rewarded when they exceed their contractual hours. She's designated as the ward manager so I think we could consider her eligible. And, before you ask, it isn't an entitlement available to medical and other clinical staff.'

He is smirking at me and rocks a little, back and forth in his chair, perhaps facilitated by his short legs not touching the floor. 'While you're here, I am told you have begun some research. Gallstones, isn't it?'

'Yes, that's right. We think they may be caused by a bacterium and, if so, we may be able to prevent them re-occurring after we dissolve them or even stop them happening in the first place.'

'I see. Do you realise that the Trust is paid £3,600 for every gallbladder removed and that the operation earns us a total of nearly £200,000 every year?' I didn't, but it seems an answer from me is not required as he continues quickly. 'While you're busy trying to undermine our revenue stream, it is imperative that you do not lose sight of your primary role.'

I know I shouldn't, but this man has got under my skin. 'And that is?'

He scowls. 'And that is helping the Trust to meet its clinical targets.' Based on our earlier exchanges, I am in no doubt that this is not the same as providing excellent patient care.

'I would point out, Mr Lytle, that every year I see more new outpatients than the majority of my physician colleagues and that the various endoscopic procedures I perform generate considerable income for the Trust.'

'Glad to hear it.' He doesn't sound it. He regards me with a self-satisfied expression, lacking in any warmth. 'Well, I think we understand each other better now,' he states sardonically.

I hold his gaze and reply, 'Yes, we do.'

24

There is something invigorating about teaching. The questions you pose and are asked in turn often stimulate a fresh assessment of a case and identify lacunae in your knowledge. Not that the students have much information to impart yet, but what is that saying about fools being able to ask questions even the wisest man can't answer? They certainly aren't fools. They all have good minds. The trick is to encourage them to use them. Not that today is a problem. It is the last day of their six week "firm". All present and keen to impress, just before we grade them.

Four girls and two boys, or rather four young women and two young men, since they are all in their early twenties. The gender distribution is an accurate microcosm of today's medical student demographics. Medicine has become less popular with boys, who increasingly are attracted to more lucrative occupations with quicker progression. A Porsche by the time you're thirty isn't going to happen with a medical career. Fortunately, women still want to be doctors, possibly even more so now that gender equality is widely observed and part-time work accepted.

We have just finished. I pull back the bed-side curtains and thank the patient, Mrs Patel. All the students echo my gratitude before thanking me - keen to tick the courtesy box before their grading? Am I growing cynical?

We move away from the bed and five of them, chattering, disperse. Kelly hangs back. Able, assertive and undeniably attractive, she should do well. What does she want?

My unvoiced question appears to be answered as she offers me a card and gushes, 'Doctor Westwood, we're all so grateful for your excellent teaching. We've arranged an end of firm party tomorrow to express our appreciation to you and our other teachers. Doctor Roberts is coming. We are hosting it together with the firm on Tulip Ward and the two consultants there are coming as well, so we really hope you can make it.'

I am not keen on these events, though on this occasion I have no competing arrangements. 'Could I let you know tomorrow?'

Disappointment descends on her face, before being quickly superseded by a forced smile. 'Of course, I'll write my mobile number on the back of the invite for you. One more thing, I still don't feel confident palpating spleens, would you mind terribly showing me how to do it again on Mrs Patel?'

I can hardly refuse. I incline my head in the direction of the patient. 'No problem.'

We walk back to the patient's bedside, gain her permission, and pull the curtains once again. Kelly takes her place next to the right side of the patient's bed while I stand opposite. I offer a few comments. She listens attentively. While I speak, I find myself appraising her afresh. Her glossy auburn hair is a testament to her youth, the bloom on her cheeks an indication of her high blood oestrogen levels dilating her facial blood vessels and, I can't help thinking, boosting her sex drive.

I gesture for her to begin. She places her right hand on the patient's umbilicus and begins to palpate sequentially upwards and across towards Mrs Patel's left side. As Kelly leans forward more, her loose blouse bows out, revealing a generous cleavage.

She chooses that moment to look up at me. I needn't have felt guilty about ogling her breasts, it quickly becomes apparent. She gives me an alluring smile, a mischievous glint in her blue eyes and in a sweet, girlish tone enquires, 'Do you want me…….to do it like this?'

The pause is unmistakeable, as is the brazen meaning it gives to her words. Breath-taking – quite literally, I notice. I am no longer wearing a wedding ring as a deterrent to her advances, though on this evidence I doubt it would have made much difference. She has always been flirtatious, but I didn't expect this. Awkwardness must be evident on my face, but it only makes her smile wider.

'Perhaps if you turned the tips of your fingers more towards the patient's ribs, rather than using the sides of your fingers, you could feel her spleen more easily.'

She isn't fooled by my bluster. 'Oh yes, that's better.' She straightens up. 'It's so good having a one-to-one with you.'

Time to draw this to a close.

'Thank you, Mrs Patel.' Fortunately, her English is limited. I doubt she has perceived the sexual tension in the dialogue between Kelly and me. A contest I have undoubtedly lost.

'See you tomorrow then?' She winks at me before turning away. Is it my imagination or is she exaggerating the sway of her hips?

I wander back towards my office, slightly dazed. I had

resolved to clear all my paperwork and e-mails before leaving, but now it is going to be difficult to concentrate.

Do I want her... to do it like this?

25

The scent of newly mown grass fills my nostrils. It was a little damp to have cut after the shower this morning but I was not going to have another opportunity any time soon. The sky is now clear and the blazing August sun has glued my shirt to my back. I sit on a bench to survey my efforts. Joan's walled garden, as always at this time of year, is tidy and filled with a conglomeration of colour, especially her beloved dahlias. (I wish I loved my new Dahlia Ward as much). Her greenhouse, though, would benefit from renovation: two of the panes of glass are cracked and the paint is badly peeling.

The cherry blossom tree looks healthy but hasn't grown much. I presume it's establishing its roots first.

A gull struts along the top of the wall at the end of the garden then stops to regard me. If Freya was a bird, what would she be? Not a gull, that's for sure. A bird of paradise? That's no good, the attractive ones are the males. Perhaps a swan? I know I have to move forward but I begin to feel guilty thinking about Freya in sight of Clare's cherry tree. What bird would Clare have been?

'A penny for your thoughts.' She chuckles. 'Not much of a deal anymore, is it? Just a penny.'

Lost in my whimsical reverie, I had not noticed Joan, now nearly eighty, appear behind me. 'Here you are. I've put some ice in it.' She hands me a large glass of water which I drink greedily.

'Thanks. Just what I needed.'

She smiles, crinkling the skin around her eyes even more. Her teeth are too good to be real. 'Your lines are straighter than my gardener's.'

I laugh. 'So where is he?'

'Gone to his sister's villa in Spain for six weeks. Marbella, I think.'

'That's a long time for a gardener to be away at this time of year, isn't it?'

'Oh, he's not a proper gardener, just a recently retired local man.'

'Don't you think you should get someone more regularly?' I hesitate a moment but I've been wanting to broach this subject for a while. 'I'd be happy to pay.'

She looks up at my face. I hope I haven't offended her. After a few seconds she says, 'You're right. I do need more help. But I'm fine for money.'

'Okay, but I just want you to know that if you ever do need a hand financially, I'll help.'

'I'm grateful Miles, but you spend your money on those boys of yours.'

'Not boys anymore.'

'No.' She looks wistful. 'Shall we have some tea? I've just made scones but we'll have to eat them in the conservatory. The gulls can be very aggressive.'

We walk slowly up to the conservatory where Joan has

laid a small table with fine China in a muted floral pattern, a plate of scones, and a choice of strawberry or raspberry jam. She goes to fetch the tea as I gaze out over the sea. She returns with a tea pot, sits on the padded wicker chair opposite me and begins to pour two cups of tea.

'So, how are your young men these days? What's Luke planning to do with himself?'

'He's still undecided.'

'I thought he was thinking of being a doctor, like you. Shouldn't you encourage him?'

I shake my head. 'No, I don't think so. The job is good. I do love it. But it's becoming harder and harder to do it well. The system is failing.'

'You mean the NHS?'

'Yes. Too political, too many managers, excessive bureaucracy and, of course, not enough resources.'

'And now you've nobody at home to share your problems with.'

I'm taken aback by her adept change of subject. 'Don't you start. I've already been nagged by Adam.'

'Good for him.'

I sigh. 'There is someone I'm interested in but I'm not sure she wants to continue our relationship.'

Joan regards me sympathetically. 'Stick in there, Miles. You're a good catch. Clare chose well.'

'So did I, Joan. So did I.'

26

'Well played, Dad.'

Luke, seemingly fresh as a daisy, vaults the net to my side of the court. I need a moment to catch my breath before I can congratulate him in return. 'You're improving,' he adds.

And I am. I'd forced a third set and only lost that four games to six. My groundstrokes are better than his and shot selection less reckless, but with his speed around the court, it sometimes feels as if I have to win the point twice. I pat him on the back.

'You okay? You did make me promise no mercy.'

'Don't you dare let me win.' And then more mildly, 'But you could do me one favour.'

'What's that?'

'Stop growing. Otherwise, I'll never get the ball past you.' He laughs and we begin to collect the balls and pack up. We walk home, chatting happily.

I sit in my study at home later that day. It's not been a bad summer, I reflect. If Freya hadn't waltzed off to Spain then I probably wouldn't have excavated my tennis racket from our loft and spent these times with Luke. Adam's not around, island hopping in Greece with his latest girlfriend. And it's done me good. Along with the extra running, a coping reaction to Freya's departure, I'm fitter than I have been for some years.

It would have been easier if she'd not left me in this limbo. Not knowing whether we can rekindle our relationship when she returns. But if she thought that was what she might want, why did she give me Kate's card? Is it a test? I'd told her I was willing to give her time. I've decided that she wasn't clear in her own mind why she did it. Or is that just wishful thinking?

For now, I just have to try and banish thoughts of a Spanish toy boy rubbing her with sun-cream before removing her bikini. Though even if she was inclined to behave like that, Lily would be an obstacle, but not an insuperable one with the connivance of Annabel.

Damn it. She's not mine and may never be.

27

"I sit in Alan's office waiting for him to return with our coffee for what is becoming our regular Friday lunchtime meeting. The door onto the courtyard is open and the scent of the flowers in the tubs outside wafts in. Since my last visit a new filing cabinet has appeared and is labelled "bili". A good sign, though I wonder how long it will take us to fill it with paperwork. Not too long if the NHS has much to do with it, but we are aiming to keep the hospital's involvement to a minimum.

It does me good to come here, leave the clinical hurly burly behind for an hour and discuss our plans. Alan is proving to be a highly efficient, as well as a congenial, colleague. After what he told me about his late wife, his determination for our research to succeed is beyond question.

'There you go'. He pushes aside some microbiology report forms, puts a mug of black coffee in front of me and settles himself into his chair. His face assumes the affable expression I am becoming familiar with. 'You know, I don't mind meeting in your office sometimes, say alternate weeks'.

'Thanks, but it's too small and I can't ask Andrew

Roberts to vacate it while we meet. Anyway, this is where the action is.'

'Okay and that's something, I want to discuss with you today.'

I'm intrigued. 'Go on.'

'Well, as you and Freya are proving so successful at raising money, I think we should aim to appoint two research scientists, not one. I've already advertised, by the way. I hope you don't mind.' He halts to try and discern if he has offended me. I smile and nod encouragement. 'And we're going to need a full-time technician, in addition to the two part-time ones we already employ.

Also, we should have our own equipment as much as possible, rather than renting time on the hospital's.' He pauses again and regards me intently to gauge my reaction before hurtling on. 'So, we need more room and it seems to me the best way to do this would be to have a separate space for the research activities. I've been looking into the cost of a prefabricated building and it's not that expensive. I realise that we haven't enough money yet but we'll need to gain the hospital's permission and planning consent, so we should be thinking ahead to avoid future delays. What do you think?'

I've never seen him so animated before or heard him speak so rapidly. 'Thinking big, eh? Must be hard for a microbiologist.' I immediately wonder if this wasn't the moment for my dubious sense of humour and am relieved when he laughs. 'Seriously, I think it's a great idea. Let's do it'.

'Really?'

'Absolutely. Let's compile what it's likely to cost and ...'

Alan reaches inside one of his desk drawers and passes me a sheet of A4 paper. 'Done,' he says proudly.

I scan the document briefly. There is a long, detailed

breakdown of our proposed expenditure and a bottom line exceeding our current donations. 'Well then, I suppose the next step is for us to make an appointment with the finance director.'

'I agree and took the liberty of enquiring with his secretary. He could see us Tuesday lunchtime. I know you've a morning ward round and afternoon clinic.'

'Sounds good to me.'

I'd like to talk to Freya about expanding our income generation but she's still incommunicado. She might have made time to attend the meeting and used her feminine charms to gain the finance director's agreement. Alan is unaware of my difficulty. What the hell. 'Come on Alan, let's really go for this.'

We chink our coffee mugs together in celebration, gently since we've been too engrossed to drink much of it. Alan sits back in his chair, looking relieved. He takes a gulp of his coffee and then jumps up before opening the small fridge in the corner of his office. Does he want more milk in his drink? But it proves to be nothing so mundane.

His right hand is wrapped around the object, obscuring my view of it. He places it on the desk in front of me and, with a small flourish, like a magician, reveals it. I see a Petri dish, a shallow, circular, plastic container, part-filled with what I know to be nutrient jelly, on which is growing a dirty green bacterial culture.

Is this Helicobacter bili? Any doubt I may have had is dispelled as I look up at Alan's beaming countenance. How pathetic the bug looks here. Something you could destroy with detergent and a cleaning cloth. Not so easy, of course, when it's inside you.

'Well done.' And it is. Finding the right blend of nutrients to permit the growth of a particular bacterium can be tricky. 'Have you had a chance to determine antibiotic sensitivities yet?'

'Of course,' he replies, a little smugly. 'Most strains we've tested so far are sensitive to amoxycillin, clarithromycin, metronidazole, ciprofloxacin and tetracycline.'

'Similar to Helicobacter pylori then?'

'Yes, indeed.'

It is what one would predict. What I'd hoped. Yet hoping and predicting are not the same as knowing. Now we can expect to rid people of the bacterium but there is still a long way to go to determine if it causes pancreatic cancer and gallstones. To enable that we have to first discover a non-invasive way of detecting it. A blood test would be ideal. Until we can achieve that, we're not going to make much more progress.

Alan is watching me, a contented expression on his face, almost motionless now, his anxiety and excitement abating. He must realise what I'm thinking and confirms this with his next statement. 'With two research scientists, we should develop a blood test to detect it quicker than with just one.' That seems logical. Let's hope he's correct.

'Okay. In the meantime, I'll keep collecting blood samples from appropriate patients so we have plenty to work on, once you and your scientists succeed.' We have to be positive and it's not just flattery. Alan fills me with confidence.

He glances down at the photographs on his desk and then offers, 'You know, if we find that bili is the cause of pancreatic carcinoma then it should spur others to put more effort into investigating bacteria and viruses as potential causes of other cancers. I really hope so. It frustrates me how little work seems to be happening on this. Most of the focus is on treating cancer, not enough, in my view, on preventing it and understanding the fundamental causes. Sometimes you can't put the genie back in the bottle. Better not to let it out in the first place.'

'I have sympathy with the point you're making but what alternative is there to treating the unfortunate people who develop cancer?'

'Sure. I'm just not certain we have the balance right.' He shakes his head a little. 'Look, the last-ditch chemotherapy Alison had was hugely expensive and perhaps gave her an extra month or two of poor-quality existence. I really believe that she would rather have seen the cost of those drugs spent on basic research into ovarian cancer. Something that one day might prevent one of our daughters going the same way.'

'I understand. The problem, of course, is that there is little or no kudos for politicians in diverting scarce treatment resources into cancer-preventing research.'

He shrugs. 'Well for now, I think the best we can do is get back to work.'

'Talking of which, I won't be able to meet next Friday. I'm obliged to attend a day-long course on how to talk to patients with cancer.' No consultation as to whether the course was likely to be useful to me. The management clearly has a target to fulfil, a tick-box exercise to enhance its credentials, regardless of the cost involved and the disruption to clinical work.

Alan laughs. 'How long have you been doing that?'

'Twenty-five years. But there's no escape. All the physicians and surgeons have to do it. Otherwise, Graham has advised us he won't sign off our annual appraisal.'

His mirth evaporates and a troubled expression appears on Alan's face. 'I didn't know he had to.'

'Oh yes, new this year. Didn't you hear that our esteemed medical director wouldn't authorise two of the surgeons' appraisals until they agreed to sign the new consultant contract?'

He shakes his head. 'But that's awful. Appraisals are meant to be for the individual's benefit.'

'A good intention, but, at least in this Trust, they've become just another method of management subjugation.'

28

I emerge from my en-suite bathroom, naked after a shower. 'Ping'. My mobile is on the bed-side table. It pings again when I don't pay it immediate attention. The message reads: 'Hi. I'm back. Freya'.

What am I meant to reply? I toss the phone on the bed. A few hours later, I text back: 'Hi'. I almost add "hope you had a good holiday" but it may seem to her an unpleasant echo of my last remark in the coffee shop. Besides, I don't want her to have had too good a holiday. I want her to have missed me. Let's see if she's willing to make the next move.

Time seems to pass slowly and I sleep restlessly as I wait expectantly. Three days later I find a new message on my phone. 'Can we meet for lunch to discuss the research?' Lunch, an upgrade on coffee.

I arrive early, as before. Should I have chosen an outside table? The early September weather is still warm and fine, and the light has an indefinable, attractive quality at this time of year. She arrives wearing a white, short-sleeved top and white leggings. Virginal? A signal of her good behaviour in Spain?

No, just better to display her tan. And the figure-hugging outfit is hardly an aid to keeping a man's thoughts pure. I stand and give her the standard no body contact embrace and an air kiss.

'You look well,' she offers. Her smile is warm.

'So do you'. I pour her some sparkling water. 'How was your holiday?'

'Restful, a chance to reflect. And it certainly did Lily good. Her friend, Cassie, has been there so many times that she knows loads of other kids for them to be with.'

'Did you get on okay with Annabel?'

'Yes, she's easy and, with all her friends and acquaintances there, she wasn't dependent on me when she wanted to go partying.' A slight pause, perhaps to allow me to absorb the implications of her answer. 'And you? What have you been up to?'

'Not much. I've started playing tennis again, mainly with Luke. And helping to teach him to drive. That's a bit scary.'

'Not seen Kate then?' She watches my face intently.

'No. No way.' She continues to stare at me. 'Ask her yourself if you don't believe me.'

The corners of Freya's mouth twitch in a hint of a smile. 'She's not talking to me anymore.' She nods, almost imperceptibly.

'How's the research going?'

I tell her about our plans to appoint two scientists and a technician and, later, create some dedicated premises. 'But despite your colleagues' generosity, we will need more money before we can start building.'

'Then I have some good news.' After a pause of a few seconds for dramatic effect, she continues, 'I already have more money for our research, another £105,000.'

'Wow! How come?'

'Well, people talk and at least one member of the audience recorded your presentation and has been playing it to others. I've hardly been able to do any work this week with colleagues coming to me, wanting to donate and sign up. I'm even getting enquiries from outside the bank. There'll be more yet.'

'That's astonishing. I never imagined this sort of response. Well done.' I raise my glass of water in a toast to her.

'No. I've facilitated but it's you that's done it. Particularly that bit about "many of us already carry the seeds of our eventual destruction within us". What a soundbite! It really got to them.'

We are smiling at each other. An opportune moment. 'Freya, perhaps you would let me take you out for dinner? To celebrate our fund-raising success.'

She laughs. 'Well in that case, Miles, how can I refuse?'

****

I awake. Early autumn sunlight pierces the gaps around the sumptuous dark red curtains of the bedroom. My body is cupped around Freya, her buttocks warm against me. She is still asleep, her breathing soft and regular. My hips begin to push towards her. My right arm moves up and cups a breast.

After, we lie together, her head on my chest, my left arm around her, sated. At least I am and she had an orgasm, I think, so hopefully she is as well. What's certain is that I can't manage it again for now. Three times since dinner last night, I didn't think I was capable of that anymore. How long since Clare and I made love three times in a night? The thought triggers immediate feelings of guilt. A new relationship is bound to be more exciting than a long established one.

And what about Mark? I didn't want to sit on his bench

but here I am, sleeping in his bed yet again. "Love conquers all," Virgil claimed. Suppresses all your scruples more like.

Do I love Freya?

Some might caution it is too soon to know for sure but I am not in any doubt. It's not just her beauty and the intensity of our passion, I feel comfortable as well as enlivened by her, made whole again. In some respects, I have less in common with her than with a fellow doctor like Clare, but increasingly nowadays, I am glad to leave medicine behind when I escape from the hospital. Hearing about Freya's job is fascinating, a financial 'world' entirely novel to me.

But it's too soon though to tell her how I feel. I don't want to frighten her away. I recognise that my situation is easier than hers. Adam and Luke are semi-independent. Lily, only thirteen I've learnt, now has only her mother to depend on. Freya arranged for her to sleepover at Cassie's last night to enable us to be together in a congenial atmosphere.

'How do you cope?' she murmurs into my chest. Is she asking how I am coping without Clare? 'With all your sick patients, their suffering, death?'

I just do. But such a profound question deserves a more analytical answer than that. I presume she's been thinking of Mark. 'You become used to it to some extent. Learn to distance yourself from the patient's suffering so you can think unencumbered about their illness. Otherwise, you can't do your job properly and fail to give of your best to them.'

She lifts her head and stares at me. Her expression is sad. She has been thinking about Mark. 'But you still care? About them?'

'Yes. Yes, of course. It's how I am, how most doctors are. And the patients can tell if you care.'

I'm warming to my subject and there is no doubt I have

her attention. 'It's not always easy. Take Outpatients where I see around twenty patients in quick succession, you first have to listen to what they have to say. There's a well-known saying: "listen to the patient, he's telling you the diagnosis". But I've learnt that there's another reason for listening, even when what the patient is saying is probably irrelevant, because unless he or she feels they have been heard, then they may doubt that your diagnosis is soundly based.

Even then, it's not enough to listen and empathise, you have to be a social chameleon, talk to each patient in a manner that's appropriate for their age, sex and intellect. Otherwise, at the end of the consultation, you may have made a clever diagnosis but if the patient doesn't like you and trust your judgement, he or she may not comply with your treatment and you've failed.'

Freya regards me a few moments longer then caresses my face, before leaping out of bed. 'Come on, I'm famished,' adding in that mischievous tone of hers I'm coming to know, 'I can't think why.'

After breakfast, we sit drinking more coffee on her terrace, enjoying the beauty of her garden and the morning sun. Freya's post-coital tristesse has cleared like early morning mist and the sparkle is back in her eyes. She favours me with a radiant smile. 'I wanted to ask your professional opinion.'

I assume a more serious expression. 'Fire away.'

'It's to do with Lily. She's been offered vaccination against cervical cancer. Is it a good idea? It's just that you read horror stories about children becoming brain-damaged when they react badly to a vaccine. And her mood's still fragile. Perhaps it could wait a while?' Her voice tails off.

From my perspective, it doesn't require much thinking about, but I pause before answering, not wanting to appear too hasty. Maybe Freya misinterprets my hesitation. She looks sheepish. 'I'm being silly, aren't I?'

'No. No, you're not. You just want to do the best for her and why not discuss it with me? That's sensible. So, yes, I think the vaccine is a good idea. It's very effective at protection against many strains of the human papilloma virus that causes the cancer, particularly the current vaccine on offer. The government originally chose the cheaper but less effective alternative but were pressured by the medical community into changing their mind. They haven't been persuaded to immunise boys yet, so I've given it to Adam and Luke.'

She tilts her head to one side and a lock of her blond hair falls across her eyes. 'Okay, if you've given it to your sons then you've convinced me that it's safe, but I'm not really with this. I understand that cancer of the cervix is a sexually transmitted disease. But Adam and Luke? Are you just being philanthropic vaccinating them?'

'No. Not really, though it may stop them passing one of the cancer-causing strains of the virus to their partners or wives in years to come. You see we now know that the virus can cause at least some cancers of the mouth, throat and nose, and I think possibly some others as well. Fundamentally, I'm doing it to protect them.'

Freya pouts. I don't think I've ever seen her do that before. 'You can catch it from oral sex as well?'

'Yes, it's a scary thought but the oral sex you may have at, say, sixteen can give you cancer decades later.' Another soundbite? I hesitate but decide to press on. 'Going back to Lily, I appreciate she's still a girl now but they change so fast in early adolescence. And, well you know this, girls tend to like older boys and the boys often put pressure on them to have sex, even if the girl is not yet sixteen.'

Freya glances away towards the garden, looking rueful. 'You're right. So before too long, Lily may meet a boy and if she really cares about him, while she may not be willing to go all the way, she may consent to oral sex, rather than risk losing him.'

'Exactly. And you have to bear in mind that with her height, she looks older than she is and she's clearly going to be very beautiful, like her mother.'

'Umm. The mother you may have just given a cancer-causing virus to.' The playful tone in her voice leaves me in no doubt that she is saying this tongue in cheek.

I open my arms wide and shrug. Guilty as charged. 'Or vice versa.'

She laughs. I like that. I'm not sure why, it's hardly a funny subject. Laughing in the face of death, perhaps?

'So', she says with a mock serious expression, 'if I don't want to increase my risk of cervical cancer in the future and I don't want to become celibate, then I'd be sensible to stick with you.'

If this is a declaration of commitment, it's the strangest, most morbid one I've ever heard, but I'm not complaining. I grin. 'And vice versa,' I reply again.

It doesn't have the same ring to it as "I love you too", but for now it will have to do.

29

I groan in frustration.

It is around seven pm and sustained by a cup of strong coffee, I am checking – or, rather correcting, - my letters to general practitioners and patients, dictated after a recent outpatient clinic. They are now outsourced for typing to India, a cheap option that enabled the cull of consultants' secretaries, even though the consultants complained forcefully that their secretaries fulfilled other important duties besides typing. Much harder now for a patient to speak on the telephone to a person familiar with their case and receive the words of clarification or reassurance that are sometimes necessary.

The turnaround time from India is commendable but the quality of service is very variable. The typist of these letters has reproduced faithfully almost all the difficult words I dictated but has altered liberally the pronouns and verb tenses. Forensic attention is required to render the correspondence intelligible. I reflect wryly that this process would be a false economy if the extra correction time required by the consultants was paid for. And this batch of letters contains the best, or should that be the worst, typo I have seen for some time. My dictated words of: "her bowel habit is erratic" has become: "her bowel habit is erotic."

My mobile rings and even though I am not on call, my heart sinks a little at the thought that it may be a request to see a severely ill patient immediately. So, my delight is even greater when I see "Freya" displayed on the caller identification. This is earlier than the call that we nowadays make to each other most evenings. I slide accept. 'Hi. How are you?'

'Hi. I'm on the train home.' I can hear that in the background.

'Lily phoned this afternoon and I've agreed to her staying at a friend's tonight, some joint school project. So would you like to come round?'

That must be the most ridiculous question I've been asked this year. 'I'd love to.'

'Great. Have you eaten yet?'

'I should be so lucky.'

'Okay, I'll ask Teresa to prepare us something. Come any time after eight.'

'I won't be late. See you soon.'

I send Luke a text message telling him not to expect me home and set to work on finishing my out-patient letters. A quick check of my e-mails and I can make my escape. I log on. My recent read e-mails appear momentarily before being swept down and then off the screen by a deluge of new ones, an inexorable tsunami of trivia. A harsh assessment. I am not blind to the value of instant and paperless communication but most of these would probably not have merited a letter to me. As expected, most can be rapidly scanned and deleted and only just a couple require answers. Seven forty-five. Perfect, I can be at Freya's house in twenty minutes, traffic permitting.

Freya looks weary as she opens her front door to me but her smile could not be more welcoming. Barefoot but still in business attire of a cream blouse and tight blue pencil skirt, her blonde hair held back by a black scrunchy. She opens her arms to hug me, before kissing me briefly. What would I give to be greeted like this every night? Entering the grand hall of her house, its spaciousness, the sweeping staircase, and the ornate plasterwork are a joy, almost surreal. compared to the shabbiness of my office.

'I'm ravenous. Shall we eat straight away?' she asks. Needing no persuasion, I follow her into her splendid dining room. Two bay windows look out onto her delightful rear garden. The large mahogany table is set just for two. A crystal chandelier enhances the room's grandeur but this evening it is not illuminated. A more intimate ambience has been created by some side lights and two candles in a silver candle-stick holder on the table.

Freya presses a button on the wall and the sumptuous emerald green curtains close automatically. My amusement at this must be evident on my face. 'Sorry,' she says. 'I know it's ostentatious. It's the only room in the house like this but Mark wanted it to impress our guests.'

I laugh. 'Freya, Mark could have invited me to a shack and I'd have been impressed that he had you.'

She moves towards me, lays a hand on my stubbly cheek and kisses me gently. 'You do say some cute things.'

'I mean it.'

'I know.' She pauses a moment. 'It was a problem.'

'I don't understand.'

'Do I have to spell it out?'

I shake my head a little. 'Sorry, I'm tired.'

'Okay. It's simple really. The men Mark invited here did

look at me rather too much and their wives didn't like it. No matter how good an evening we tried to give them, we were hardly ever invited back.'

'Maybe they felt awkward that their house wasn't as splendid as yours?' I wonder if that was the right thing to say.

'Perhaps, but they could have taken us to a restaurant. That never happened. And it's the same with women on their own, some obviously just don't want to be around me. I have very few girlfriends.'

'But you can't be sorry you're beautiful?'

'Of course not. I'm just explaining it comes with a cost.'

She shrugs. 'Come on, let's sit down. Wine?'

Freya pours us both a glass of red, a Rioja with an expensive-looking label. I doubt we'll finish the bottle. I've never seen her drink much and, after what happened to Clare, my consumption has become even more modest. 'I'll ask Teresa to start our steaks. Medium, isn't it?' We're beginning to learn each other's preferences.

'Yes, thanks."

After a few minutes, Freya returns from the kitchen with a bowl of salad and one of steaming boiled potatoes. Shortly after, Teresa appears bearing our steaks. She is small, olive-skinned, her dark hair streaked with grey, probably mid-fifties with a Mediterranean accent that I suspect is Greek. She doesn't linger and almost maternally, exhorts us to eat our food before it goes cold.

'She's a marvel,' Freya declares. 'Been with us since soon after Lily was born. I couldn't manage without her.' A sad look descends on Freya's lovely face. 'I sometimes feel guilty that she is more of a mother to Lily than I am. And now Lily's lost her father …' Her voice trails off and her sentence remains unfinished.

Too easy for me to make a trite response, continuing to listen seems best. Freya sighs. 'Ideally, I'd like to work part-time but the bank can be ruthless. They were really good with me after Mark died but often any hint of an inability to cope or less than full commitment and you're out, sometimes with no warning.'

I reflect that for all my mental whinges about the NHS, I do enjoy considerable job security. 'Freya, you're doing your best. It's the most any of us can do.' I recollect that I said something similar to Mark on the day he died, but I'm sincere, then and now. She looks grateful. I want to put my arms around her but there is a dinner table between us.

We progress onto less emotive matters and share our day's experiences. Freya is under pressure to complete some work for Monday and apologises that she will have to spend most of the weekend finishing it. While disappointed, I have my private practice on Saturday and the research is generating plenty of paperwork for me to deal with: protocols, Ethical Committee submissions and preliminary analyses of our early results. Not something I have time for on a weekday. Research is ostensibly part of my job description but, in reality, there is little or no time for it.

Freya takes a sip of her wine and regards me over the top of her glass. 'How's Lily?' I venture.

She looks away and when she turns to face me again, her eyes are moist. 'I'm really worried about her.' Her voice is trembling and tears begin to flow.

Taken aback, I pick up my chair, place it next to her, and grasp one of her hands in both of mine. 'Tell me.'

'Oh Miles, it's not right that I should burden you.'

'Tell me.'

She pulls a tissue from the sleeve of her blouse, wipes

her eyes and looks at me intently. 'Okay. Thank you.' She gives a deep sigh. 'Lily is just so difficult and moody since we returned from our holiday.'

'I'm no expert on this, but isn't that fairly common in girls of her age?'

'Perhaps, but what really worries me is that she's lost weight and she's very skinny now.'

Alarm bells begin to ring in my brain. 'Go on.'

'She's become obsessed by food. Is really picky about what she'll eat. I'm trying to have meals with her whenever I can but she does her best to avoid it, claiming she's eaten already or is not hungry. And when we do eat together, she just mopes, cuts her food into tiny pieces and pushes it round her plate.'

'So how much does she weigh now?'

Freya exhales deeply and shakes her head. 'Was that a battle! It's perverse because I can tell she uses the scales in my bathroom every day. She's not tidy like me and I can see they've been moved. But when I insisted I look myself what she weighed, she adamantly refused. I tell you that was the nearest I've ever come to smacking her.'

'I understand.'

Freya gives a brief, harsh laugh. 'You might not when I tell you what happened next. I grabbed her by her hair, dragged her to my bathroom, and forced her to stand on the scales. She was crying and screaming at me, but I was at the end of my tether and I wasn't going to let her win.'

It's not my place to judge and am I sure I wouldn't have done something similar? 'What was her weight?'

'Seven stone four and she's five foot eight. I Googled her BMI and it's only 16. The website said she's at moderate health risk.'

'Have you taken her to your G.P?'

'Yes, but he wasn't much use. Sorry, but he wasn't. He just referred Lily to a dietician and when we went, Lily lied to her. The dietician recommended some high calorie and protein drinks but I think Lily pretends to take them and actually pours them down the sink. It's head banging. It really is.'

'Freya, these sort of,' I stop myself saying "cases", 'situations are hugely problematic. She needs specialist help - and urgently, before her pattern of behaviour becomes too ingrained and she loses more weight. I can recommend someone. Lily would have to see her privately. There's no time to be lost waiting for the NHS.'

Freya shifts in her seat, withdraws her hand from mine, and affects to look round the room. 'What sort of specialist?'

'A child psychiatrist.' Freya looks doubtful. 'I know one who's excellent and really caring,' I persist, 'You couldn't ask for anyone better.'

'What's she going to do; talk to her? I've done that 'til I'm blue in the face and it doesn't work.' Her tone and demeanour have suddenly become combative and aggrieved.

'Look, I'm in no doubt that you've done as much as any mother could have done. And yes, of course, Doctor Godwin will talk to her but, perhaps more importantly, Lily may engage in a more therapeutic dialogue than she does with you. No offence, sometimes it's easier to confide in a stranger.'

Freya pushes out her bottom lip. 'And what? She'll conclude that Lily has been upset by the death of her father. It hardly takes a genius to realise that.'

I'm beginning to feel like I'm back in Outpatients but at least my experience has taught me to keep calm in these sorts of situations. 'Well, she may decide to do more. From what you've told me Lily is down. Understandably so,' I hasten to add.

Even in the subdued candlelight, I can see the flush

appearing on Freya's cheeks and neck. 'I'm not an idiot. I can see where this is going. It's not enough to want me to have my daughter labelled mentally ill, now you're implying she may need an antidepressant. Well, I'm telling you, she's not.'

'Why?'

She gives me a withering look, as if the answer to my question should be obvious. 'I don't agree with altering people's minds with chemicals.' Except wine, I think wryly. 'And I've read that antidepressants can make children suicidal.'

'I'm not convinced of that. I think it's more likely that the kids who are most depressed and therefore at greater risk of suicide are the ones given the antidepressants.'

'You're not convinced.' Her mocking tone is hurtful. 'It's my daughter's life you're talking about here.'

I hold her gaze and take a deep breath. I don't like doing this but, as she has just acknowledged, the stakes are very high. 'Freya, if we agree that Lily has anorexia then the mortality of her illness is at least ten per cent and her suicide risk about fifty times increased.'

She looks at me in horror and slumps a little in her seat as the fight goes out of her. She waves both her forearms outwards, as if to bat away the unwelcome information and knocks over her half-full wine glass. The red stain on the white tablecloth slowly spreads and seemingly captivates her attention. We sit there in silence until eventually she asks plaintively, 'How come anyone dies when you can feed them artificially in hospital?'

I sigh. 'It's very difficult to make anyone do something regularly that they don't want to do.' I think back to a young anorexic patient of mine, being fed by a tube down her nose into her stomach, who used to pour the contents of her liquid feeding bag out of the ward toilet window. It was only when a colleague complained about the recurrent stains on his new Mercedes in his assigned parking spot below the window that we realised this. It wasn't an anecdote I wanted to share with Freya.

'Look, I'm not asking you to rely on my opinion but please take Lily to Doctor Godwin without delay. I'll email you her contact details.' I attempt a reassuring smile. 'I'm confident she can help her.' Freya regards me bleakly.

'I think it's better I go.' I stand and lean down to kiss her on the forehead before showing myself out.

The following evening Freya rings me. 'Hi, how are you?"

'I'm fine. More importantly, how are you?'

'Okay. Lily and I are going to see Doctor Godwin tomorrow.'

'Good.'

'I have to confess, it's a relief. I'm tired of battling with her alone.'

'How did Lily take it?'

'Sullen acceptance is probably the best way to describe it.' She chuckles. 'Since I dragged her by the hair, she seems wary of arguing with me. And talking of which, I'm sorry we argued.'

'So am I. At least you didn't pull my hair.' She laughs. It's good to hear.

There's a pause in our conversation. 'Miles, with Lily being so fragile at the moment and her not reacting well to you that time she came home early from her friend's, I think we have to be circumspect about meeting. Please, I do want, I do need to see you, but I don't want Lily to know - or if she does, at least not to flaunt our relationship. Could we do that?'

'Yes, I understand. Getting Lily better has to be your first priority.'

'Thank you.'

30

'Thanks for coming to see her with me. She sounds pretty sick.'

'No problem.' And it isn't. I would much rather see a seriously ill patient early. It is Tuesday and my next ward round is on Friday, too long to risk the patient being given suboptimal treatment during those intervening days, particularly in this sort of case.

Erin and I are walking along one of the long hospital corridors. Maybe I should buy a pedometer and measure how many miles I walk around the hospital in a week? For now, I have slowed my usual walking speed, otherwise Erin has to scurry to keep up with me. She is petite, perhaps five foot two, with lustrous dark red hair, pale skin and freckles.

She is a second-year specialist registrar. After the reorganisation of so-called junior doctor grades, registrars had become specialist registrars, arguably an unnecessary aggrandisement of their title since there seemed to be no non-specialist ones.

'How old did you say she was?' I ask.

'Eighteen.'

'On a geriatric ward.'

'Apparently, a care of the elderly bed was the only one left when she was admitted last night.'

I note how Erin has tactfully reminded me of the current politically correct term for the medicine of old age.

Well, we are here: Poppy Ward. It's a pleasant enough name and trips off the tongue, though as my mind makes the association of morphine being derived from poppies and its use to alleviate end of life suffering, I wonder if it is such an appropriate name for an elderly care ward. Of course, a manager might not think that way and the medical staff had had no input into their wards' names, but one would expect a manager's mind to link poppies and the remembrance of people who died in wars, some of whom are likely to be erstwhile relatives of these elderly patients.

Erin and I enter the office and introduce ourselves to the ward sister who is doing paperwork, in between picking at a box of chocolates. We take the patient's notes and, seated at a desk, begin to read them together. The case history is simple: Zoe Jones. Eleven days of increasingly severe diarrhoea, accompanied by blood. Previously well, her investigations indicate active inflammation or infection.

We emerge from the office into an old Nightingale ward, a cavernous rectangular space lit by high arched windows, like the interior of a large church. Two long rows of beds, no side rooms and bathrooms at the far end.

Zoe Jones is not difficult to spot. She is about halfway down the ward returning to her bed, probably after one of her many trips to a toilet. She weaves her way round two old women making slow and unsteady progress in the opposite direction on their walking frames. Her youth is strikingly incongruous amid the otherwise elderly residents of the ward. She flops onto her bed as we approach her.

Small, with short black hair, elfin features, and wearing a brief pink nightdress, she looks as though she has strayed from a fairies' gathering. Her full name and that of her consultant is above her bed. The new chief nursing officer's experiment with confidentiality has not survived substantial negative feedback.

'Good morning. I'm Doctor Westwood and this is my registrar, Doctor Murphy. We're going to be helping look after you.'

She looks scared and very vulnerable. I hope Erin's presence will somehow reassure her a little. I don't want to loom above her and I'd better not sit on her bed in case she has gastroenteritis. Luckily, there is a chair handy.

I ask about her symptoms. She is probably tired of relating these, as I am likely to be at least the fourth doctor to have enquired about them since her admission yesterday. Nevertheless, it is always better to corroborate the patient's history personally. My diligence is rewarded as it emerges that she has been noticing small amounts of blood intermittently with her stools for at least a month. Unfortunately, this favours a more chronic process like the onset of a colitis rather than an acute infection.

Erin and I pull the screens round Zoe's bed. I examine her abdomen and am pleased to see that it is not distended. Even so, I ask Erin to order an urgent abdominal x-ray to ensure her colon is not dilated and in danger of perforating. I explain to Zoe that she may have ulcerative colitis but that we need to be more certain by having a little look inside with an endoscope later today. Her lower lip quivers as she begins to cry.

'Look,' I say, attempting to sound both sympathetic and

reassuring, 'we will take good care of you. First of all, we are going to transfer you to our ward where you'll be in a side room with your own toilet.' She looks a little happier, almost inevitably so. In her condition, trekking half the length of a long ward and possibly queuing for a toilet, risking incontinence at any moment, is hardly likely to enhance her morale. 'We'll see you later.'

I've already determined what is necessary to fulfil my promise and, as we walk away, I explain this to Erin. 'We need to move Mrs Green out of her side room. She doesn't need to be there anymore and, as we planned to discharge three patients on the ward round yesterday, that shouldn't be a problem.'

'I'd better check with the bed manager'.

I stop and look at her. No doubt my usual benign expression has deserted my face. 'Move Zoe Jones to our side room this afternoon. You can tell the bed manager afterwards, not before. Clear?'

Erin nods her head in acknowledgement, a shocked look on her face. 'Clear.'

She's not heard me snap before, a rare event. But I've implicitly asked Zoe Jones to put her trust in me and I'm not going to let her down. I'm certainly not risking a possibly officious bed manager with no understanding of the clinical priorities interfering in her care.

****

Erin and I sit by a computer and watch as two nurses wheel Zoe on a trolley out of endoscopy into the recovery area. I have just performed a gentle and limited endoscopic examination of her rectum and lower colon. I had given her a generous quantity of sedation with midazolam, so she was barely aware of the procedure and, due to the amnesic properties of the drug, will probably not remember it at all. There is no longer any doubt that she has ulcerative colitis. The surface of the bowel we had seen was inflamed and raw, weeping blood from the damaged mucosa, as if it had been scrubbed with sandpaper.

'So shall I start her on oral mesalazine and intravenous steroids now?' Erin asks.

'Yes, fine, and intravenous ciclosporin, please.'

Erin tilts her head quizzically which she probably considers more prudent than an oral question after my earlier abruptness. I understand that she wants to know why I am deviating from the national guidelines and that's very reasonable.

'Okay. I'm not in complete agreement with the guidelines.' This is accompanied by a slight shrug of my shoulders that is intended to be self-deprecating. I have no wish to appear arrogant. 'You see guidelines are formulated by committees. I'm sure you know the saying that a camel is a horse designed by a committee. They're arrived at by consensus, so some of the experts may well agree with me but they have to compromise with those who do not. And the process may seem balanced and democratic but it is crucially dependent on perhaps just one individual who decides which experts are going to be selected in the first place.'

This is becoming a diatribe. I decide to change tack. 'Let me try and convince you. Pretend you're the patient. The guidelines stipulate that you should be given intravenous steroids for three days and if you are not improving you are advised to have your colon removed, or if you've not deteriorated too much, you can be given an additional medication such as ciclosporin. But if I paraphrased this to you – in your role as the patient - saying, "We are going to give you the second-best treatment and if you don't get better after three days, we'll take your colon out or if you are not too bad by then, give you the best treatment. What would you say"?'

Erin laughs then answers, 'Why can't you give me the best treatment now?'

'Exactly. So that's what I do.'

Erin volunteers to go and discuss the endoscopic findings and the treatment with Zoe later on the ward when she has "come round" from the sedation. It may be preferable I'm not there. Zoe may find it easier to talk to Erin alone.

31

'We have a problem,' Erin announces. It's lunchtime the following day. She has sought me out in my office to give me the bad news face to face. I appreciate that. I gesture to Andrew Robert's vacant chair and try to smile encouragingly. 'Go on.'

'Well, yesterday evening, Zoe Jones was seen by a surgical registrar. It seems that the admitting team requested this consult at the same time as asking us. Anyway, he seems to have advised her to have her colon removed. She and her mum are freaking out, but worse, her dad has totally lost it, harangued the ward sister, accused us of playing Russian roulette with his daughter's life.'

I sigh. 'We'd better go and see her then.' We set off for our new Dahlia Ward, inefficiently sited at the opposite end of the hospital from my office.

Part way down a long corridor, my mobile rings.

'Miles, its Graham.' The medical director, the most senior doctor in the hospital and the only one with a seat on the eleven-person trust board. 'I need to discuss a complaint about one of your patients with you.'

A moment of apprehension as I try to think who this can be. Whoever it is, complaints are a fact of a consultant's life and normally communicated by letter or e-mail, not a phone call from the medical director. Time-consuming to investigate and reply to, particularly as the response often requires multiple consultants' input. Some are justified, others involve misunderstandings, a failure of appreciation by the complainant of the facts or the realistic limits of medicine, and most often, a manifestation of a bereavement reaction. Perhaps illogically, the unjustified ones were usually the more vituperative and insidiously destructive of consultants' morale.

'Which patient?' I ask.

'A girl with colitis.'

'Zoe Jones?'

There is a pause. He probably hasn't taken note of her name. I hear a rustle of paper. 'Yes, that's the one.'

'I'm just on my way to see her now. I think it's better I do so before coming to see you. Then we can discuss the up-to-date situation.'

A short silence. Graham has been medical director for a decade. Used to power, immediate acquiescence to his wishes is the expected response. 'Okay, but don't be too long. I have an important meeting at two.'

Erin and I reach Dahlia Ward and look for Jean, our new ward sister. I'm keen to hear her account of yesterday evening's events with Zoe's parents, but she is not to be found. Her predecessor, Marian, had resigned after the debacle with the hasty ward move. After nearly twenty years working in the hospital, her leaving party was a sad affair.

Zoe is lying in bed. I'm pleased that her mother is with her. She is small, like her daughter. Slumped in an armchair, she wears a tired, harassed look and crumpled clothes, probably slept little last night.

I introduce Erin and myself, and then enquire how Zoe is doing. There is no discernible change in her condition. Predictable, given that she has been receiving specific treatment for less than twenty-four hours and it usually takes three to four days for its benefits to begin to become apparent. At least, she is no worse. I explain the nature of ulcerative colitis to her mother and again to Zoe, stressing that we need to give the medical treatment time to work and only if it doesn't, in my opinion, would Zoe need to have her colon removed.

'I don't want an operation,' Zoe protests. 'I'm not having a bag.' I am glad to hear evidence of a fighting spirit but am obliged to remind her that, as a last resort, surgery may be necessary to save her life. She looks deflated.

Her mother interjects. 'Do you have to send many patients for an operation?'

'No, rarely these days.' It's probably four or five years since I last did so. I'd like to believe it's because I treat more aggressively than the guidelines but maybe I've just been lucky. If the latter, I hope it continues for Zoe's sake.

Her mother gives me with a wan smile. She looks "on side". Mrs Jones turns to her daughter. 'That's good, dear, isn't it?'

Zoe looks unconvinced and makes a dash for her toilet. This emotive exchange is too much for her fragile bowels.

'Is there anything else you'd like to ask me, Mrs Jones?'

'No. No, I understand. You've explained it well.'

'Thank you. I'd liked to have explained it to your husband in person but I presume he's at work.' A minor error, I realise. I should have said partner, not husband, or - better still - Zoe's father.

'Ex. Ex-husband.' She drops her eyes briefly, before continuing, 'I'm sorry about the fuss he caused yesterday. He's a difficult man.'

'I'm sure he's very worried about Zoe and just wants to ensure she gets the best treatment. Perhaps you could phone him and say I'd be pleased to see him this evening, six or six thirty, here, on the ward, when he's finished work.'

'Yes. Yes, I will,' she replies enthusiastically. I realise she's glad to leave this task to me.

****

On my way to Graham Giles's office, I glance at my watch: one thirty. He should make it to his two o'clock meeting on time. It's raining heavily as I hurry across the internal road to the new management block. Gleaming, spacious, carpeted and, above all, quiet. There's none of the hustle and bustle found in the rest of the hospital. No budgetary restrictions here, it seems.

Doctor Giles' personal assistant, the one not at lunch, is typing with fierce concentration when I arrive and give my name. She gives me a cursory look, appearing irritated to have been disturbed. 'Go in. He's expecting you.' She waves a hand to go through her office into his.

There is a room with a table and six chairs, obviously to enable small meetings. Beyond this, separated by a large plate glass partition, is a large office containing a huge wooden desk and our medical director on the phone. It seems courteous to sit at the table rather than intrude on his phone call.

The walls of the meeting room are decorated with photographs of his hunting and fishing prowess. I cannot comprehend how he reconciles killing animals yet saving human lives. Graham Giles - G.G. Shouldn't horses be his sport? I reflect flippantly.

I hear him put his phone down then his office door opens. He stands there, about five foot ten, probably in his late fifties, receding salt and pepper hair and a face wearing a stern look. A physician, like me, but a rheumatologist. He takes a seat opposite me at the table and puts down the paper he is holding.

'Okay' he begins, though his tone suggests he does not regard the situation as okay.' No time for pleasantries either. 'What are we going to do?'

Who are "we"? But it would be unnecessarily provocative to voice this thought. I would have preferred "how is she?" and decide this is where we must start. 'She's stable. She only started on medical treatment yesterday evening and we need to give it more time to work.' As concise a summary as I can manage but nevertheless, he is drumming his fingers in irritation on the tabletop.

'Hmm. You know her father is kicking up a big fuss?' I nod. 'Threatening to go to the papers. The Trust can't afford bad publicity just when we are applying for foundation trust status.'

In one respect, I have some sympathy with this. Because of patient confidentiality, it is very difficult to counter publicly any allegations of malpractice, no matter how outrageous. 'I understand, but you know how it is with some relatives. They get upset, make ill-founded and sometimes conflicting demands. We can't be bullied by whoever shouts loudest. The patient's best interests have to be paramount.'

'And what about the Trust's best interests?'

I am conscious of blinking excessively. Why do you do that? Have I heard correctly? But there is no mistake. He is staring at me, perhaps anticipating that prolonged eye contact will intimidate me?

I'm not playing ball. Enunciating each word clearly, I state, 'I am NOT prepared to recommend a premature colectomy to MY patient.'

He sits back in his seat and covers his mouth with a hand to better hide his displeasure but this is evident from the narrowing of his eyes. After a few moments, he declares, 'As medical director, I think it would be beneficial to have a further opinion and I've asked Klaus Walter to see Miss Jones.'

Beneficial to whom or rather what? And it seems he had decided to do this even before he'd heard what I had to say. No point arguing, better to try to persuade Klaus to my point of view. But Graham has stacked the odds against me. Klaus is a surgeon, not a physician and gastroenterologist.

****

Erin and I are waiting for Mr Jones to appear. Jane received a phone call from his ex-wife confirming he would come at six thirty. He's very late.

We stand by the nursing station. The ambience on the ward in the evening is strikingly different to that during the day. It's largely down to the visitors, of course. They cluster round their relatives' and friends' beds, chatting, laughing, often with forced cheerfulness, determined to keep their loved one's spirits up, hugging them hard and long, perhaps unsure if they will ever have the chance to do so again. A few visitors are less animated, largely silent, perhaps shocked by events, unable to comprehend the gravity of the situation. Some, no doubt, are privately wishing to be away as quickly as decency permits, keen to leave the sickness and sorrow behind, return to a normal life untroubled by these intimations of their own mortality.

And what of those few without visitors, watching the spectacle around them or pretending to read? How do they feel? Is it more difficult to recover if you are alone, no one to care whether you live or die?

Erin and I are about to leave when he makes his appearance. Medium height, a belly, but stockily built. The broken veins on his cheeks proclaim him as a drinker.

I greet him and lead the three of us into the cramped confines of the ward doctors' office. It has a few hard-backed chairs and a couple of flat plywood surfaces attached to the walls bearing two computers, one purchased by the Gastroenterology Trust Fund. With this degree of proximity, there is no mistaking the alcohol on his breath.

I attempt to explain Zoe's predicament while enduring his truculent expression. I keep it simple, use everyday words but he doesn't appear to be listening.

Then he blurts out, 'The surgeon said if she doesn't have operation, she'll die.'

'I don't think that's right,' I say gently.

'How would you fucking know? You weren't there when the surgeon saw her.'

He leaps to his feet, now even more plethoric than before and glares at me, fists bunched.

I stand, my arms slightly raised, ready to block a punch, meeting his gaze.

After a few seconds, he lowers his eyes and moves a pace towards the door. 'Fucking quacks.' He slams the door behind him.

Erin has shrunk into a corner of the room. 'Are you okay?' I ask.

'Yaa.' It sounds like a gargle.

- UNDER CONTROL -

****

The following morning, we see Zoe Jones at the beginning of the ward round, so as to be better prepared for when Klaus comes. Jane, my trusty spy, has determined that he does a ward round like me this morning. Zoe is much the same physically but appears more cheerful.

I hardly know Klaus Walters, as he only moved from another consultant post to our Trust a few months ago. He has a reputation as a man of firm convictions, perhaps a little inflexible and not someone who suffers fools gladly. Leaving Zoe's notes at the nursing station for him, we take the notes trolley and proceed with the round. We have nearly finished when he arrives. Tall, thin as a scalpel, with a tongue reputedly as sharp, trailing three junior doctors in his wake. Leaving him to it, we see our last patient on Dahlia Ward and wait for him to emerge from Zoe's side room. He walks towards me.

'Good morning, Miles.' He still has traces of an accent. 'I trust you will forgive my intruding.' The hint of a smile appears at the corners of his mouth. 'It is tempting to say that I am only obeying orders but us Germans don't like to use that phrase anymore.'

I am taken aback. Not what I expected, let alone the self-deprecating humour.

He is serious now. 'Her condition is stable. Immediate surgery is not required.' He looks pointedly at his juniors. Was it his registrar who recommended Zoe have her colon removed? He addresses them. 'It is not enough to be technically adept. A good surgeon must learn if and when to operate.' He turns towards me again. 'I am around. Any problem, call me personally.'

'Thank you.' The only words I've contributed to our dialogue.

- JOHN THORNTON -

'Oh yes.' An after-thought, he leans towards me conspiratorially and lowers his voice. 'Leave Graham to me.'

32

I grin, remembering yesterday afternoon. I had called in to see Zoe Jones following my private clinic. She is so much better, a joy to see the happiness writ large upon her face. Her mother ebullient and wreathed in smiles, not content with verbal gratitude, hugging me hard, fortunately not tall enough to kiss me.

I check my watch. I'm in plenty of time for our Sunday lunch date. Discourteous, I feel, to let Freya arrive first.

The young couple at the adjoining table are both lost in their mobiles. I haven't heard them exchange a word yet.

The restaurant is new. That's good. I'd rather not bring her to one I've eaten in with Clare, and have memories of a previous visit intrude into this one. A little illogical or, at least inconsistent, I realise, since we plan to adjourn to my house afterwards. It's Freya's idea. It would be surprising if she wasn't curious about where I live but, ostensibly, it's because she's not sure what time Lily is returning from her friend's. Teresa will be there when Lily comes home so we're not under too much time pressure.

- UNDER CONTROL -

I'd spent the majority of yesterday afternoon and early evening busily cleaning, tidying and re-arranging, much to Luke's amusement. 'Perhaps a little to the right, Dad?' He's agreed to make himself scarce for the afternoon and early evening, though with the strong wind today he'll probably have to revise his plan to play tennis.

My bedroom, inevitably, was the most poignant. I'd long since donated Clare's clothes to a charity shop: Cancer Research seemed appropriate. But the photos on the walls had to go. I've moved my favourite to my study. Freya does not subject me to ones of Mark in her bedroom. Come to think of it, I can't remember any there, even on the day of the fund-raising event. I smile wryly.

Nevertheless, I think our first time in my bedroom may be awkward, so I'm attempting to dispel this by displaying a poster I've bought of the goddess Freya on one of the walls. A tasteful one, not a bare-breasted Valkyrie. This is an image of her dressed in a diaphanous white gown against the backdrop of a garden. Nothing my Freya (is she mine?) could object to.

'What are you grinning at?' Lost in thought, I hadn't noticed her arrive. 'That buxom young waitress, perhaps?' She gestures with her head in the waitress's direction. Her face is unreadable and I don't know her well enough to judge whether she is serious or just teasing me.

I stand hurriedly. 'No,' I protest. 'Actually, I was thinking of you.'

'Of course you were.' A hint of a smile.

'I like your dress.' Navy blue in a gently clinging soft fabric, Jersey or cashmere, I presume. A compliment for the woman I want to complement my life.

'Thanks.' We sit down opposite each other. The buxom waitress appears beside us, enquiring what Freya wants to drink. I avert my eyes.

When she has gone, I persist, 'I was thinking about you. And your eponymous Norse goddess. I Googled her.'

'I see.' She is really smiling now.

'According to the myths, you should have two daughters.'

'Oh, spare me. One's as much as I can cope with right now.'

'How's she doing?'

Freya sighs. 'It's hard to say. She's no worse.'

'And Doctor Godwin?'

'Yes, Lily seems to have taken to her. Hey, what you didn't warn me about was how much she'd want to interview me.'

'Sorry. Was it very intrusive?'

She shrugs. 'Necessary, I suppose, and I find her okay. She's not like you though.'

'Why's that?'

'Well sometimes she answers my questions with ones of her own.' I laugh. 'But it is good not to be carrying the burden alone anymore.'

'You've got me to help as well.' I reach across the table to hold her left hand. She no longer wears a wedding ring and her large diamond engagement ring has moved to her right hand.

'I know.' There is a slight catch in her voice. 'You have helped me already with your advice and giving me someone to talk to, but you trying to help Lily directly…Well, I think it could be counterproductive.'

'I didn't mean that and I understand.'

'Do you?'

'Are you ready to order?' The waitress, bright and breezy and, with masterful timing delivers Freya's glass of white wine and stands beside our table. Can a woman be masterful?

- UNDER CONTROL -

Mistressful doesn't sound right.

'Could you give us a few more minutes?'

'You see,' Freya resumes, 'I haven't told you before but my father left us when I was eight. Went back to Germany. I've never seen him since and, quite frankly, I don't want to.

My mother was in her thirties and still attractive. She had a succession of men friends. Some of them were okay, but I resented them all because they weren't my dad.' She looks away, her expression troubled. 'What was worse was that I often felt in the way and, at times, wondered if my mother resented having me. So, you see, I don't want Lily to feel that way.'

'Sorry and yes, I get it.' Freya takes a sip of her wine. 'Have you never discussed it with your mother since?'

'No. What's the point? And it certainly wouldn't be easy. She's a rather cold and self-absorbed woman. To be fair to my father, maybe that's why he left her. Maybe she was unfaithful? I was too young to know.'

'But you do see her sometimes?' I wonder why I'm being so persistent. Is it because at least she still has parents and the opportunity to attempt reconciliation?

'Rarely. She's still in Sweden, living with a younger man whom I've never met. And now she's in her seventies, has announced that she can't cope with airports anymore. That was her excuse, anyway, for not coming to Mark's funeral. So, you see, I would have to go to her and particularly at the moment, I don't have the time or the inclination.'

Now I think I know the answer to my next question but want to be sure. 'Do you not have any brothers and sisters then?'

'No, just me.' So, no nephew to buy a card for all those years ago.

Freya begins to grin.

I smile in return. 'What?'

- 200 -

'I was thinking about one of my mother's more serious boyfriends, Sven. He used to boast that he was the biggest producer of Herrgardsost cheese in Sweden, so I used to call him the Big Cheese to my friends. He was rich and, after they'd be going out for about a year, he took the three of us to Majorca for a week in summer.

After a few days, my mother developed gastroenteritis and had to stay in her room for a day, so Sven and I went down to the beach together. I was thirteen at the time and self-conscious enough at that age. He spread his towel too near mine and tried to chat but I just buried my head in my book. But out of the corner of my eye, I could see he was staring at my newly acquired breasts, so I turned over. After a few minutes, he suggested my back would burn and that he ought to rub suntan oil on it. I wasn't letting him put his dirty hands on me and told him not to bother as I was going for a swim.' She pauses a moment to check if I'm paying attention but I am rapt.

'I decided he was a pervert. Harsh perhaps but, as you may have noticed, thirteen-year-old girls are not given to nuanced judgements. Anyway, I resolved to pay him back. So, on the last full day of the holiday, when Mum and Sven were swimming, I took one of the two key cards for their room from the beach bag and went back to the hotel. This was one occasion I was glad Mum was so bossy. I knew she would have insisted on choosing the number for the safe in their room and she always picks the same one. I found Sven's passport at the back of the safe, took it and hid it inside the little bag I was carrying. I went back to the beach, replaced the key card when they weren't paying attention and waited until it was beginning to go dark and Mum and Sven had left. Then I walked down the shore to a little cove, by then deserted, and buried Sven's passport in the sand above what I thought would be the high tide line.'

She starts to snigger and it's infectious. Once she regains her composure, she resumes. 'Well, the next morning we were due to fly home. I was packing and began to hear angry voices from their adjoining room, so I went to listen better outside their door. Sven was accusing Mum of moving and somehow losing his passport and she was vehemently denying it. It turned into a deliciously vicious row. Of course, mum and I had to leave Sven behind and best of all, she never saw him again.'

'And your mother never suspected you?'

'No way. Just to make sure, I hammed it up, saying things like "poor Sven" and what a nice guy I thought he was.'

I sit there stunned. She looks gleeful at the memory. Eventually, I say, 'Freya, that's appalling.'

'It is, isn't it? You should be honoured, though. You're the first person I've ever told. I wouldn't have dared tell Mark and needless to say, I don't want you spreading the story around.'

'Don't worry, your secret's safe with me.' Just as Mark's is.

'You're a good listener, you know.'

I give a rueful laugh. 'I should be. I get enough practice.'

We are drinking coffee now and have passed on desert. I am conscious that I don't want to be too full for my post-prandial exertions. 'How's work?' A safe subject I think but a troubled look descends on Freya's face.

'Pretty good. Busy, of course, but I'm used to that.'

'So, what's the matter?'

She shakes her head. 'I can't hide much from you.'

'Do you want to?'

'No.'

'That's good.'

She drinks the last of her coffee and puts down her cup. She glances at the couple on the adjoining table but they are still too engrossed with their phones to pay attention to each other, let alone attempt to overhear our conversation. Nevertheless, she lowers her voice. 'Yesterday morning I met with a girlfriend, Ayesha, who works at another bank. She told me she had learnt that some of her colleagues were ...' Freya pauses to select her words carefully, 'Behaving disreputably.'

Bankers, whoever would have thought such a thing. But I don't voice this and try to keep my face straight. 'What have they been up to?'

'Well, do you remember the Libor scandal?'

I look out of the window to one side of our table as I think for a few seconds. A few drops of rain spatter against the pane. 'Yes, vaguely. Something to do with fiddling interest rates?'

'Yes, that's right. Libor stands for London inter-bank offered rate. It's the interest rate at which banks in London lend money to each other and it underpins trillions of pounds of loans and financial contracts.'

'I can't get my head round trillions of pounds.'

'No, me neither. But what it signifies is that even a tiny change in the rate has huge financial consequences. And as the rate is calculated every morning based on information the banks provide; the temptation is for a bank to give an interest rate that is favourable to them. When it emerged that some traders in some banks were indeed doing this and rigging the rate for their own benefit, there was an investigation. The guilty banks were fined and a few heads rolled.'

'Ah, I remember now. The chief executive of Barclays.'

'Yes. He was one of those who got sacked.'

'Not in the proper Anglo-Saxon way.'

She looks puzzled, as I thought she would. 'I don't understand.'

I sit back in my seat and start to explain. 'Sacking was originally an Anglo-Saxon punishment for unfaithful wives.

The offending woman was put in a sack, sometimes with a snake for good measure and thrown in a river.'

She protests: 'You're kidding me.'

'No, I'm not. They had better ways of keeping women under control in those days.' I'm struggling to keep a straight face.

Freya attempts to glare at me but fails woefully and we both burst out laughing at the same time. As our mirth subsides, I enquire, 'Okay, so what's Ayesha's bank has been doing?'

'Essentially the same scam as with Libor, but this time with overseas interest rates. At least, that's what she's heard. And that some other banks are doing the same.'

I ponder this for a few moments. Freya looks again at the couple next to us but they are still seemingly caught up in their electronic worlds. 'What I don't understand is, if bankers have recently been caught rigging Libor, why would they risk getting caught with a similar fraud?'

Freya smiles and simultaneously shakes her head. I realise she probably thinks my question is naïve. 'Because the profits are huge and the possible fines are modest in comparison.'

She hesitates and then asks, 'I want your advice. I'm wondering what to do and considering talking to Sue. You remember her? In charge of compliance. The one who thought you were dishy.'

'As well as Kate.'

She looks irritated by my provocative remark. 'What do you think?'

'Can I get you the bill?' It's uncanny, the timing. The bill is already in her hand, and to be fair, the restaurant is full and we have been here a long time. I pass the waitress my credit card.

Once she's gone, I ask Freya, 'Let me think about it a bit. Shall we go?'

****

The poster has proved a success. Freya thought it demure and teasingly asked if that's how I wanted her to behave. My answer is easy to guess. Now, she is lying on top of me and my right hand is leisurely stroking patterns on her back.

'About what Ayesha said …,' I murmur, 'I don't think you should do anything.'

She rolls off me and sits up on the bed. 'What, nothing?'

'Nothing,' I confirm. 'Why should you? You're not in the compliance department and you're not involved personally, even if some members of your bank may be rigging rates. Better to keep your head down.'

She stares at me and takes a few deep breaths, causing her breasts to rise and fall distractingly. I realise that, if this becomes an argument, it's going to be harder for me to think coherently with Freya naked, but she just gives me a disappointed look and walks off towards my bathroom.

33

'The coffee's good,' I say.

'Thanks. By coincidence one of my daughters and my brother both gave me coffee machines for my birthday so I brought one here.'

I put my drink down on Alan' desk. It's so battered that he doesn't seem to mind if the hot mug makes a mark. 'So how old are you now?'

'Fifty- two.'

'Congratulations.'

He smiles ruefully. 'Not that I feel it. I don't know where the time goes. The years seem to fly by so fast.'

'Maybe that's because you're having fun,' I suggest, to try and divert Alan from his introspection, though, on reflection, given the death of his first wife, that may not be an appropriate remark. I continue rapidly, 'And you're certainly using it well at present. I'm very impressed by how quickly you have developed the antibody blood test for bili. Really commendable.'

Alan shakes his head. 'I can't take any credit. It's all down to Ravi and Aaron. They're highly experienced scientists who have done this sort of thing before. And not being too constrained financially has helped.'

Alan leans back into his office chair and gives a self-satisfied chuckle. 'Since it was bankers' money, it seemed appropriate to offer them a bonus, one proportionate to the speed of their success.' His face assumes a more serious expression. 'But it's not just the money motivating them. They realise the importance of what we're doing and are enthusiastic about being part of the team. And, I have to say, they've worked so cooperatively'. Alan clasps his hands together, symbolising Ravi and Aaron's working relationship.

'You also chose well with Jess,' I say. 'She's a little star. Learnt how to collect bile samples in no time at all and she's really good with the volunteers, praises their contribution, jollies them along and, no offence, she enjoys the variety, not being stuck in the lab all the time.'

'No offence taken. It's very obvious she's happy in the job. She's a single mother you know?'

'No, I didn't.'

Alan nods. 'Her mother's ill. So even though her parents live locally, when she worked for the hospital, leaving her daughter with them when she was on call had become very difficult.'

I finish the story for him. 'No doubt, the NHS was not willing to give her a break from being on call until the resolution of her mother's illness?'

Alan gives a wry smile. 'How did you guess?'

I shake my head despairingly. How many times have I known of these sorts of situations, the insatiable demands of the Health Service, the unremitting exploitation of the staff's dedication, ground down until finally some could take no more and resigned. But I don't want to spoil the positive tone of our conversation by digressing into NHS problems and I'm eager to hear what preliminary results the bili blood test has revealed.

Tantalisingly, Alan is now holding a single sheet of paper and grinning at me. I reach across his desk and take it from him. Given his expression, I know I'm not about to see bad news, but even so, I hesitate a moment. All this effort, so much at stake. I take a deep breath and look.

The results are arranged as a simple table with three columns: patients with pancreatic carcinoma, patients with gallstones, and healthy subjects. Alongside each category are the numbers tested for bili by our new blood test and the percentage positive. Only a glance is necessary to assimilate the information but I find I keep staring at the numbers. Erudition abandoned, 'Wow!' is the only comment I utter.

Alan's grin has metamorphosed into an almost paternal smile. 'Wow indeed. Pretty clear, isn't it? Both diseases over ninety per cent positive for bili compared with eighteen per cent of the healthy controls. You don't need a statistical test to tell you that's significant.' He carries on, 'Of course, we've more samples to test yet. You've built up quite a collection. We haven't tested any of your banker donors yet. I wanted your opinion first.'

'Well, I should discuss it with Freya but my feeling is let's do it now, or, at least, offer it to them now, making clear that our work is still incomplete. Of course, at the moment the main downside is that, after we've given antibiotics to those who are positive, we won't be able to confirm that the treatment has worked.'

'Sure, the antibodies will still be present, but based on Helicobacter pylori therapy results, you can tell them you expect about an 85% success rate. Or they can choose to wait for treatment until we've developed a stool antigen test to confirm eradication.'

It's obvious to me what he wants to do and why. Once Freya divulges news of our early success to her colleagues, then more donations are likely to be forthcoming and our burgeoning team can expand into new prefabricated premises adjoining microbiology. The Mark Johnson Laboratory we've decided to call it. 'I think Freya will be in favour of us offering to test her colleagues' samples now.'

He looks delighted with this response.

'Alan, I want to say thank you for all your hard work and for doing so much to turn our ideas into reality. You've been, you are tremendous.' He looks embarrassed but he has earned this praise. 'What feels especially rewarding is that at present when I'm treating a patient with pancreatic cancer, I'm engaged in a rear-guard action against their illness, but now we are beginning to tackle the disease itself, really fighting back.'

'There's hope now, isn't there, that before too long we may be able to prevent hundreds of thousands of people world-wide dying of this disease?'

'It's difficult to comprehend on that scale, isn't it?'

'The death of an individual is a tragedy but the death of millions is just a statistic.'

'Who said that?'

'Stalin.'

'Well, he should know. How many deaths was he responsible for?'

'At least twenty million.'

We should move back to a less harrowing topic. 'I've been thinking ,,,'

Alan emits a loud guffaw. 'I'm not sure we can cope with any more of your ideas just yet, however worthy they may be.'

'No, I appreciate that. I know how hard you must all be

working but what I'm thinking of doesn't require your input.'

He rests back in his seat. 'Go on then.'

'Okay. Our preliminary results are strongly suggestive of Helicobacter bili's involvement with pancreatic carcinoma. But it's far from conclusive that it causes the disease.'

Alan frowns. 'That's difficult. It could take a decade to prove. How do you think you can do it?'

'Because it's probably been done already.' Now it's my turn to smile at his discomfiture.

He stares at me. The two vertical furrows on his brow deepen as he ponders my response before eventually shrugging his shoulders. 'I give in. Enlighten me.'

'So, gastroenterologists have been treating Helicobacter pylori for over twenty years and confirming eradication by one means or another for most of that time. Many units keep a record of who those patients were and, in recent years, the British Society of Gastroenterology has compiled that information into a national database. You've determined that pylori and bili are often sensitive to the same antibiotics, so eradicating pylori from these patients may have inadvertently eradicated bili.'

'Yes! I see. And spared some of those patients from developing pancreatic cancer.'

I carry on. 'What we, sorry, I' He doesn't deserve teasing but in my excited state, it is irresistible. 'What I have to do is find an efficient way of collating the pylori eradication data with information from the National Registry of Births, Marriages and Deaths as to how many of those patients died of pancreatic carcinoma. In theory, of course, there should be far fewer, though we have to accept that we can't be certain that antibiotics will have eliminated Helicobacter bili in every patient, even though it worked for their pylori. And the death registry data will also include people who've died of other types of pancreatic cancer that are probably not induced by Helicobacter bili.'

Alan interrupts. 'But as the latter only constitute about 5% of pancreatic cancer cases, that shouldn't skew the results much.'

'Exactly. Also, I thought that I should study only patients five years or more after eradication treatment, in case the bacterium had already induced irreversible cell mutations that may have progressed to cancer over time.'

He is shaking his head. 'I have to hand it to you, Miles, now you've explained it, it seems so simple, even obvious. You realise, I'm sure, that even if we hadn't discovered bili, then you could have collated this data, made a circumstantial case.'

'Perhaps, though I'm far from certain that the Births, Marriages, and Deaths Registry would have cooperated based just on my speculation. Now, I'm confident they will do. And as all the information is computerised, a quick result may be possible.'

'You seem to have it all worked out then.'

'No, not all. But I will.'

He nods and pronounces sagely, 'That's an important part of this, isn't it: the will, the will to succeed?'

'One more thing. Along the same lines. You know how microbiologists criticise general practitioners for supposedly over-prescribing antibiotics.'

He regards me warily but nevertheless gives the expected reply. 'Of course. The development of bacterial resistance to antibiotics is a major concern. They have to be used more sparingly, not given for minor infections that the patient would recover from without any intervention.'

'Yes, but have you ever considered that some of those minor infections will be with Chlamydia pneumoniae, the possible cause of atheroma we were discussing when Adam had his coronary angiogram, and that treating those infections with antibiotics probably prevents the organism becoming established in artery walls. Therefore, the general practitioners your colleagues malign may well have inadvertently protected their antibiotic-treated patients from future heart attacks and some types of strokes and dementia.'

'If so, it follows that the declining prevalence of vascular disease may not be due entirely to statins and smoking cessation.'

Alan is frowning and remains silent.

'It's possible, isn't it? Consistent with the opinion that you propounded to me?' I prompt.

'It's possible,' he concedes, 'But that really is heresy.'

One for Clare.

34

Friday evening. Excited by our results, I'd phoned Freya before calling round at her house. We are sitting on opposing sofas in her lounge with neglected cups of coffee between us. She seems distracted and isn't as thrilled by my news as I'd expected.

'Is it Lily?'

'No.' A silence descends and I wonder if she is going to say any more. 'No. Lily is making progress. She's eating better, her BMI is up, and she's not as morose.'

'That's great.' I try to sound upbeat but I'm puzzled as to what's happening here.

'And you might as well know, she's taking an anti-depressant.' Her tone is distinctly surly.

'If Doctor Godwin thought that was for the best.'

'Well, we agreed, Lily, me, and the good Doctor Godwin that we'd try with just counselling but that if Lily didn't improve and gain weight within three weeks, we'd start the medication. So, you were right.'

'Surely all that matters is that Lily is getting better, it

doesn't really matter how.'

'Sensible, as always.' She begins to gaze out the window.

'What is it? What's bothering you?' I try not to sound exasperated.

She shrugs and turns her head to look at me again. 'I spoke to Sue.' Then more defiantly, 'I know you told me not to, but I did.'

'Freya, I didn't tell you what to do or not do. I offered my opinion. The opinion you asked for.' We stare at each other. I don't want to argue. I've come to share good news. 'Look, if that's what you felt you needed to do, fair enough.'

'Huh, I may as well not have bothered, for all the good it did.' Then she adds, 'So you were right again.'

This is just what I need on a Friday evening. With exaggerated patience I ask, 'What did Sue say?'

'She said she was unaware of such a problem at Statesbank.'

'And anything else?'

'That was it. Except for advising me to concentrate on my own work.' She looks disgusted.

I pick up my coffee cup. A displacement action that I reconsider when I realise the coffee has gone cold. 'Hey, you've done what you thought was right. I'm proud of you.' Her look softens.

She stands up abruptly and begins to pace the room. As much to herself as me, she declares, 'Ayesha said she was almost certain some traders at Statesbank are rigging foreign rates. Sue just doesn't want to know or, at least, acknowledge she knows.'

Freya turns towards me. 'When I first mentioned this to you, I don't feel you took it very seriously.' My protestation is on the tip of my tongue before I realise she is correct. She seems to detect my unspoken contrition.

'You can be forgiven for not automatically appreciating that Libor is the base interest rate on which private finance initiative hospitals make repayments. If the rate is dishonestly inflated, they have to pay more and, as you've told me, the hospital management's response to a shortage of money is often to close a ward.'

I stand and move towards her. 'I'm sorry. You're right, I hadn't thought through what you told me, the human cost.' I take her in my arms and hold her tight. I feel her body relax against me.

Soon after, there is a knock at the lounge door and we pull apart. Teresa enters and asks if we want more coffee or for her to prepare an extra meal for me. Freya looks at me quizzically.

'No, Teresa. Thank you, but I'm not staying.' She closes the door softly behind her.

I offer Freya a smile. 'Whatever the true situation is at the bank, your conscience should be clear.' I think this is the end of the matter but she looks sad. 'What?'

'Should it? Should both our consciences be clear?'

'I don't understand.'

She shakes her head at my perceived stupidity. 'Haven't you thought? The money we've raised for the research. Some of it has probably been corruptly earned. If the bank's profits hadn't been as large, then the bonuses wouldn't have been as generous and nor would the donations.'

It's my turn to start pacing the room. 'Well?' she enquires when a response from me isn't forthcoming.

Obviously, I can follow her train of thought but it seems to me unduly sanctimonious. I stand still and look at her again. 'Accepting you're right …' That seems the safest start. 'Isn't it better their money is spent on our research and not, say, on Bentleys or designer handbags.' Not that five or ten thousand pounds will go very far towards buying a Bentley. A terrible thought flashes into my mind. 'For God's sake, you can't be thinking of giving back what we haven't spent?'

She looks at me forlornly and I'm relieved when she slowly shakes her head. 'No.'

'No, we can't.' I have to hammer this point home. 'We're on the brink of something really important now and we have responsibilities to others. That money, apart from anything else, pays the salaries of our two scientists and three technicians.' Other potential arguments occur to me, such as is she sure that her house and lifestyle haven't been partially funded by Mark making ill-gotten gains, but I could never be that callous. And she already looks so sad.

'Don't worry. I won't do anything stupid and I will keep trying to raise more. I just can't shake the thought that the research has been funded with tainted money.'

35

Alice looks tired.

Perhaps I do too, but I don't feel it, for all the pressures of the long day. The thought of meeting Freya for Sunday lunch tomorrow is too enlivening, filling me with seemingly boundless energy. My watch shows ten thirty and, fleetingly I have a fond memory of my father whose watch it was originally. There is still one more patient we need to see on Intensive Care.

Alice's shift theoretically finished at eight pm but she will have to hand over to the night registrar before leaving, no small task after the day we've experienced. I'm fortunate to have had Alice's assistance. She's an experienced and conscientious registrar, and I know from working with her previously that her judgement is good. With a less able colleague, my task today would have been near impossible.

Our job has been made more onerous by the management's latest ruse. Patients in Accident and Emergency are supposed to be seen and then discharged or admitted within four hours. This is a crucial target affecting the Trust's star rating. Now, when a patient is about to breach the four-hour limit, he or she is sent for a chest X-ray or some other form of imaging, regardless of whether it is necessary or not, and then not allowed back into the A&E. Not only does this add to the imaging workload but more seriously, these unstable patients loiter in X-ray corridors with little supervision while a bed is sought for them. They are also harder for Alice and me to locate, wasting our limited time.

Sadly, this is only one of a number of such devious tricks and undesirable practices I am aware of management employing in attempts to be target compliant. It is difficult to avoid the unsettling thought that a few of the seemingly best-performing trusts may be just more adept at fiddling their figures.

The long corridor is quiet and empty, a marked contrast to its daytime bustle. The lighting is dimmed, creating a strangely intimate atmosphere despite its cavernous extent.

'How many have we admitted today, then?'

She consults her computer-generated list, heavily annotated in black biro. 'Forty- seven. And I've been called to three cardiac arrests. All died.'

I detect a trace of bitterness in her tone. Her considerable efforts and emotional expenditure at resuscitation unrewarded. Illogical perhaps, but all too human. 'That's what it's been like today.' she continues, 'Numbers aside, so many of them have been really sick.'

'A greater proportion usually is on Saturday and Sunday.'

'Do you think so? I've noticed that.'

'Yes, I'm convinced. As I see it, at the weekend, the patients who are very unwell call an ambulance but others who aren't as poorly decide to wait to ring their GPs on Monday, hoping their own doctors can deal with their problem. But then, the GPs still send many of them to hospital. That's why Monday is often the busiest day of the week for emergency admissions and a major reason why emergency mortality is higher at the weekend.'

She chuckles. 'That's not what the papers say. Apparently, more patients die at the weekend because you're on the golf course.'

'I should be so lucky.' It seems the appropriate response, though I'm not a golfer. I should qualify my flippant reply. 'To be fair, if there are some hospitals which, unlike this one, don't have enough consultants working at weekends then that needs to change.'

I laugh as a heretical thought occurs to me. Alice waits for me to enlighten her on the reason for my amusement. 'Paradoxically, the best way to reduce the disparity in emergency admission mortality in hospitals between weekdays and the weekend is to oblige GPs to provide a weekend service. That way, the less sick patients who currently delay until Monday will see a GP and then be admitted on Saturday and Sunday. Just as many will die at weekends but they'll be a smaller proportion of the total admissions on those days.'

'I see, so conversely, the percentage of emergencies dying at the beginning of the week will increase because the less sick patients haven't delayed coming.'

'Yes, but you're not likely to hear about that in the papers, or from the government, for that matter.'

'Why not?'

'Because they'll highlight that the proportion of patients dying at the weekends has fallen and is now similar to that of weekdays, vindicating their campaigns and initiatives. The details, whys, and wherefores will be lost in the headline message.'

'So, the apparent, if not real, fall in weekend mortality will look as though it's a consequence of making consultants curb their weekend golfing proclivity.'

'Unfortunately, yes. And you'll be one of us lazy consultants soon,' I add.

'Can't wait.'

She sighs before resuming. 'You know the other thing that really got on my wick today is the bed manager. She's kept ringing me up asking if I know of any beds. It's her job to find them. And calling me to suggest I go and see two little old dears who I don't know and decide whether they're fit to go home, only for me to find that their own teams reviewed them yesterday and concluded that they would have to wait for a package of social care to be put in place.'

It seems Alice has slipped into complaint mode. But my responsibilities to her are not only to listen but also to educate, particularly the things she can't learn from books and journals. Our progress down the corridor had slowed some time ago but now I stop completely and turn to face her fully.

'There's no doubt that it would help if social services could facilitate us discharging more of the elderly patients who are medically fit. Nobody disputes that. But even then, we would still need more beds. You know in the time I've been a consultant here, the management have closed two medical wards. That's nearly sixty beds.'

'Sixty! What I wouldn't have given for half of those today.'

'And you're right. When they briefly opened one of the closed wards last year, A&E became half empty most of the time as there was no wait for a ward bed. It made such a difference, much quieter, less hurly burly, easier for the staff to think and work, and much more reassuring for the patients.'

'No longer like a war zone, then?'

'No, not at all, considerably less stressful. As things are now, it's hardly surprising so many A&E. staff leave. I wish the management could see that.'

'So, why do you think they've closed these two wards? Is it money?' she asks.

'Money is almost always the bottom line in the NHS, but it's more complex than that.'

'Firstly, the management will always claim a ward isn't open because of a shortage of nurses. In other words, it's not their fault. Otherwise, they are liable to clinicians suggesting they reconsider their financial priorities.'

'Fewer managers?' she offers provocatively.

I smile. 'That would be likely to be one of our suggestions. But the management don't seem to appreciate that even claiming the reason is insufficient nurses is at least partly their fault. When the wards, as with the A&E. are full to bursting, it's more stressful for the nurses and some leave which, of course, only makes matters worse for the rest of them. And, to cap it all, some of the money saved by closing wards is then squandered by having to pay for expensive agency nurses to replace those the management are inadvertently driving away'

'Surely, somebody could explain that to them?'

'Do you think they would thank you for it?'

'Okay, probably not.'

'There might be a small chance of persuading them, but the situation is more complex than that. You know, of course, that the latest reorganisation of the NHS has given the money to the GPs, who are meant to commission services from the hospitals. The money follows the patient, or so the apparently sensible, if somewhat facile, theory goes.'

'Doesn't it work then?'

'Not that well. GPs always insist on under-purchasing emergency admissions. Consequently, emergencies generate a financial loss for hospitals. Since we can't bar the doors of

A&E, once we've filled our quota of purchased admissions, the only way to prevent what is euphemistically called "over performing," is to announce to the other local hospitals that we are full and try to divert emergencies there.'

'But what if all the hospitals did that?' asks Alice, looking a little alarmed.

'They sometimes try to. So, you see, it wouldn't be enough for some brave doctor to persuade the management to open another ward here because it would rapidly fill with emergencies diverted from outside our catchment area. Then we'd spend even more money on those out-of-area patients which would never be reimbursed, the trust would appear to be financially mismanaged and the chief executive and finance director might be sacked. So, there is a bizarre logic to the management's behaviour after all.'

Alice looks at me, clearly attempting to comprehend the inanity of the system. Then, surprisingly, she grins again. 'I feel like Alice in Wonderland.' Her smile grows even wider as she enjoys her joke.

'You look more like you're auditioning for the role of the Cheshire Cat.'

'Maybe and I could think of one or two suitable people to play the Mad Hatter.'

I have to laugh at that. 'More than one or two, Alice. More than one or two.'

36

Tranquillity, so infrequent and precious in my hectic life. The last few months have not been easy as Freya and I have met surreptitiously to avoid endangering Lily's recovery. But now Freya has decided we can be more open in our relationship.

We are walking the two or three miles back to Freya's house after Sunday lunch at a pub. The path runs flat and straight between fields of sprouting wheat, a sea of green rippling in the gentle breeze. The May weather is unseasonably warm, allowing Freya to wear shorts displaying her long, shapely legs. A few wispy clouds float in a pale blue sky, reminding me of the day we first met many years ago. How strange that she has no recollection of that encounter. One day I must tell her. But not yet. When the time is ripe.

For now, we walk hand in hand. How remarkably satisfying it is, arguably more indicative of our being a couple than having sex. We stroll, temporarily in silence, relaxed enough in each other's company not to have to fill each moment with words.

We may be silent but Luke and Lily, ambling along twenty

paces or so ahead of us, are certainly not. Their chatter is incessant, interspersed with an occasional giggle from Lily. I wonder how they are finding so much to talk about. But there can be no doubt they are enjoying each other's company. Lily now looks properly nourished and healthy, and had eaten normally at the pub. Luke repeatedly leans down a little towards her and the radiance on her up-turned face matches that of the sunny day.

I had hoped that bringing Luke today would facilitate breaking the ice between Lily and myself. So far, so good. I was slightly surprised that he had agreed to come so readily. Perhaps it was curiosity, wanting to check out Dad's girlfriend. Odd calling a woman of Freya's age a girlfriend but is there an alternative? Partner? Doesn't that imply more of a shared life, living together?

I would like to spend more time with Freya, have even considered suggesting that we go on holiday, but Lily accompanying us might lead to conflicts and Freya's passport anecdote is enough to make the most ardent suitor wary. Leaving Lily behind is not a realistic option, either. Wouldn't that be seen as my stealing her mother from her?

A terrible thought enters my mind, not by any means for the first time. Better to voice it now than allow it to fester. 'Freya.' She turns from contentedly regarding Lily and Luke towards me. 'Do you think?' This is hard. She looks disconcerted by my sudden, apparent change of mood. 'Do you think Lily believes I let Mark die so …' How to phrase this? 'So, I could be with you?'

She stops in her tracks and a look of horror passes over her beautiful face. 'No! No, no. You must never think that. Yes, she was very close to her father, but she is slowly coming to terms with it, and I've told her many times that you and the other doctors did everything possible for him. And, of course, she knows about the research you're doing.'

I persist. 'It's just that children can sometimes harbour strange ideas. And with what she said to me in your hall ...'

Freya puts both her hands on my cheeks. 'That first time you met, she was lashing out. At things she didn't fully understand. And you were there, in the firing line.'

I know about this in my professional life. It's easier to blame a tangible doctor than fate or any god, and much harder for me to endure when it's so personal.

Freya pulls my head towards her and kisses me fiercely, seemingly uncaring if Lily should turn and see us.

****

I lie in bed, reviewing the day. Sadly, my own bed, not Freya's. It hadn't felt right to send
Luke home alone in a taxi while I stayed behind. Not only for him, but better not to intrude into Lily and Freya's evening together.

I remind myself that today was always intended as an investment in the future. A future together with Freya seems to hold the promise of immense happiness. She appears to think the same, so what is preventing it? Mark died over a year ago, Clare more than a year and a half. Decent intervals, the time for grieving should be over, Freya and I should both move on.

Am I too cowardly, unable to face the possibility of her rejection? Faint heart never won fair lady. Maybe, but somehow, now does not seem the optimum time for me to propose to her.

Lily's antipathy is a significant factor, one that I hope her pleasant experiences today will help to erode. What does she really think about me now?

Freya has sought to reassure me that Lily knows about the research I've initiated, assuming she must perceive this as virtuous, but my analytical brain unkindly has presented alternatives to me. Lily may see it as a way for me to atone for allowing her father to die. More plausibly, though the two possibilities are not mutually exclusive, she may regard it as a device to facilitate my becoming close to her mother. The former I would reject but the latter would be more difficult to deny. It is irrefutable that our shared quest has brought, and hopefully is continuing to bring, Freya and me closer together. But it is a bonus, not the fundamental reason I embarked on the research.

And why did I? Undoubtedly, Freya's scorn at my, and my colleagues', impotence in saving Mark and the poignancy of my final conversation with him had been catalysts, but like sparks on tinder, there was a ready substrate for them to act on.

I had abandoned my research activities just before achieving my consultant post, disillusioned by the theft of my ideas. Though, as this disenchantment faded with time, it was countered by an increasing burden of work and family responsibilities. If I was to devote sufficient time to Clare and the boys, the only way to find the time to pursue research was not to practise privately. But without that income, I couldn't pay the mortgage or school fees.

Now, my situation is more permissive, though that still does not address the question of why I feel impelled to do it. I have no desire for fame, influence, enhanced status. There is, of course, an intellectual satisfaction to discovery, solving a puzzle, particularly one so important. Primarily though, I feel a sense of duty. No longer a very fashionable concept but hardly so unusual. Altruism seems to be encoded in most peoples' genomes, probably a necessary adaptation to facilitate social cooperation.

    Whatever the explanation, for the time being, at least, I feel better, more fulfilled by our early successful efforts.

37

Hospital corridors, the site of many impromptu meetings, offering a chance to exchange news, facilitate referrals, enhance relationships. Congenial encounters unless you are late and your colleague loquacious. But I sense this one will be different.

It has to be Klaus coming towards me. Tall, thin, well dressed, his head is drooping so much I can't see his face. And where has his confident, long stride gone? He is shuffling along, almost as if he is drunk.

'Klaus, are you alright?' How do I manage to say such stupid things? He's obviously not alright. He raises his head and his eyes slowly focus on me, as though he's just woken from sleep. Does he have narcolepsy? Can you sleepwalk if you're narcoleptic? Ridiculous ideas that the look on his face belies, one of shock and desolation. Did I look like this when Alan found me waiting during Adam's cardiac catheterisation?

'Oh, Miles,' he struggles to utter.

'What's wrong?' He looks off into the distance and does not answer. Without conscious thought, I have put a hand on one of his upper arms and am squeezing it gently. He turns his gaze slowly towards my hand but makes no attempt to shrug it off. 'Come, come on, my office is nearby.' I steer him gently in the correct direction. Andrew Roberts is in outpatients. We will have it to ourselves. What is the matter? It must be one of his family, ill or died.

'Have a seat.' His lanky frame collapses onto a chair which creaks under the strain.

'Do you want a drink? A cup of tea?'

'Ha,' a brief derisive sound. 'I do not think my predicament will respond to your traditional English remedy.' His obvious distress renders this remark inoffensive.

I try again. 'Tell me, then.'

Klaus regards me for a few moments before making an almost imperceptible nod. 'So.' He pauses, perhaps to gather his thoughts or is it that he does not want to verbalise his situation, acknowledge that it is real. 'I am suspended.' He almost spits this out. 'Just now, by Graham and that human resources' woman, Owen.'

Though I expected him to tell me something terrible, this is difficult to comprehend. Klaus was recently made clinical director of surgery: an indication of the high regard the Trust must have held him in at the time of this appointment. One of our best surgeons and by all accounts a man of impeccable character. What can he have done to deserve this?

'But why?'

He grimaces. 'There is why and why.' I don't understand but after a brief pause, he continues. 'Graham and Mrs Owen claim they are suspending me because of concerns about my surgical practice and, in support, cite a patient of mine who died of a stroke post-operatively. He was in his seventies with a history of heart disease, a high-risk case. I do not remember anything wrong with the operation. I made a potentially curative resection of his bowel cancer.'

The stress of surgery and an anaesthetic can precipitate unpredictable complications in patients with vascular diseases. This is well known and even the subject of gallows humour: "the operation went well but the patient died." It does not sound to me as if Klaus is culpable. 'What about the notes?' I am trying to be practical. What is written in the operation record and case notes could be crucial.

'They had them on the desk in front of them but would not let me see, taunted me, told me there will be time enough for me to examine them in due course. I think "in due course" will be many months. Damn them!'

'Did the relatives complain?' I'm still trying to get my head round this, searching for something that might have prompted this apparent over-reaction by the management.

He shakes his head. 'No. I spoke to the patient's wife immediately after his death and again, together with a daughter, a few days later. They were very understanding. Thanked me for my efforts. I remember the conversations well. Strange what people say sometimes. His wife looked so lost when she told me she had already bought his Christmas present.'

This is not right. 'So, was this last year?'

'Ja, November.' That is over six months ago.

If the management have concerns, why have they only acted now? A grim possibility surfaces in my brain. 'What is the other "why", Klaus?'

'The other why.' He turns towards the window but I doubt he is looking at the view, his focus is inward. I sit there quietly until he is ready to resume.

'Eamon Keane.' It is barely more than a whisper.

Mr. Keane is an upper gastro-intestinal surgeon, a few

years from retirement. I had never taken to him, found his manner shallow and supercilious. Consequently, I send appropriate referrals to his two younger sub-speciality colleagues.

Klaus turns to look at me again. 'I had heard things. Not good. When I became clinical director earlier this year, I began to investigate his operative morbidity and mortality. Stealthily. I was not going to accuse a man until I was sure of my facts.' He shudders. 'But it is dreadful. Truly dreadful. I searched through many notes of patients he had operated on and found eight serious adverse events this year alone, including what I consider to be three avoidable deaths.'

This is appalling. Could Klaus be mistaken? But I cannot believe that. He has a reputation for being meticulous and, by his words just now, has shown he is not a man to jump to premature or ill-founded conclusions.

As if he can read my mind - or perhaps my thoughts are discernible from my expression, - he states, 'I know. It is hard to believe. And there is more. I have not had time to fully investigate earlier years but already I have found other disasters. It became clear to me that there is a trail of bodies waiting to be discovered - if we care to look. I can't understand why it has taken until now to find out. How can that be, Miles?'

'I don't know, Klaus. I don't know.'

He shakes his head. 'It is difficult to hide much from the juniors, so last week I spoke to my registrar, in strict confidence. Confidence I am now breaking by telling you, but someone else should hear this. They have a nickname for him. It's Killer, Killer Keane.'

I shut my eyes but I cannot block out the horror of what I have just heard, or my nascent insight into Klaus' suspension.

I hardly need to hear the rest.

Klaus resumes his sorry tale. 'I would have wished to continue my investigation but I realised that it would be indulging myself and that I had to act now to save future patients of Mr Keane's from harm. I quickly wrote a detailed report of my findings so far and ...'

'And gave it to Graham, who no doubt promised to deal with it immediately.'

'Ja, you understand.'

'I understand.' Too bloody right, I understand. My shock is being superseded by fury. Klaus, his story told, looks deflated. He musters a brave smile.

'I must go. I am not meant to remain in the hospital. Thank you for listening.' He rises from his chair and opens my office door.

'I will do more than that, Klaus.' I don't know what, but the urge to assist him is almost over-powering.

'No, you cannot help me. I fear no one can.'

I struggle for something to say. He raises a hand in salutation, leaves my office and begins to walk away but his progress is quickly halted by the security doors guarding the consultants' offices. He has swiped his card ineffectually three times through the scanner. The bastards have deactivated it already. I go and open the door for him with mine.

****

What should I do? The question batters round my brain like a pinball in an arcade machine. Angry as I am, it is still obvious to me that demanding to see Graham and protesting at Klaus' mistreatment would achieve nothing, other than perhaps my own suspension.

Alan. I must speak to Alan. He is at his desk, scanning microbiology reports. His door ajar, I knock and walk in. My agitation must be obvious to him. His perceptiveness is wasted on his bugs. He gestures towards the chair next to his desk and says simply, 'Tell me.'

So, I do. He listens attentively, never interrupts, though inevitably his expression clouds, the more he hears. At the end, gazing out towards the flowers in his courtyard, he sits there stunned. We sit in silence for a while. I need to give him time to absorb the awful information, eventually asking, 'What should I do, Alan?'

He stares at me, shakes his head a little and then more vigorously. 'No, you shouldn't do anything. You can't, can't do anything effective to help Klaus. The management are all powerful, you realise that.' I don't know what I expected him to say, but not this.

'But it's wrong, so wrong. They are ruthlessly destroying Klaus's career for their own selfish ends. And it's not just Klaus, more people will be harmed and die unnecessarily if Eamon Keane is allowed to continue operating.'

'Miles, that's the management's responsibility, not yours. Perhaps they will deal with Keane in their own way?' His latter sentence is not stated with any conviction. I feel my anger rising again.

'I don't buy it. You don't really believe that do you? By their actions, the management have made it plain that all they care about is their own interests, avoiding a scandal. Patients are just disposable commodities to them, plenty more available.'

'What if it was one of your family Keane had killed?'

He winces. That was cruel of me. Pertinent, maybe, but cruel, nevertheless.

'I'm sorry. I shouldn't vent my frustration on you.'

'Look, we are so near now. Near to achieving something of major importance that could save thousands, hundreds of thousands of lives. We have to stay focused on the research. Try to fight wars on two fronts and you are likely to lose, lose everything. That was Hitler's downfall. Surely you can see that?'

'Yes, but while we're on wartime analogies, we should remember Winston Churchill saying: "All that is necessary for evil to triumph is for good men to do nothing".'

38

Under a leaden sky, I pick my way carefully through a morass of human misery. All around, people sit or lie upon the ground. Some groan or cry out in pain, a few in the grip of fever ramble deliriously. A boy, glistening white bone protruding from his right shin, tries to stand on his left leg but collapses again in a pool of his own blood.

I walk on, side-stepping an elderly woman who is sobbing as she kneels and clutches a hand of an inert man. Up ahead is brilliant sunshine but, barring my way, is a huge wrought-iron gate set between two gigantic yew hedges. People clutch at the gate, shaking its bars and plead with two beefy men to be allowed in. "Security" is stencilled across the chests of the men's lurid yellow uniforms.

'I'm a doctor, let me through,' I shout above the hubbub.

A cliché but nevertheless the crowd fall silent, turn to me in wonder and make room for me to pass. I can now see a small, locked gate in the much larger one. I repeat my hackneyed incantation for the benefit of the security guards but this time the only response is an indifferent shrug from the larger of the two.

'I'm a doctor. I can help,' I plead.

'This is the patients' entrance, mate,' says the older of the two.

'How do I get in?' frustration all too evident in my tone.

'At the doctors' one. How do you think?' He turns towards his fellow guard, smirking. 'Cor, Sam, I thought these doctors were meant to be clever.' But their mirth is halted abruptly by an imperious voice.

'Let him through. And three more.' Instantly, their demeanour changes as they rush to do the voice's bidding. A figure appears around the corner of a hedge. A red floor length dress of sumptuous velvet, hennaed hair beneath a crown. Even from the side I recognise the Red Queen. But when she turns towards me, it is the puffy face of Max Lytle wearing crimson lipstick.

'Welcome to the Looking Glass Hospital, Doctor Westwood. Please pardon my uncouth staff but they have an unpleasant task keeping that rabble at bay.'

'But ...' I hesitate, considering how to address her. She perceives my difficulty and interjects.

'"Your Majesty" is the correct mode of address. And I do not like the word "but".'

I try again. 'Your Majesty, that rabble, as you call them, is patients.'

She gives me a withering look. 'Perhaps the guard was right and you doctors are not as clever as you believe. They,' she gestures towards the gate, 'they are NOT patients because they are not in the hospital. It is simple logic, is it not?' She shakes her head at my stupidity and her crown wobbles precariously, its diamonds and rubies sparkling in the bright sunlight. She continues to berate me. 'And have you no conception of duty? I would certainly be failing in mine if I allowed the uncontrolled admission of that horde to disrupt the orderly function of this hospital.'

'Come, I will show you how a hospital should be run.'

She leads me round a corner of a large yew hedge. Stretching before us is a long wide grass path bounded on either side by deep flower beds with further tall yew hedges behind them. Patients in hospital beds are interspersed regularly among the flowers. 'You see,' she asserts proudly, 'order. Order and efficiency. These are the foundations of any viable organisation.'

Just behind me, I hear a squawk of protest. I turn to see an elderly woman being bundled into a large wheelbarrow by Eamon Keane, dressed in gardening clothes. He sneers at me before trundling his burden away. Two peonies beside the now vacant bed metamorphose into nurses and begin to change the bed sheets, and more ominously, remove the patient's name from over the bed.

I turn to face the Red Queen. 'Your Majesty, where is he taking her?'

'For composting.'

'Composting?' but even as I parrot the word, I understand her sinister meaning. She looks at me as if I am a pupil beyond hope of enlightenment.

'Of course, how else can we begin to accommodate at least a few of that rabble without some re-cycling. And we have our targets. Follow me.' She sweeps away.

I trail obediently in her wake. We pass through a gap in a yew hedge. Before us are three large archery targets secured in a concrete base, a bound and gagged person, dressed in a hospital gown, is tied to each of them.

'Begin!' commands the Red Queen. Three archers clothed

in green and brown start to fire.

'No. No, stop!' But they ignore me. Arrows thump into the captives. Blood gushes from their wounds, staining the concrete and the immaculate lawn. They attempt to cry out but no sounds emerge. I turn away in sorrow.

'Do you not approve of my bed facilitators' actions, Doctor Westwood? Without them, the hospital could not possibly begin to meet its targets.'

'Bed facilitators. Is that what you call them?'

'What else would you propose?' she asks in a voice laced with scorn. 'They are clearly facilitating the turnover of beds. Besides, it is my prerogative to give them any job title I wish.'

'But you can't hope to get away with this. There are records, case notes.'

She glares at me. Her cheeks are flushed, almost matching the colour of her dress. 'I have warned you, no "buts" are allowed. And what a pathetic objection.' She turns towards a yew hedge and crooks a finger towards her. Three sets of patient notes float out of the hedge. She straightens her finger and makes a stabbing motion towards the records which disappear in puffs of white smoke.

'There. You see how easy it is to make records disappear.' She sighs. 'You seem to have no appreciation of the onus of senior management. Difficult decisions have to be taken if the organisation is to thrive.'

'And always we must be mindful of the numbers.' A hint of a smile crosses her face. 'I do so like numbers. Such malleable creatures. Six is my favourite.' With a flick of her wrist, the Red Queen conjures up a girl, dressed in a white one-piece suit emblazoned with a red number six. The girl cocks her head enquiringly.

'Yes, yes, girl. Do your stuff.' She stands on her hands

creating a number nine. With another flick of the Red Queen's hand, girl number seven appears. Looking a little bemused, she positions herself on the other girls' right creating the number seventy- nine. The sky darkens abruptly, lit only by a solitary star.

'No, you stupid creature,' the Red Queen screams. 'Would you have us in special measures? Are you trying to commit regicide? The other side. Stand the other side.' The trembling number seven opens her mouth as if to protest. 'Don't. Don't presume to tell me where you think you should stand if you want to keep your head. You go where I please.'

Number seven moves into the place she is ordered. Four more bright stars appear in the sky and the gloom is dispelled.

'You see! Ninety-seven, that's the sort of percentage we need as a centre of excellence.' She glares at the numbers. 'Enough, away with you both,' she orders disdainfully. The numbers vanish and the sun reappears.

'I hope you begin to understand, Doctor Westwood, as with so many aspects of life, reality must take second place to appearances.'

Come. I will show you the public face of my hospital: the rose garden.' Around us appear beds of roses, all in bloom with deep red flowers. The Red Queen picks up a pair of secateurs and begins to remove dead or dying flowers.

'They need constant attention. And, at times, if their growth becomes unruly, as with any part of this organisation, vigorous pruning is mandatory.'

She gives me a brief, wistful look. 'It is a shame you are not a team player and that your sacrifice has become necessary.' Her small secateurs have grown into large shears with blood-stained blades. She advances towards me with a determined expression.

39

'In conclusion, we have discovered a bacterium, Helicobacter bili and found it to be present in the bile of over ninety per cent of patients with pancreatic adenocarcinoma compared to around twenty per cent of healthy people. Furthermore, we have demonstrated that antibiotic treatment, likely to have eradicated this bacterium, led subsequently to a much-reduced incidence of this cancer'.

I can remember every word. Almost hear myself again addressing the thousands of my world-wide peers packed into the huge auditorium. But I was not prepared for what happened next. Some of the audience stood and clapped enthusiastically, with even a few scattered cheers of "bravo". Not, in itself, such a remarkable event, routine at a theatre show but I'd never seen it before at a medical conference.

We doctors are normally so self-restrained and our presentations, as mine had been, are matter of fact, devoid of hyperbole. Strange how I'd felt, not just elation but also relief, relieved to have performed well in front of the watching Alan and Freya. And, as the applause subsided, a fleeting, foolish wish that Clare could have been there to see me as well.

Much more emotional than yesterday when I had presented our gallstone results. These strongly support our hypothesis that both Helicobacter bili and bile supersaturated with cholesterol together are necessary for stones to form. I suppose it's because most of the audience perceive the work as of academic interest only.

The relevant surgery is now so skilful that it has swept away all attempts at medical treatment.

Why wait six months for your stones to dissolve and risk their probable recurrence when you could have keyhole surgery to remove your gallbladder instead? Except that a few patients did experience complications from the operation or the anaesthetic, and around a quarter were no better after surgery because the gallstones had not been the cause of their pain in the first place. Many peoples' gallstones do not cause them any symptoms but such uncertainties don't seem to bother some surgeons. Perhaps now we can develop a pragmatic alternative treatment.

And from now on, even if the patient had their gallbladder removed, then he or she was going to want their Helicobacter bili treated. Who would want to harbour a bacterium which might in the future give them pancreatic cancer? A potential disaster waiting to happen.

Today, after the presentation, I couldn't stay at the meeting, feeling cooped up, too restless to sit still, unable temporarily to concentrate on anyone else's lecture. Freya and I had made our escape into the autumn sunshine, walked the length of the Ramblas - immersed in the throng of tourists, revelling in the spectacle, thoughts of bacteria and disease banished temporarily. A late, leisurely lunch beside the Barcelona quayside and then, ineluctably, back to our hotel room.

Is sex in the afternoon more enjoyable? It certainly has a tinge of decadence about it, hedonism at a time when many people are working. Now, I am sitting on our balcony, savouring the last of the day's sunshine, gazing down on the view of the city below me. From my elevated vantage point, I can see over all the old town, dominated by the soaring spires of Gaudi's cathedral, to the enveloping hills beyond.

I still find it hard to believe what we have accomplished and in only nineteen months. It's an awful thought but this would never have happened if Mark had not died or even if he had presented to another consultant. And would I have been as susceptible to Freya's grief and vituperation if I'd not had that brief relationship with her? Or if Clare had still been alive?

It's all so seemingly random. From what I've been reading lately about Norse gods and goddesses, the early Scandinavians would have had no such dilemma. It was Mark's and Clare's destiny, no question. They had to die so others could live. Nonsense, of course, but if events had not played out as they did, how many years before someone else hit on our ideas? How many people would have died in that time? People we can now hope to save.

I rise from my chair and look down at the people bustling along the pavement below, oblivious to the many bacterial and viral dangers lurking inside of them, the pathogens just waiting for the opportune moment to strike. Perhaps ignorance is bliss? Thinking like this, unless you can alter the situation, is not the road to happiness.

Oh, come on, Freya. She is still busy, preparing for our dinner with Alan and his second wife, Amy, beautifying herself even more. Or, as she might see it, repairing the damage I had inflicted on her hair and make-up. If she doesn't get a move on, we'll be late.

'I'm ready,' trills Freya from the bedroom. Good. As always, she looks fabulous and is wearing a figure-hugging black dress cut just above the knee which leaves her shoulders bare. Her cheeks are still a little flushed from our afternoon exertions.

It's only a very short walk across the square to our chosen restaurant, bursting with customers. The atmosphere is lively, almost festive. There is a spectacular view over the Barcelona harbour, a host of lights, their reflections dancing on the placid water.

Alan and Amy have already arrived and are drinking champagne. She is small, slightly overweight with dark hair, cut short, and wearing a turquoise dress displaying a generous cleavage. Perhaps a decade younger than Alan, vivacious, and even now a little tipsy. Incongruous perhaps, as of the four of us, she has had the least involvement and therefore cause to celebrate. She pours Freya and I some champagne and then raises her own glass. 'Well done, guys. You're a great team.'

We duly drink a toast, then Alan observes, 'Part of a great team.' His mobile pings. 'Talk of the devil,' he laughs. 'It's Aaron, one of our scientists', he explains for Freya's benefit as he enters his password. For a moment, he looks puzzled then shows us his phone revealing a brief cryptic message: "Fame?"

Freya and I glance at each other in bemusement.

'There's an attachment, darling. Here, give it to me. He's not good with it,' Amy says disloyally. She activates the attachment, clearly a clip from this evening's BBC news and holds it so we all can see.

'British doctors today announced that they may have discovered the cause of pancreatic cancer and it's a bacterium, treatable with antibiotics.' I groan but the others ignore me as the scene shifts to a presenter outside our hospital. After a few further details of our research, the camera pans back to reveal Max Lytle, complete with a self-satisfied expression.

'A remarkable achievement,' the presenter prompts.

'Yes. It is indicative of the ethos we have engendered at this Trust, placing excellence at the heart of all our activities, whether that be providing clinical care, or our commitment to and support for our ground-breaking research,' he declares smugly.

'Thank you, Mr Lytle.'

The attachment finishes and for a few moments, we regard each other, slightly dumbfounded. Amy breaks the silence, 'What a slimy git.'

Freya casts a disapproving glance at her, perhaps just because of the coarse turn of phrase, but I could drink to that assessment.

In vino veritas.

40

Back to reality.
My first day of clinical work since my return from Spain and already I feel tired. Maybe the apprehension before the meeting and the stress of performing has taken more out of me than I'd appreciated. Still, it has been a particularly busy day.

The ward round was only just achievable in the time available. Since the latest move of gastroenterology to a smaller ward, we are obliged to see more referrals, scattered hither and thither throughout the hospital, patients who should have been accommodated on our ward in the first place. It's not efficient and it's less safe. At least I'd made the management aware that was likely to be the outcome, even if it hasn't made any difference.

Outpatients is little better. Seemingly regardless of the number of patients I indicate to the booking department that I am capable of seeing in a session, more and more are crammed in. Are the booking clerks told to do this, to comply with the relevant waiting time targets? What is certain is that I couldn't have worked any faster in this afternoon's clinic. Not without denying the patients the time with me that they deserve and have often waited so long for. I've learnt how to curtail a garrulous patient's discursive history diplomatically and have the experience to cut a few corners safely, but there are limits.

Unfortunately, my new specialist registrar is a first year and still very slow. I was obliged to see some of the patients on his list, in addition to my own. An unexpected bonus was Joyce Briggs walking, albeit slowly and with a walking stick, into my consulting room. I remember endoscopically banding her bleeding oesophageal varices a year or so after I arrived here. Her liver disease has been so well controlled by treatment that I have not seen her since her discharge, way back nearly fourteen years ago, as I attempt to devote my time to the sickest patients.

Nearly finished now. A nurse bustles into my out-patient room.

'That's it, Doctor Westwood.' Welcome news. She plonks four sets of notes on the desk with a thud. 'These are the DNA's. What would we do without them? I'm off now, supposed to have finished at six. I've left a trolley outside for you.'

'Goodnight. Thanks for your help.'

She pauses in the doorway, turns, and gives me a warm smile. 'A pleasure, Doctor Westwood. Don't stay too late.'

Tempting as her advice may be, the reality is that I must dictate letters to the general practitioners about the twenty-two patients I've seen today and refer a couple of them urgently on to other consultants. There was no time to do this during the clinic this afternoon. There rarely is. I will have to do it this evening while my memory are still fresh.

Helen, the nurse who helped me today, knows I don't like to dictate here in a soulless and deserted outpatient suite and would rather do so in my office. At least there I can make myself a cup of coffee and consume some of my stash of chocolate. Too many notes to carry back to my room, hence I am obliged to wheel a trolley full through the hospital, like the pickings from a supermarket of disease.

Helen is right, I muse. How would we cope without the DNA's? Blithely and ignorantly condemned by health "experts" as a source of wasted expenditure, we rely on there always being a few. If there weren't, I would have to make greater efforts to limit my clinic template and therefore no more patients would be seen, though there may then be a statistic apparently demonstrating greater efficiency. What is that saying about statistics and lies?

****

I wake suddenly. It's the middle of the night. I stretch out an arm before I remember that Freya is not next to me and I'm back in my own bed, alone. What am I going to do? I so want, so need to be with her every day. It would have been good to have had her to talk to yesterday evening, share our latest experiences with each other. Perhaps then I wouldn't wake so often as my brain processes my hectic days' events.

My mind jumps "laterally", as it so often does. How? How could I be so stupid? I pride myself on my intelligence and yet I didn't see it. A solution may be achievable. D.N.A. "Did Not Attend" in outpatient parlance but, in any other context, deoxyribonucleic acid.

What an idiot I am.

41

The restaurant is quiet, cosy, and elegant. A candle flickers on the table between us, the soft glow erasing the minor wrinkles on the classical features of Freya's face.

'How's Lily?' How many times in recent months have I asked that question?

'Better.' Freya is nodding in affirmation of her assessment, causing her diamond earing studs to sparkle in the candlelight. 'Definitely improving. You know, I still feel hurt about what she said to you, the first time you met her.'

'Oh, Freya, it's history. Anger is a normal part of grieving.'

'But I want you to know she doesn't dislike you.' She laughs. 'She thinks you're quite cool, particularly as you're Luke's father.' That was the plan.

'Luke made quite an impression on her. All of a sudden, she's developed a passion for tennis.' I laugh. 'You may laugh but it's costing me money, I'll have you know, kitting her out with all the gear, club membership, and weekly lessons. And she demanded two rackets. One wasn't enough.' She sighs. 'But it's hard not to indulge her at the moment.'

- UNDER CONTROL -

Freya leans towards me confidingly. 'She tells me she has designs on Luke when she's a few years older. Young girls have these silly ideas. But he is such a lovely boy.'

'He liked Lily too.' Though not as much as he approved of Freya, I decline to mention. "She's seriously hot, Dad." I was grateful he hadn't called her a MILF, a term I find seedy and one that would have been unsettling under the circumstances. What was the male equivalent? Hardly surprising you didn't hear that acronym bandied about.

I had asked Luke to keep in touch with Lily. "No problem, Dad. She's a cute kid. I've already accepted her friend request on Facebook" was his reply.

'I meant to ask you at the time,' Freya says. 'Why did you groan when you heard the news report on Alan's phone?'

'Ah yes. Well, I thought the headline message was accurate but its brevity rendered it ambiguous. I'm sure some patients with pancreatic cancer or their relatives hearing it will think that they may benefit from antibiotic treatment. I expect that very soon I'll be flooded with GP referrals for these desperate patients, many from outside the hospital's catchment area, whose hopes I will have to dash.'

'Are you sure it won't help?'

'I really don't think so. Of course, the only way to be sure is to try it in some patients. I won't be able to avoid that as they will argue it can't do much, if any, harm to try antibiotics. Inevitably some will have a placebo response, feel it has helped them and in no time at all will have Tweeted, Facebooked, or by some other electronic means, spread news of the treatment's supposed success around the world.'

Freya pulls a face. 'Don't you think you're being a bit cynical?'

'Sorry if I've come across that way and I'd use more diplomatic language if it wasn't you I was talking to, but really, is it kind to raise false hope in these people? And my NHS clinics are already bursting at the seams.'

'I understand. Well, one advantage of the news report, at least, is that we're not going to have any difficulty raising more funds. Have you thought that some of the patients, even if realistically you can't help them personally, may be inclined to make bequests to our research?'

I raise my eyebrows. Why didn't I think of that? 'No, I hadn't but you're right.'

'Money is part of my job, darling.' Freya blows me a kiss across the table. I like the "darling" and have no ego issue in conceding that a commercial lawyer is more fiscally aware than most doctors. And there are no ethical issues in accepting donations for our research from patients or their relatives. I'm relieved Freya hasn't raised the issue of our potentially tainted bankers' money again.

As the smile slowly subsides from her face, Freya says, 'On another matter, when we were listening to Alan's talk in Barcelona about bili, he mentioned that it is believed that many people with Helicobacter pylori probably acquire the bacterium as a baby from one of their parents.'

'Yes, that's right.'

'So, we must presume Mark had bili and therefore he may have given it to Lily?'

'Yes.' Her logic is sound. I'm glad she's raised this, otherwise I was going to.

'So, shouldn't we test her? And me as well?'

'Yes. Good idea.'

'And while we're on the subject, shouldn't you test yourself, if you've not already done so?'

'Sure.'

Perfect.

42

This is overdue. I should have made time for it before now, though I wonder how many of our other colleagues have visited. Colleagues are not necessarily friends, of course, but don't we share the same purpose, have an obligation to support each other in that aim? Or am I being ridiculously altruistic?

I can attempt to excuse my omission on the grounds of our research. Alan may have been correct that before was not an appropriate time for me to be distracted but when will be? There is still so much to do. "Ars longa, vita brevis". The art is long, life short, as Hippocrates said, and it certainly hasn't become an easier task in the two thousand years or so since then.

I am grateful for my BMW's satnav as I make the convoluted journey to his home. The house is large, rather rambling, clearly an amalgam of the original and at least two extensions. A weeping willow's branches dangle towards the stream that runs along one side of the house. Two bay trees in large grey pots stand guard by the entrance. The garden is neat, all ready for winter. It should be. He has plenty of time to attend to it now. Not for nothing is suspension euphemistically termed "gardening leave".

I make a dash from my car through the driving rain to his front door and ring the bell. 'Good afternoon.'

'Miles. What a pleasant surprise.'

He certainly appears surprised to see me. He also looks disproportionally older than the last time I saw him. I presume it's the stress.

'Sorry. Probably should have rung and made some arrangement with you, but I wasn't sure what time my private practice would finish today.' Not an entirely satisfactory excuse but I didn't want to give him the opportunity to refuse to see me, perhaps too proud to relish me witnessing his diminished status. I realise, belatedly, that my being dressed in a suit while he is wearing dark blue chinos and a grey sweater may emphasise this.

'Not at all. You're very welcome. Come in. Come in out of this foul weather.' He leads me to a large room overlooking his back garden as I brush the raindrops off the shoulders of my jacket.

He musters a smile. 'Tea? Coffee?'

'A black coffee, please.'

He disappears into the adjoining kitchen. I hear water beginning to heat in a kettle and the rattle of crockery. The lounge is immaculately tidy apart from a large pile of documents on a side table with a few sheets scattered on a sofa, along with a pair of reading glasses. There is a piano in the corner, black and burnished, exuding a faint whiff of lemon polish, with framed family photos gracing its top.

Klaus returns bearing two mugs and passes me mine. He picks up one of the photographs and shows it to me. 'My wife, Ingrid, and our two children.' He corrects himself.

'Hardly children anymore, both at university now. Seems no time at all since they were little.'

'I know. I have two sons, only a little younger than yours.'

'But your wife, she died last year.' He gives me a brief, sympathetic look.

I sigh. 'Yes, a stroke, no warning. At least it was quick.'

'Ah, I remind myself, often these days, that we all have problems of some sort, and to count my blessings as you say. Ingrid has been very supportive, never a word of recrimination. She's at the supermarket, by the way, or I would introduce you.'

I nod then gesture towards the piano with my free hand. 'Do you play?'

'Yes, mainly Beethoven and Bach. Every day now. It is a comfort to me. A tranquilliser, if you wish.'

'How's it going? Are you making progress?' He knows what I'm referring to. No need to use unpleasant words like suspension.

'Ha, progress. Regressing more like. Look there.' He points at the pile of documents. 'Paper, paper, and more paper. They are trying to drown me in it. Refuse to communicate with me or my representative from the Medical Defence Union by e-mail. Probably too quick. Posting letters, second class, incidentally, imposes delay. I won't be returning to work any time soon. If ever,' he adds gloomily.

'Haven't you been able to refute the management's accusation based on the case notes?'

He shakes his head and looks away briefly towards his rain-drenched garden. 'I've not seen the notes. They have gone missing, would you believe?' A rhetorical question, if ever I've heard one. 'And they have made another charge. I am accused of bullying my juniors. It is preposterous.'

I can believe he is strict with them but he strikes me as a fair man, not a bully. 'What evidence do they have for that, Klaus?'

'A junior complained about me. She wanted my support to enter registrar training in surgery but I refused. I had watched her carefully in the operating theatre many times, tried to teach her but she lacked the necessary spatial ability.'

'I understand. I had a registrar once who just could not grasp how to perform ERCP. Not a disaster for him as he could do simpler endoscopies and colonoscopies and still become a gastroenterologist.'

'This woman was never going to make a good surgeon. She wouldn't be safe.' He pauses. 'I am aware that diplomacy is not one of my strengths but I was gentle and kind. Tried to make it plain to her that I was trying to help. Told her that she is a good doctor but would be better choosing a different career to surgery.' He is shaking his head now. 'No good. She still complained. Said it was sex discrimination.'

'I don't see that as bullying, Klaus. You should be able to give her your honest opinion about her performance, providing it's delivered sympathetically, without any repercussions.'

'The management may think the same, but for now it is convenient for them. Another stick to beat me with.'

I take a token sip of my coffee. Now, it's time for the vital question I want to ask. 'Klaus, do you still believe that the management suspended you because you were investigating Eamon Keane?'

He nods. 'Yes, I am certain. They do not want the bad publicity, particularly while they are applying for foundation status for the Trust.'

Hardly a revelation. He must have ruminated on his situation almost incessantly. 'For what it's worth, I agree with you. What I don't understand though, is that when we spoke before, you told me that you had found the problem with Keane's performance went back years. So have you had any further thoughts as to why it wasn't discovered before?'

'Good question. I think it had. Soon after I began my investigation, I went to see George Briers, my predecessor as clinical director of surgery, to ask what he knew.'

'And?'

'And he was unhelpful, not at all forthcoming. At that point, I realised I was on my own. I had to press on, could not leave it. It would have been an abandonment of my principles, a negation of who I am.' He looks embarrassed. 'Do you understand?'

I am convinced that he is usually a private, proud man and am touched by the insight he has allowed me into his feelings. 'Yes, I do. You did the right thing. I hope I would have had the courage to do the same.'

'You are kind, Miles, though I think there is a fine line between courage and foolishness.' This is becoming too philosophical. It may help Klaus's morale but it's not going to be of practical value to him.

'Have you tried speaking to George Briers again?'

'No. Under the terms of my suspension, I must not enter the hospital or contact any of its staff.'

He is clearly in no hurry for me to leave, glad of some company. Ingrid, I learn, works full time as a teacher. She offered to give up work to alleviate his weekday loneliness but he refused. His present situation must be a stark contrast to the busy life he led before. We talk for a while longer, mainly reminiscences about his life, almost as if he is terminally ill. His suspension has clearly fomented a form of bereavement reaction.

How appalling for the management to have wrought this damage on such a fine man.

43

I am not bound by the restrictions that the management has, advantageously for itself, imposed on Klaus.

If I am to help him, this is obviously the first step. George Briers has an outpatient session on the same afternoon as one of mine. I'll try and see him after he's finished his clinic. He probably has similar habits to me, going back to his office to try and maintain control of his workload. It would be a good time to talk. The secretaries will have gone and we are less likely to be interrupted by clinical calls.

I knock on his door and am pleased to hear him call, 'Come in.'

His shared office is a little larger than mine and better decorated, not that the latter is difficult. A plastic model of a knee joint sits on top of his bookcase. I take a perverse pleasure in seeing piles of patients' notes on his desk and floor. I have yet to see a consultant's office that is not littered with them.

Technophiles, of course, would claim that electronic records are the answer and are probably correct. But without the physical reminder, it would be easier to delay completing the task the notes are there for. Out of sight, out of mind.

George stands to greet me then waves me towards his colleague's vacant chair. Stocky, strongly built, with a lantern jaw and a nose that has seen better days. An ex-rugby player? But that is long behind him. Even without my knowledge of his impending retirement, his sparse grey hair and a slight tardiness to his movements would lead me to suspect as much.

'Caught me. But you won't be able to much longer. Six more weeks and I'm out of here for good,' he says cheerfully. Demob happy.

Just as well I didn't leave this any longer. Some small talk first would be helpful. I don't want to plunge right in and we don't know each other well. George is an orthopaedic surgeon and we have had little clinical interaction, though we have chatted on social occasions a few times.

'Are you going to continue with private practice when you leave the NHS?'

'No, had enough. Angela and I have a villa in Portugal. Vale do Lobo, do you know it?'

'Yes, been once.' An expensive resort on the south coast of Portugal, heavily populated by the English. Home from home with sunshine and no need for a foreign language. Because of the frequency of degenerative joint problems in our ageing and increasingly overweight society, along with the Health Service's inability to cope with the demand, orthopaedic surgeons enjoy a buoyant private market for their services. Hardly unexpected that he can afford a villa there.

'Well, that's where we're off to spend the rest of the winter. Golf for me. Tennis for her. So, Miles, do you need an orthopaedic surgeon? Anything broken?' he enquires in a facetious but affable manner.

'No, though you could say I'm here to keep it that way,' I reply enigmatically. 'You see I told Klaus Walter I would help him at the time he was suspended and I'm trying not to break my promise.'

George looks serious now and stares at me appraisingly. 'Very noble I'm sure, but if you'll pardon my asking, what's it got to do with you?'

I'm not offended. It's an understandable point of view, though not one I share. 'It's easier, isn't it, to pass by and tell yourself it's not your problem? But in Klaus's case, I think it is partly my problem. Mine, yours and all the consultants in this hospital.'

I take a deep breath. 'You see Klaus believes he was suspended to silence him because he was investigating Eamon Keane, and I agree. He told me that this year alone, Keane has had eight serious adverse events including three avoidable deaths. Those three people, whether they're killed with a scalpel in an operating theatre or stabbed on the street, they're dead just the same.' Melodramatic perhaps but incontrovertibly true.

George looks shocked on hearing this, as well he might. 'Even putting aside Klaus's situation, we all have a duty to prevent Keane killing or harming any more patients. That's what the General Medical Council instructs us. You agree, don't you?'

He nods. He can hardly do otherwise. I'm conscious I've been preaching and become a bit heated. It would be wise to back off a little. I don't want to antagonize him. It's his co-operation I seek. 'Klaus thinks you knew about Keane's problems and doesn't understand why you didn't do anything about them.'

George drops his eyes. 'I did. I did know and I did do

something. Like Klaus, I investigated, wrote a report, and took it to Graham.'

This is an outrage. How can the most senior doctor in our hospital knowingly shelter a serial killer, apparently doing nothing to stop Keane wreaking havoc? I need to keep calm. 'What happened?'

'Graham told me to leave it with him, particularly as it wasn't long before my clinical directorship finished. I objected, said I wanted to remain involved, but he was insistent.' George stops abruptly then gives a rueful look. 'Graham praised my supposed achievements in the director post, told me I was in line for two clinical excellence points and that he was sure I wouldn't want to jeopardise them.'

This is abhorrent: bribes as well as bullying. Carrot and stick. Two so-called clinical excellence points will add about five thousand pounds a year to George's pension, a hundred thousand in total if he lives another twenty years. I am silent but presumably my disgust must be evident on my face.

'Look, I'm not proud of caving in but I just don't have the fight in me anymore. Waning testosterone levels, I suppose. And I really believed Graham would do something.'

"But he hasn't.'

'No, and from what you've just told me, matters are getting worse.'

'What is it that Keane's doing wrong, do you think?'

'Ah, it's complicated. One of the problems is that he's trying to develop a new technique, though he doesn't appear to have informed management about it or the patients he tries it on. He clearly sees himself as a pioneer and perhaps considers some of these adverse events as part of a learning curve. In some of his other disasters, it appears to me that the surgery he attempted was too aggressive. The heart of the matter, I think, is that he lacks insight. He's over-confident, believes he is a better surgeon than he really is.'

'And uncaring?'

'Well, empathy is decidedly not one of his strong points.'

'George, we need to stop him. Will you help me? And help Klaus?'

He bobs his head from side to side a couple of times. A strange action, but also expressive, as I presume he is weighing the pros and cons. 'Okay. If truth be told, it has been bothering me. Yes, count me in. Anyway, what the hell can they do to me now?

The management can't revoke his two new clinical excellence points, I think cynically. 'Good. Thank you.'

'What do you want me to do?'

'Well, for now at least, do you still have a copy of your investigation of Keane?'

'Yes.' He taps his nose with a finger. 'But only on paper and at home, not here. I thought if I left it in my office, it might disappear. I'll make another copy and, if you give me your home address, I'll post it there.'

What is this place coming to?

44

Saturday morning. I have to tell her. I've put it off far too long and with what I know now, I can no longer pretend to myself that it may not be necessary.

We are sitting at the island in Freya's capacious kitchen, fashionable pale grey wooden units, black granite surfaces and gleaming cream floor tiles, rendered luxuriously warm beneath my bare feet by the under-floor heating. Lily has just gone swimming with a friend. Freya and I are sipping at our second cups of coffee. We made love this morning. It's a good time. As good as I'll get.

'Freya.'

'Umm.' She raises her head from the Financial Times and smiles at me.

'There's something I want to tell you.'

She puts down the newspaper, sits a little straighter, and cocks her head to one side. As sometimes happens, I find myself mesmerised by the beauty of her remarkable speckled blue eyes, but I force myself to escape their spell and press on. 'We met before Mark became ill, many years ago.'

'I know. When you came into my hospital room by mistake, as I was recovering from my car crash. We've had this conversation. Surely you remember.'

'Yes, I do but I mean even before that.' She regards me quizzically, seemingly a little perturbed. 'On the day before your crash, in the afternoon, we ... encountered each other in the card shop on the High Street.'

'Where we bumped into each other after Mark had died?'

'Yes, but that time it wasn't a random meeting. I saw you and followed you into the shop.' I don't think it's necessary to be entirely honest, that I'd been waiting outside her house and trailed her into town.

'You wanted to see me, even though I'd been such a bitch to you?' She grins.

I laugh. 'Yes. Yes, I did.'

She considers this for a few moments, before giving a slight shrug of her shoulders. 'Well, of course I'm glad you did.'

We've digressed. 'You don't seem to recall the first time we met there. You told me you were choosing a card for your nephew.'

'My nephew? I don't have a nephew. How could I when I don't have any brothers or sisters? You know that.' She looks annoyed. Does she think I'm making this up?

'I know that now, but not then. Honestly, we picked a card with a train on it, one that made a choo choo sound when you pushed a button. You couldn't stop giggling.'

She looks away, perhaps trying to retrieve her lost memories. Surely, she'll believe me. She turns to face me again and sighs. 'I found that card in my handbag when I was discharged from hospital, thought it had been put there by mistake. I remember it well because I wished I had a little boy, a son, to give it to.' She takes a deep breath. 'Go on, then, tell me the rest.'

I try to relate the events accurately but part way through she interrupts. 'Hang on, you're saying that, having taken off my wedding ring, I started talking to you on a pretext in the card shop, led you down the river to a pub where I proceeded to drag you into a bedroom? I seduced you.'

'I wouldn't put it like that. I didn't need much persuasion.'

But my diplomatic effort fails woefully. She looks horrified. 'I've never done anything like that before. Truly.'

'I believe you. Neither have I. Apart from that time with you, I was never unfaithful to Clare, but we were going through a bad time together. Sorry, I shouldn't try to justify my behaviour.'

'And I was just available, was I?' She looks hurt now, stands and starts to pace round the kitchen. This isn't going as I'd hoped. I stand up as well and hold her by the shoulders at arms' length.

'No, Freya. No. We really clicked and I thought you were wonderful, heaven-sent.'

She gives a wry smile. 'It doesn't sound as if I'd get into heaven behaving like you've said.' She seems mollified.

'Go on, what happened at the end, did we both decide to go our separate ways, chalk it up as a one-night stand? Maybe we weren't that impressed with one another?'

I close my eyes briefly, as if by doing so it will shut out the painful memory of when we parted. 'No, that's not how it was. It would have been better if it had been. I did think you were amazing and, if I had been single, I would have done almost anything to see you again. But that wasn't the case. And yes, it's a cliché but I did love Clare and of course, Adam and Luke too. I told you I couldn't risk losing them by seeing you again. You were upset, more than I would have expected. At the end, I'm ashamed to tell you, I just walked out. I'm sorry, I didn't know what else to do.'

She is shaking her head in wonder. 'I just don't remember any of this. It's as though it happened to another person.'

'There's more.'

'Oh.'

'The day we parted, you had the car crash. And when I came to your hospital room a week or so later, it wasn't by mistake, I wanted to see how you were, that you were making a good recovery.'

She's never looked at me like this before, as if she's scrutinising my soul, judging me. 'Is that what this is about? Your guilt. You want me to forgive you?'

'No, but that would be welcome.'

'What's the point, then?' she snaps and backs away from me a little.

'The point, Freya, is that I'm Lily's father.'

'What?' She stares at me, wide-eyed.

'I'm Lily's father.' It sounds strange on my tongue. 'The possibility never occurred to me until recently because you told me at the time that you were taking an oral contraceptive. But then I realised you probably missed some of your pills after your crash.'

Freya is silent for a few moments, probably doing the maths and, then in a slightly calmer tone says, 'Okay. I agree it's possible but how can you be so sure?'

'Because I checked her DNA, along with yours and mine. You see, when we had blood tests taken to determine if any of us were infected with Helicobacter bili…'

'You sent some of our blood for DNA analysis.'

'Yes.'

'That can't be legal.'

'No, it's not. Under the Human Tissue Act 2004, a person with parental responsibility has to give their signed permission to test a child under sixteen and, of course, testing you without your knowledge is illegal as well.

The idea only came to me a few weeks ago. I couldn't get it out of my head. I had to know and didn't want to risk you and Lily refusing to be tested. I reasoned that if the test was negative then I wouldn't tell you, and if it was positive, then it's better that we found out.'

'And that I was hardly likely to report you to the police, particularly if you were the father of my child,' she states with more than a hint of sarcasm.

'Yes.'

She opens her mouth as if to speak before closing it again and pausing to think for a few moments longer. 'What I don't understand is why you tested me. You can't think I'm not her mother.'

'No, of course not, but testing the mother's DNA makes the result more accurate.'

'So how conclusive is it?'

'Realistically, it's certain.'

Her eyes are moist. She lifts her arms to waist height, palms outstretched towards me. 'I need a while to try and take this in.' She backs out of the kitchen door.

I slump back down on a seat. Well, what did I expect? Should I have said anything differently? I told her the truth. I can't tell her why she behaved how she did back then. We'll never know and can only speculate. If we are to have a future together, then this was too big a secret to keep hidden from her any longer. Another volley of rain batters against the windows, typical weather for the end of November.

After a while, I go to look for her and find her downstairs in a back room. There are shelves of books, a desk, two comfortable-looking leather armchairs. She is gazing out of the bay window, sitting on the window seat. I sit opposite her, ignore the cold, draughty situation and wait.

Before long she starts to talk, softly but clearly. 'I must have lied to you. I could play along with the explanation you suggested about missing my pills after the crash but I don't want there to be any secrets between us. The truth is that I wasn't taking the pill. I'm sorry. Sorry for deceiving you, anyway.' Not for conceiving Lily.

'In fact, Mark and I been trying to get me pregnant. After nearly two years, we went for tests. I was fine, but Mark had a low sperm count and what there was had poor mobility.' Her eyes are unfocused, not required for seeing the past. She gives a rueful smile, presumably as a memory surfaces. 'He tried to joke that his sperm needed a swimming coach, a pity he couldn't hire one. It was a lesson for him, for both of us, that money wasn't the answer to every problem. To his credit, he did everything he could think of to help. Found time to take more exercise, gave up alcohol, became obsessional about his diet, began taking all manner of supplements and vitamins. But it made no difference.'

She gives a wry smile before focusing her gaze on me once more. 'Mark was the sort of man who thought that, with enough endeavour, any problem could be beaten. When his efforts weren't rewarded, he began to nag me to adopt his new health regime.'

'I bit my lip, didn't turn on him and say my fertility had passed the tests. I went along with it but, of course, not with the same zeal as him. And he began to find fault, insisting that I mustn't eat sugar and chocolate, that I could only eat gluten-free bread and other products, demanding my assurance that I'd taken my zinc tablets. They were so big, Miles. He knew I had trouble swallowing them.'

I nod in acknowledgment of her past ordeal. She returns to her story.

'Inevitably, our sex life didn't escape Mark's attention. He announced that it had to be improved.' She draws in the air with her fingers the quotation marks around the final word. 'He reasoned that we shouldn't do it too often to give his sperm count time to accumulate and that we should be well rested when we did. So, every Sunday afternoon, after our spartan, non-alcoholic, sugar-free, gluten-free, enjoyment-free lunch and supervised supplement consumption, we had sex.'

'And he'd read that women were more likely to conceive if they had an orgasm. Not such a burden to bear, you might think. But being Mark, he extrapolated from this: that if a woman didn't, then her body was unwilling to become pregnant. Before long he began to talk about giving me an orgasm as "breaking down my defences", as if it was my fault. If I didn't come then the atmosphere for the rest of the week was soured. Of course, at times I tried to fake it but he wasn't fooled every time.'

She frowns. Tears are streaming down her cheeks. There is a catch in her voice as she continues. 'Then, suddenly, he changed. His vivacity returned. I heard him humming in the shower. The obsessions were abandoned, the Sunday afternoon ritual discarded. In fact, sex became even less frequent.'

I know what's coming. One would hardly need to be particularly perceptive after Freya's account, but Mark had told me in his death-bed confession.

'I accused him of having an affair but he denied it. I didn't believe him.'

She is breathing deeply, eyes narrowed, expression fierce, probably reliving their confrontation. After a few moments, her anger appears to subside and she looks deflated. 'I tried to understand, rationalised that the temptation of uncomplicated sex had proved too much for him, sex where the woman didn't want him to make her pregnant.'

I am not so sure about that. The possibilities cascade through my consciousness. A rich, good-looking, relatively young banker. The other woman may well have hoped to conceive, might have lied to Mark that she was taking the pill, eventually might even have cynically become pregnant by another man and told Mark it was his. What would he have done then? These are not thoughts I need to share with Freya and she is talking again.

'I was so unhappy and was about to leave him when my car crash happened. He was very supportive, visited me in hospital every day. I could see he still cared about me and then, as if by magic, I was pregnant. I presumed Mark and I must have had sex just before the crash and I couldn't remember. It changed everything. He couldn't do enough for me. Started calling me darling again, buying me flowers and, ironically, chocolates. And I was pretty dependent just then, with a broken arm and a wonky brain.'

'By the time I was better, Lily was about to be born. Once she was, Mark adored her. It was Lily this and Lily that and all the plans he had for her. She brought us closer together, gave us a shared goal. And I was... content.'

I couldn't take her away from him. It would have been too cruel. And I didn't want Lily growing up without her father.' She gives me a rueful look. 'Or who I thought was her father.'

'Lily was everything we could have wished for. A happy child, precociously self-assured, at least until Mark's illness disrupted her life. And so bright. Mark was fond of saying that Lily had inherited my looks and his brains.'

She looks out the window. She stands up suddenly. Her arms are making little purposeless waving movements in front of her, unwittingly mimicking those of the branches of the trees outside as they are tossed around by the frenzied wind.

'Miles, I'm sorry, really sorry. Sometimes I think I'm so stupid, behaving the way I do, and I've fretted that I'll drive you away.'

I rise from the window seat and take a pace towards her. 'Well, you'll have to try harder than you have done so far.' I take her in my arms and hug her tight. She gives a small sob and I feel some of her tears begin to run down my neck.

45

I've recruited George Briers to the cause but I don't know who else would be useful.

It shouldn't be this way. There ought to be someone or some regulatory body to take our concerns to. In theory, the Care Quality Commission would be appropriate but in practice, from what I've learnt, they're not fit for purpose, as the vogue phrase goes. And what might they do, ask the hospital management to investigate? Probably take a year or two about it and eventually issue some dubious report that would never be acted on.

In the meantime, Klaus would still be suspended, his surgical skills atrophying and his private practice lost. And I could end up joining him. Not the answer.

In reality, the management are only accountable to the government. Klaus could try and enlist the help of his Member of Parliament but I can't see him getting very far. The politicians are clearly desperate to keep any problems with the NHS out of the news. It's as if they have given hospital managers tacit approval to suppress any scandals, though of course they would profess otherwise.

What to do? No matter how many times I turn it over in my head, I keep concluding that I, or rather we, the doctors, need to help ourselves. Unfortunately, we have so little power. No that's not correct, fortune doesn't come into it. Margaret Thatcher apparently decided we had too much power and commissioned the Griffiths Report in 1983 to curb it. A bit before my time but surely, it's been overdone, the pendulum swung too far.

There is no denying that we don't make our situation any easier. Too busy with our clinical commitments, most of us have little inclination to become distracted by management activities. Paradoxically, one of our strengths, our independent mindedness, is under these circumstances, a weakness. Easy for the management to divide and rule.

****

It's early evening and I've ventured into the gynaecology department. I knock on the partially opened door of his office and poke my head around it. 'Miles. Come in. Have a seat.'

'Thanks.' I perch myself on a battered upright chair.

He swivels on his chair away from his computer screen and faces me. 'I presume you want to be a candidate to succeed me as chairman of the consultants?'

I smile at his perception. Paul White is a big, avuncular man with hair that is now in keeping with his surname. Hard not to like him. 'How did you guess?'

He smiles back at me. 'Well, you've left it a bit late, only five days to the deadline but that's not a problem. Shall I tell you a bit about the job?' I nod but barely listen to what he has to say. I have my own ideas as to what to do with the post and they're quite different to Paul's.

'Well, I've prattled on enough. There are four other candidates by the way but that said, I think you've a good chance. Your newfound prestige will help.'

I make a dismissive gesture with my hands. I'm not fond of flattery but he's probably right.

'But most of all, you have a reputation for talking straight, no bullshit. People like that.'

'Thanks, that's very encouraging.'

He stands and offers me his hand to shake. 'Good luck.'

****

The process is all very informal, too much so. I'll change it if I'm elected. There are no ballot papers sent out. This would also enable each candidate to attach a brief resume of what he or she intended to achieve in the post. If you want to vote, you have to attend the next Consultants' Committee meeting and raise a hand for your preferred candidate.

I've canvassed shamelessly. As much as I'm able in the limited time available. I stop and talk to any consultant I come upon in the hospital corridors, target others at clinical meetings, eat leisurely lunches in the canteen and impose myself on my colleagues there. Keeping up with my admin. is temporarily more difficult but this is necessary.

My pitch is simple: we need to be more assertive with the management.

I'm astonished at how receptive my potential electorate is to this message. Many of them regale me with their own grievances and tales of dissatisfaction with our current rulers. Some report management bullying - ironic considering the latest charge made against Klaus. All seem to agree that our already limited influence has declined even further since the new chief executive took over.

I'd not realised quite how low morale had sunk.

I encounter some scepticism that I will be able to live up to my rhetoric but most of my colleagues seem inclined to believe in my willingness to try. Others are enthusiastic, delighted that one of their number is prepared to upset the powers that be, with all the sanctions that could entail. No more clinical excellence points for me. No great loss: my self-respect is worth more than money.

Now, the meeting has just concluded. In the end, something of an anti-climax. Paul White, chairing for the final time, announced that three of my four rivals had withdrawn. I'd heard rumours of this. Apparently, I was expected to win easily and these three didn't want to risk receiving a humiliatingly low number of votes.

Paul didn't even require me and the other remaining candidate to speak. I needn't have bothered writing my mini manifesto and then learning it. Still, better to have been prepared.

A pity I'd not given any thought to a brief acceptance speech. When almost every hand in the room was raised on my behalf, I found the powerful emotions my overwhelming victory engendered made it difficult for me to think clearly. I said the first thing that popped into my head: that I would try hard to be worthy of their trust. It felt right at the time, even with the benefit of hindsight. And my colleagues, with working lifetimes behind them of evaluating people, could have been in no doubt that I was sincere.

The atmosphere is almost festive. I accept a succession of individual congratulations. There is no escape from this and it would be churlish to try. Maybe I should want to bask in my victory but I don't want to be drawn into specifics as to how

- JOHN THORNTON -

I intend to implement my currently vague campaign pledges. My intentions are more radical than any of my colleagues would ever imagine.

46

Freya is pleased. She perceives my election success as a justified reward for our research efforts. Alan is more circumspect. Outwardly complimentary, I surmise that he is annoyed, seeing my new role as an ego trip and a distraction from our work together. It is tempting to enlighten him as to my plans, though I conclude that this may only make matters worse. It hurts, but for now I must endure his displeasure.

It's a little like adultery, I reflect. Better to keep the secret to yourself rather than confiding in friends.

Even if I told Alan and Freya my plans, they would probably both inform me that the risk is too great and that I'm crazy. Or is it that I'm sane and no longer prepared to work in an organisation that has become crazy? A Trust you can no longer trust.

Well, here goes. I square my shoulders and knock on Graham Giles' door. This time I am admitted into his inner sanctum and we sit with his desk between us, rather than at the small conference table. His manner is certainly more welcoming than the last time I was here. I worry that he may secretly record our conversation. I'm probably being paranoid but I have been surprised repeatedly by the management's skulduggery, so I resolve to choose my words with care.

'Congratulations on your appointment, Miles. What can I do for you?'

'Thank you.' I pause but there is no point beating about the bush. 'I want to talk to you about Eamon Keane.'

In a flash, his amiable look is gone and replaced by a hostile expression. We sit in silence while he considers how to react. Perhaps his first thought was a response like George Briers' but now that I'm the consultants' chairman, arguably any consultant issue is my concern.

To some extent, my new post is what I choose to make it and one thing's for sure, I don't intend to preside over a toothless talking shop.

'Yes,' is his only belated reply.

Of course, he isn't aware of the extent of my knowledge and wants me to reveal this. 'Keane has a grossly excessive operative morbidity and mortality. What have you done about it?'

A flush of annoyance suffuses his face. 'I think your recent successes have gone to your head. You forget yourself. I'm the medical director of this trust. It's not your place to question me.'

'But I am Graham. Whether you like it or not. What have you done about Keane?'

He stares at me and I look back at him steadily. He appears to decide that since intimidation is not working, he should try diplomacy. I thought these were usually employed the other way around but I presume this inversion is indicative of his long-standing, largely unfettered power. 'Eamon is a highly skilled surgeon. I have spoken to him about his results and he has explained to me that the cases he operates on are often more complex and higher risk than those his colleagues take on.'

He would, wouldn't he? I restrain myself from verbalising this platitude. I don't want to provoke Graham into terminating our meeting. I've much more to say yet. 'Did you test his claim?' I had discussed this possibility with both Klaus and George Briers and neither had found any evidence to support Keane's assertion.

'Look, Eamon may not be the easiest of characters but I know him to be a man of integrity.' 'Yes. I understand you know him well, have been friends since you were at medical school together.'

'That does not affect my professional judgement,' he snaps back.

'Nevertheless, it is possible for Eamon to be a man of integrity, as you put it, but for him to be mistaken.' The logic of this is indisputable and Graham does not respond. I continue, 'Klaus Walters found that just this year to May, Keane had eight serious adverse events and three deaths which Klaus considered to be avoidable.'

A distinctly malevolent look descends on Graham's face. 'You seek to accuse me based on the word of a disgraced, suspended surgeon? Haven't you considered that Walters' assessment has been warped by his situation, an attempt to distract attention from his own problems?'

A fine example of management's dark arts, twisting timelines to confuse and obfuscate.

'My understanding, Graham, is that Klaus investigated Keane before, not after, you made accusations against him. He believes ...' it's probably wise to keep my view undisclosed for the moment ... 'that you suspended him to keep him quiet while the Trust was applying for foundation status.'

'That's outrageous. How dare he say such a thing?'

Maybe I don't look convinced by his bluster and after a few moments he continues in a less agitated manner. 'I accept that Walters' allegations were made at an awkward time for the Trust. If the assessors had given them any credibility, then they would have sunk our application. Phew, they'd have blown it out of the water.'

'And how is the Trust's application progressing?'

His scowl disappears. 'We've just learnt it's successful. Max is going to announce it officially tomorrow. I can't begin to tell you how much work it's been, seemingly endless forms, data collection, visits, and inspections. Now, though, we'll have much more control over our future and greater financial independence.'

As well, I think cynically, as less supervision of any sharp practices and the ability for the managers and medical director to award themselves pay rises on the grounds of increased responsibility. 'So, the end justifies the means, does it, Graham?'

'I don't know what you're talking about,' he replies huffily.

'I think you do. Oh, yes, I think you do. You see, I spoke to George Briers and I have a copy of his investigation into Eamon Keane's previous operative disasters.'

He sits there, seemingly transfixed. His right hand grips the edge of his desk. I pull the document with a flourish from the folder I brought with me, evidence for the prosecution, though the judge and jury are still to be determined.

'How did you get that?' he demands.

'George gave it me.'

'But ...'

'But what?'

'He told me he'd given me the only copy.'

I struggle to smother a smile at Graham's dismay that George had lied to him, that only one side should break the rules. 'And you tried to keep it that way, didn't you? George told me his computer had experienced massive data loss almost immediately after he gave you the report.'

'That's a coincidence. You can't believe I had anything to do with it?'

'But I do, Graham. Human Resources and I.T. have access to all the hospital's computers. As you've just pointed out to me, you're the medical director. They'll do what you tell them to do.'

'George's report,' I tap it for emphasis, 'clearly demonstrates that Keane has had problems for years, that patients were suffering and dying needlessly.

You,' I stress the pronoun but manage to restrain myself from pointing a finger at him, 'obliged George to relinquish responsibility for his investigation and took charge. That may well have been appropriate but you did not implement any effective action. Surely you can see that the minimum you needed to do at that point was to forbid Keane from operating while he was investigated further?'

I wait for a response but none is forthcoming so I press on. 'If you'd done that you would have prevented Keane's latest disasters. At least three patients have died this year because of your inaction, Graham. They're not just a statistic. They were people's mothers and fathers, husbands and wives.'

He squirms a little.

'The duties of a doctor in hospital management are clearly defined by the General Medical Council. You've failed in your duty of care and, when I report you to them, I've little doubt that they'll strike you off the Medical Register. And your despicable treatment of Klaus has extinguished any opportunity you may have had to defend yourself by claiming an error of judgement.'

He seems to have shrunk in his seat. 'You wouldn't do that.' His voice is almost a whisper.

'Why wouldn't I?'

'Err, we could come to some arrangement about Klaus. Get him back to work,' he pleads.

I shake my head and simultaneously realise that he wouldn't have made his last remark if our conversation was being recorded.

'Miles, come on, I have been the medical director here for over ten years and throughout that time I have worked tirelessly in the best interests of the Trust …' His hands are shaking. He babbles on and on until a stress-induced, dry voice forces him to stop and take a long drink from the bottle of water on his desk.

It's quite extraordinary to witness his normally imperious demeanour disintegrate like this. I stare at him fiercely. I need him to believe that I am implacable.

'Why, Graham? Why did you do it?'

He shuts his eyes briefly, perhaps to give himself a few moments respite. 'I had to. Max told me to do it. Don't you understand? If I didn't, he'd have sacked me as medical director and appointed a new one who would do his bidding.'

I understand only too well. What I hadn't been sure about was whether I'd be able to extract this confession from him.

'I don't accept that, Graham. You could have made a stand, tried to enlist the support of the chairman and non-executive directors, sought help from your colleagues. And even if you'd failed, you'd still have had your consultant post.'

A silence descends on the room. I don't fill it.

'I'll be finished if you report me to the GMC. I'll never work again,' he says with a mixture of incredulity and alarm.

'So, how do you think Klaus felt as you and your crony, Max Lytle, set about ruthlessly destroying his career?'

He winces. I suppose that's to his credit. He's not fundamentally a bad man. How has he let himself be led astray? I'm finding it hard. There is a degree of grim satisfaction but hurting another person this way is alien to me. I must mask my feelings. This is necessary. The end justifying the means?

'Is there nothing I can do to change your mind?' He begs.

Time to cut a deal. 'Yes, there is. I will agree not to report you to the GMC but there are conditions. First and foremost, you will come to the next consultants' committee meeting and tell our colleagues what you have done. You will leave nothing out and this is crucial, you will make it explicit that you were acting on Max Lytle's instructions.'

He looks horrified. 'But Max will be there.'

'No, he won't.' I state firmly. 'He attends our meeting by invitation. I shall inform him that he and any other management representatives are not welcome.'

Graham's mouth drops open, amazed that I should dare to do such a thing. 'Even so, he's going to hear what's happened.'

'It's that or the GMC.' I find I've put both my arms in front of me, palms upward, for emphasis. One hand or the other, weigh the alternatives.

Graham raises both his hands in a defensive gesture. 'Okay, okay. I'll do it.'

'Good, and you don't need to worry about Keane being there. I've learnt that he's just flown off to Barbados for a fortnight. He never comes to the meetings anyway.'

'Secondly, you will apologise to our colleagues and

inform them that you will be resigning as medical director.'

'Okay.' He sighs.

'But before you do, you will instruct Human Resources to withdraw the allegations against Klaus and re-instate him.'

'I will but Max won't agree.' I'm tempted to say, "leave Lytle to me" but think better of it.

'Just do it. And I want those patient notes you're keeping from Klaus.' He nods.

'Lastly, I'm sure that on reflection you'll realise that your continued employment here is undesirable. You will leave the Trust as soon as possible, no later than one year from now.'

'Miles, it's not easy to find another consultant job at my age.'

'Maybe, but it's not impossible by any means. You have an MBA and many years of management experience. You shouldn't find it too hard to gain employment in a medically related industry.' He offers no further objection and looks at me with loathing. 'So, do we have a deal?'

He looks away then after a few moments turns to face me again. 'Yes.'

'Well then, I'll convene an emergency meeting of the consultants' committee later this week. In the meantime, you say nothing of this to anyone, especially not Max Lytle.'

'Understood,' he mutters.

'Now what about those notes?'

He rises from his chair, opens his door, and beckons with a hand for me to follow him. We proceed down a corridor of the management building to a door at the end. Graham fumbles with a bundle of keys before selecting one and unlocking the door. Inside is a large room almost entirely fitted with shelves stacked with box files of documents and a large number of patient notes. Graham exhibits no hesitation, quickly locates the relevant set and hands them to me. They are emblazoned with a stamp: deceased. I look at him but don't need to ask.

'We took them without completing the tracking document or computer log. Medical records have no access to this room. We've never told them it exists.'

How many secrets, other scandals even, lie buried here?

47

There's certainly a good turnout, and a buzz of excitement and anticipation as we gather in the postgraduate centre. Have I stirred a hornet's nest? That's not a good analogy. I can't even think of a time when we have "stung" the management. We've been completely emasculated. Careful, can't use that word. Not gender correct. Nearly half my consultant colleagues are female and I don't want to risk upsetting any of them. Imperative tonight that we are united.

I'd confronted Graham on Monday and called this emergency meeting of the consultant's committee for Thursday evening of the same week. Very short notice but speed is essential. I can't give management the time to make a pre-emptive strike against me.

The e-mail and letter I had sent to all the consultants had only indicated the need to discuss a matter of utmost importance. No specific agenda. Nothing to enlighten them or the management, though as I'd made plain to an affronted personal assistant of Mr Lytle that he was not invited. He must realise that "the natives are restless".

It is past the time the meeting should have started but there's still a steady trickle of latecomers. Preferable that all those present tonight hear everything, the full case for the prosecution, to enable them to make the most informed decision. Besides, it's still too disorderly to begin as some people are still hunting for chairs in adjoining rooms. I've never seen one of these meetings as packed as this.

George and Graham are seated either side of me at the head of the long rectangular conglomeration of small tables we have created. I would dearly have liked Klaus to be present but he is barred from the hospital's premises. George is chirpy. Retiring in a few weeks, he's going out with a bang. Probably cathartic for him too.

Graham, unsurprisingly, is subdued and looks pale. He avoids eye contact and busies himself picking tiny specks off his jacket. But he's here. Even though logically this option is, for him, the lesser of two evils, I had begun to fret that his nerve would fail.

Am I right to spare him referral to the General Medical Council? Then again, isn't what I've agreed with him akin to plea bargaining by the Crown Prosecution Service, making a deal with a lesser offender in order to secure the conviction of a greater one?

Too late for moral qualms now. Time to begin. I call for order. There is a final scraping of chairs as they settle. My colleagues are keen to learn why I've called them here.

I start with a few words of gratitude for their attendance at short notice and that the reason for this meeting is to consider what I regard as seriously flawed actions by our management. That is key. I don't want any of them drifting away when we start discussing Eamon Keane's operative problems in the mistaken belief that this is the principal subject for discussion tonight.

I ask George to summarise his investigation into Keane's disasters and how Graham responded, or rather failed to respond in any effective manner. I feel a pang of guilt that we are accusing Keane without him being present to defend himself, but that would have been a distraction from the meeting's primary purpose, and Keane will have the opportunity to explain the deficiencies in his performance once he returns from holiday. George gives a concise account, a little too succinct as he omits the part about his clinical excellence points, but that is not vital. He has started the ball rolling.

I invite Graham to continue the narrative.

He begins hesitantly, pleads an error of judgement in his response to George's report, but then is commendably frank about his mistreatment of Klaus and describes graphically the pressure Max Lytle put him under to behave that way. He apologises for succumbing, labels his behaviour unacceptable and states he will be resigning as medical director. At the finish, he turns to me.

I nod. He has done enough.

Briefly, the room is remarkably silent before a clamour to ask questions begins. I allow a few, especially as most seek further confirmation of Max Lytle's role in the events. I want them in no doubt of that. But there is no merit in allowing Graham to be torn apart and I need to focus their anger effectively. I tap on the table. Silence gradually ensues and over a hundred pairs of eyes regard me.

I wait a little longer than necessary before I speak. 'I share your outrage. Are there any here who feel the management's actions are excusable?'

A pause for a reply is required but it would be an imprudent man or woman who sought to make a case for the defence right now. I had considered one or two management loyalists might claim Mr Lytle should be here to try to justify himself but that challenge does not materialise.

I resume, speaking slowly and firmly, as befits the gravity of my words. 'Then I propose we should vote on whether we, the consultants of this trust, have confidence in Mr Lytle's leadership.'

A commotion ensues as my colleagues absorb the implications of my statement. Paul White looks at me in amazement. Nothing remotely like this happened during his anodyne chairmanship.

'I want no part of this.' Sandra Robins, a dermatologist, has risen to her feet.

I daren't let her initiate an exodus. 'Are you just going to slink away, Sandra? Abrogate your responsibility to others? This is a time to stand up and be counted.' It is withering and she takes her seat again. But I realise that I may have overstepped the mark. I don't want to be bullying her.

Alan quips, 'Couldn't we vote sitting down, Miles? It would be more comfortable that way.' A poor joke but under the circumstances it provokes some amusement and the tension eases, as Alan no doubt realised it would.

I nod my appreciation to him. No-one else gives any indication of wanting to leave. The numbered ballot papers I have prepared are quickly distributed. This is too important for a show of hands and I want a permanent record of our decision. I instruct that these should not be signed as I surmise that there will be more anti-management votes if anonymity is available. The choice on the ballot papers is between:

"I have confidence in Mr Lytle as chief executive officer of this Trust." and

"I do not have confidence in Mr Lytle as chief executive officer of this Trust."

Clear and fairly worded, I believe. After a few minutes, it's apparent to me that almost all have voted and I encourage the stragglers to decide. I co-opt Alan and Sandra to act as tellers. I hope she views this as a gesture of reconciliation. Or am I just binding her more tightly to my plan?

They begin to divide the ballot papers into two piles. An obvious disparity between their sizes rapidly becomes apparent. Murmurs grow louder, the atmosphere electric. Are my colleagues astonished, appalled or euphoric at their temerity? Perhaps all three?

I announce: 'There are sixteen votes expressing confidence in Mr Lytle and one hundred and forty-three that do not. I therefore declare that we do not have confidence in Mr Lytle as chief executive officer of this trust. I will communicate your decision to him.'

****

It feels surreal as I walk down a dark, empty hospital corridor towards the management building. Sensors activate lights immediately ahead of my progress. Is that what I'm doing? Bringing light into the darkness? But such fanciful notions are not sustainable. Where does my plan leave the victims and relatives of Keane's disasters? It does not encompass enlightening them, does not provide them with any attempt at financial compensation. Surely, it's wrong if they never learn the truth. The moral burden is almost overwhelming. Why should I be the one to decide?

No more. These are considerations for another time. My tasks today are not yet complete. Better I do this now, if possible. Keep him off balance. Carpe diem has never seemed more apt. Not that there is any daylight remaining at around eight o'clock on this December evening. I doubt he would have gone home without learning what had happened at our meeting. One from which I had unprecedentedly barred him from attending.

He will have waited on site to hear the outcome. Maybe at this moment, one of his tame consultants is informing him by telephone, ratting on his colleagues. At least that may have been that consultant's plan, hoping to gain favour. But now? Aren't rats supposed to desert a sinking ship?

The gentle rain on my face is enlivening as I cross the internal road to the management block. Good, the lights in his office are on. I have borrowed Graham's swipe card. The doors are no barrier to me today. I climb the stairs to the top floor, my footsteps silent on the carpeted floors.

Am I stalking again, though this time with malevolent intent?

His door is slightly ajar. I make a peremptory knock and enter uninvited. He is standing with his back to me, jacket and tie discarded, looking out over the hospital. I doubt he can see much other than blurry lights through the rain-spattered, plate-glass window.

He turns abruptly, shocked by my entrance. His podgy face is suffused and contorted with rage. He knows.

'Who the fuck do you think you are?'

I am pleased how calm I feel in the face of his anger. Unlike Graham, I have no pity for this man.

'How fucking dare you?' Spittle flies from his mouth. 'I'm the chief executive officer. I'm not responsible to you and your mob.' He glares at me.

I lock eyes with him. His rant, at least for now, appears to be over. I move nearer to him to show I am not intimidated. Jane was correct, I reflect, when she observed on his arrival that he is far from an impressive figure of a man. And his pathetic tricks with a raised chair and platform are of no use at this moment. I am at least six inches taller than him.

It is time for me to speak. 'I have come to tell you that tonight at the Consultants Committee meeting, sixteen consultants expressed their confidence in you as chief executive and one hundred and forty-three did not.'

He flinches on hearing the latter number. Probably his informant was not brave enough to tell him the scale of his defeat. 'So what?' he snarls defiantly.

'So, you should resign.'

'I'm not going.'

A brief derisive laugh escapes me. 'What do you think you're going to do? You can't suspend one hundred and forty-three consultants. If the vote becomes public, your career is over completely.' Was the latter a foolish statement? There are too many people involved to facilitate secrecy, but in his intemperate state, he seems to have accepted it.

'You can't go to the media. Once you mention that idiot Keane, you'll be committing libel.'

'Not if the allegations are true.'

'And before you know it, you'll be breaching patient confidentiality,' he tries instead. That's a better point.

'I could go to the police.'

Momentarily, he looks shocked, before rallying. 'The police! You really are out of your fucking mind.'

But I can tell it's bluster. If that truly is his assessment of my mental state, he should realise that it may make me even more dangerous to him.

'I consider that there is a strong case for prosecuting you for corporate manslaughter. Be under no illusions, Graham will testify against you to mitigate his part in your sordid scheme.' The colour has drained from his face, just as his resistance is clearly slipping away.

'No NHS trust or chief executive officer has ever been prosecuted for manslaughter,' he responds.

A last stand? He's right though. I've checked this, as best I can. But this is not just about facts. What it comes down to, as in so much of life, is will. Is my determination and what I have initiated, greater than his power and will to resist?

'Then you will have to bear the added indignity of being the first.' I notice a relatively clear reflection of myself in the window. My appearance is gratifyingly fierce. His eyes drop. I am winning.

'You will resign. If you have not done so by twelve noon tomorrow, I will go to the police.'

He shudders. I turn and walk away, leaving him to contemplate his predicament and cast a final look over his domain.

48

Friday morning. The ward round is proceeding swiftly and uneventfully, facilitated by the presence of two of my three junior staff, as well as Jane. There's even a nurse accompanying us.

Fortunate, as my brain does not feel as sharp as usual. I slept fitfully after the tumultuous events of yesterday evening. My pager bleeps, indicating a number for me to call. I break away from the round and find a hospital phone.

'Mrs Smythe would like to see you.' Celia Smythe is the Trust's chairman. Or should that be chairperson or even chair?

'I can come after I've finished my ward round, in about an hour.'

'She is available now,' is the haughty reply.

'Well, I am not. About an hour.' I disconnect. That felt good. An indulgence but also an expression of my new authority. I need to maintain it, if I am to have any hope of effecting beneficial change here.

- UNDER CONTROL -

****

Her office is smaller and less palatial than Mr Lytle's. Fitting, I consider, as her post is only part-time. One of the walls bears a framed copy of the Trust's mission statement, the paean to excellence penned by Max Lytle. In itself admirable, but from now on we must ensure its aspirations conform to reality.

Mrs Smythe's face is tight and unsettling, the consequence, I presume, of a surfeit of botox. Nevertheless, I can still detect signs of her emotional strain. Her hair is similarly inflexible, held in place by a discernible sheen of lacquer. The grey roots could do with some attention, a sharp contrast to the jet-black remainder.

She is seated next to Mrs Owen. For moral support? Or should that be morale support? I'm far from certain about their morals. Our head of human resources, dressed today in black and with her large nose and slightly stooped posture, is redolent of a giant crow.

'Take a seat, Doctor Westwood.' No please, I notice, or other pleasantries. Mrs Smythe is renowned for her brisk, no-nonsense style but is usually a stickler for good manners.

'Max Lytle has tendered his resignation to me this morning.'

'As a consequence of your' and your colleagues' actions, this Trust has lost the services of a very able chief executive officer, one who has guided the Trust to foundation status. I do hope you fully appreciate the seriousness of this situation you have created.'

Arguably, that last sentence is not a question so I remain silent and stare at them. Calculated to be unsettling, I'm becoming practised at confrontations of this nature.

Her nostrils flare and she demands in a querulous manner, 'Why did you do it?'

I offer a thin smile and stare at her so she realises I am not intimidated. In a calm voice and measured delivery, I state, 'Mr Lytle allowed a consultant surgeon, Eamon Keane, to continue operating in the full knowledge that by doing so this would be likely to cause harm to and the death of patients. His failure is compounded inexcusably by his ordering the suspension of another surgeon, Klaus Walters, when he brought this matter, yet again, to management attention.'

'I know nothing of this,' she asserts.

Do you think I was born yesterday, Mrs Smythe? You knew. Lytle would have wanted to be sure you had his back. I raise my eyebrows but say nothing.

Mrs Owen chips in, her Welsh accent in marked contrast to Mrs Smythe's cut-glass English. 'The Trust has a clear and robust whistle-blowing policy, Doctor Westwood. I can assure you we take these matters very seriously.'

'I do not need your assurance. You demonstrated how seriously by suspending Klaus Walters.'

Her eyes blaze. 'That is offensive. Mr Walters is facing allegations of a grave nature.'

What a strange choice of word: grave. Keane is the one with grave problems, far too many. But the irony of her word selection escapes her.

'Those allegations, I contend, are spurious, manufactured to silence him while the Trust sought the foundation status it craved.' I almost spit the last few words. Calm down, squabbling with Mrs Owen will get me nowhere.

'Doctor Westwood,' Mrs Smythe returns to the fray in defence of her minion, 'that is a disgraceful and frankly incredible accusation you appear intent on asserting.'

I turn my full attention on her and speak more softly than before. After all, I am carrying a "big stick". They just haven't appreciated how big yet. 'I am considering whether to involve the Crown Prosecution Service in determining the credibility of my accusation and whether the management of this Trust should be charged with manslaughter.'

She reels back in her chair as if I've punched her. Mrs Owen's head sinks down even lower than before and she begins to fiddle with the papers in front of her in a seemingly demented fashion. I watch their distress until eventually Mrs Smythe entreats me, 'Surely that is not necessary?'

I choose not to answer that question. Let them stew while I tell them what I want. 'These events are regrettable and I'm sure you will both agree we must all strive to prevent any recurrence. Better communication and closer working between management and consultants is vital. Therefore, I propose that the consultants have an elected representative on the Trust board.'

'You have the medical director,' chirps up Mrs Owen.

'As you are well aware, he is appointed by the CEO, not elected by his consultant colleagues.'

'And I presume that representative will be you?' Mrs Smythe enquires sarcastically. Revealing. Not "proposed representative". She's going to agree, in the face of my threat, to anything reasonable I suggest.

'I imagine that's what my colleagues will decide. And that representative will be part of the selection committee for the new CEO, with a power of veto.'

She opens her mouth to speak but then appears to think better of it. Just as well, as she'll like my next demand even less. 'And the CEO will henceforth deliver an annual report and be subject to an annual appraisal by the consultants committee.'

'But that's unheard of,' she splutters.

'Maybe, but the Trust prides itself on its innovation.' I struggle to suppress a smile, remembering Lytle's assertion on the BBC. 'And I think it is essential to cement our newfound cooperation and prevent a recurrence of these tragic events.'

Mrs Smythe scowls at me. 'Anything else?' I almost feel sorry for her. Her chairmanship won't be as cosy in future with me around.

'Yes, there is. Graham Giles has managed to locate the case notes pertaining to Mr Walter's suspension and concluded that Mr Walter is not at fault. He has also decided that the other allegation is unjustified. Consequently, he will be recommending that Mr Walter's suspension is lifted with immediate effect. You will cooperate with that, Mrs Owen.'

She looks as though she'd like to peck my eyes out but instead gives a cursory nod.

Mrs Smythe asks, 'And in our new spirit of cooperation, you will drop your accusation?' She can't bear to utter the words.

'Of manslaughter? Yes, I will.'

****

I burst into his office. 'Alan, he's gone. Lytle's resigned.'

He grins. 'Good riddance, I say.'

'I just had to tell someone.' I don't know which is greater, my delight or my relief. 'Sorry, I've just been with Mrs Smythe, forgot all about our usual meeting.'

'Have you persuaded her to resign as well, then?' A hint of devilment in his voice.

'No. Better to have a compliant chairman than a new one.'

He smiles and shakes his head. 'Machiavellian as well as persuasive,' he pronounces.

I slump onto a chair. Perhaps he believes he has offended me but it is just that I am lost in thought.

'Miles, I'm sorry. It's taken real bravery to confront them. I could never have done it.'

I lift my head and smile at him. I remember Klaus' observation about fine lines. Am I brave because I have succeeded? Would I have been foolish if I had failed?

'When I was appointed here about fourteen years ago, Graham Giles was the clinical director of medicine before he became medical director and he was ...' I struggle and fail to identify the appropriate word. 'He was fine. It bothers me how he changed and how he allowed himself to be manipulated by Lytle.'

'Corrupted by power?' Alan offers.

'I suppose. I want you to make me a promise. If you ever think I'm getting that way, you'll tell me. Please.'

'Of course, that's what friends are for.'

Yes, we are friends now, more than just colleagues. I haven't many true friends. My life is too hectic. But I couldn't wish for a better one than Alan.

'Thanks. Look, I've got to go and teach now. No time to discuss our research.'

'No problem. We're on track. Nothing that won't wait.'

****

I lie in bed, my own. I haven't seen Freya since last Sunday or told her on the telephone of any of this week's turbulent events. I didn't want to worry her and she might have tried to dissuade me from my plans.

I had to do it. That's the bottom line. The desire to protect patients from Keane and disgust with our management were important parts of that compulsion, but not least was my need to help Klaus.

I recall Adam's response to my ill-considered question in our kitchen: "Dad, he's my friend. I couldn't leave him". As a parent you help to mould your child's behaviour but sometimes fail to appreciate how much the child is influencing yours.

It may be an exaggeration to consider Klaus my friend, though I believe that will change, but he is a man I like and respect. I was not going to stand by while our depraved management destroyed his career.

A divergent thought flits into my consciousness. That pop song: Won't Get Fooled Again by The Who. Came out when I was still in nappies but nevertheless, it appeals to me. Particularly the part when the music builds to a climax and the lead singer roars: "Meet the new boss, same as the old boss". Not while I have anything to do with it. We've been unlucky with Lytle. I doubt that he's unique, but there must be many able and dedicated chief executives out there, committed to enabling good patient care. We just have to find one.

And what of Keane? The Trust will almost certainly oblige him to take early retirement. Is that justice? Shouldn't he pay a greater price for the suffering he's caused? Shouldn't the harm that he's inflicted be revealed? That would do great damage to the Trust's reputation, perhaps result in the revocation its newly acquired foundation status and inevitably create a host of prolonged and expensive patient litigation. No, it will remain a cover-up.

Should I do more? How much is enough?

It will be good to discuss this with Freya tomorrow. And we need to speak again about telling Lily I'm her father, at least genetically. Should we tell her now or wait? What will Adam and Luke think when they know?

- UNDER CONTROL -

Here's a thought: should I, with their agreement, test their DNA? I'm not sure I'm brave enough to do that.

Life is so untidy.

No more. I'm exhausted.

49

My car crunches to a halt on Freya's gravel driveway as I park next to her Mercedes and the blue Audi Q3 Teresa uses to do the shopping and take Lily to school. Tiny flakes of snow drift down, caught in the beam of the headlights. The security lights have been activated by my arrival and illuminate the house. I sit for a few seconds, admiring it's mock-Georgian magnificence before climbing out into the cold, crisp air.

It feels wonderful to be free of all medical responsibilities for a whole week. I'd booked this leave at the beginning of the year to ensure I wasn't on take for emergency care on Christmas Day. My sons deserve to have one parent to spend it with and I certainly need a break, feel frazzled this evening.

Freya has invited Adam, Luke and I to spend Christmas with her and Lily. Both Adam and Freya are eagerly anticipating meeting each other for the first time. It should go well. Adam has a knack of charming women and they have their interest in the law in common. He may even be planning to enlist Freya's assistance in gaining an internship in the legal department at Statesbank. I've learnt not to pry.

I'm encumbered not only with a small case of clothes, but also with presents for the four of them which I hope to smuggle unseen below the large Christmas tree that now adorns Freya's grand entrance hall. I let myself in the front door using the key she has recently provided me with. As I do, heated voices emerge from one of the adjoining rooms.

'I said no, young lady. I mean it. No.'

Lily in a short skirt and lacy top is backing out of one of the rooms and fires a parting shot. 'You know, you can be such a bitch,' then slams the door in her mother's face.

She turns, striding away, before becoming aware of my presence and glaring at me. 'Don't. Just don't. You're not my dad,' before stomping up the stairs. I've had enough of this. I drop my baggage and bound up the staircase after her, catching her on the landing.

'Hey, that's not the way to speak to your mother. She deserves your respect. I don't know what you two were arguing about but I'm sure she's trying to do her best for you.'

She looks pointedly at my hand gripping her upper arm. I release my hold on her.

'What gives you the right to interfere?' she asks disdainfully.

This has to be it. 'I'm your father.'

'What?'

'I'm your father,' I repeat, more sympathetically this time.

She searches my face but is bound to realise this is not a subject for trickery. With less anger in her tone, she says, 'I don't understand.'

'Nine months before you were born, your mother and I had an affair. Well, not really an affair, a one-night stand. Do you know what I mean?'

She nods. Tears are beginning to roll down her flushed

cheeks and streak the make-up she is wearing.

'Of course, that doesn't automatically make me your father but when you gave a blood sample to test for the bili bacterium, I also checked your DNA and it's a match with mine.'

'Mum let you do that?' Her anger beginning to resurface.

'No, she didn't. I'm sorry. I did it in secret. I hope when you've had time to think about this, that you'll understand I had to know, and maybe it's better you and your mother do too.'

Lily looks desolate, struggling to assimilate that the very core of her being has changed forever. She opens her mouth but no sound emerges. Then, in a faint whisper, 'Luke.'

'Luke and Adam are your half-brothers.'

'So, I can't …'

'Can't what Lily?'

'Doesn't matter,' she snaps. A hint of defiance against me or fate, perhaps both.

"Can't marry Luke," I realise is the question she curtailed. An adolescent fantasy, though who can know if it might have come true? Regardless, it clearly matters, mattered to her.

Her eyes are downcast as she continues to struggle to absorb my revelation, but then she demands incisively, 'How long had you known my mum before you did it with her?'

I gulp but this has to be a time for honesty. 'I'd just met her that day.'

Lily looks shocked. 'So, you didn't love her. You didn't love each other,' she accuses.

'I thought your mother was wonderful and we were very attracted to each other,' I offer rather inadequately.

'But you were both married. That's wrong.'

'Yes, Lily. It is.'

'But you still did it. What, for fun?' Her tone is scathing. I don't know what to reply. 'You didn't want me. You and

Mum didn't mean to make me. I'm just here because of a bit of fun.' She sobs, turns and runs to her bedroom. The crash of her slamming bedroom door causes the chandelier over the hallway to rock and tinkle.

I take a deep breath. That could have gone better, though it was never going to be easy or the time perfect. More difficult than confronting a manager; at least then I held the moral high ground. I shouldn't have done it, should have let Freya tell her. But when was that going to happen? And in the meantime, I would be obliged to remain silent. Have I destroyed any hope of gaining Lily's respect and friendship and, in time, even love? A lesser concern but this is going to cast a dark cloud over the Christmas celebrations. Time to confess what I've done to Freya. I begin to walk with heavy steps down the stairs.

****

Freya and I are sitting round her breakfast table making small talk, tense, part of our minds anticipating a further clash with Lily. The smell of the toast Freya burnt lingers in the air. Perhaps Lily will hide away in her room all day. Oh no, please don't let her call her mother a whore. This could be a disaster. We hear footsteps and turn to face the door.

Lily, in pale blue jeans and a pink sweatshirt, breezes in, 'Hi, Mum. Sorry about last night.'

'Okay, sweetie,' Freya says warily.

Lily looks directly at me. 'You're not my proper dad.'

'I understand, Lily. But I'd like us to be friends. Could we try?'

She nods and smiles. The first real smile she has ever favoured me with. My daughter, my unintended consequence.

Luke appears at the breakfast room door. He must have heard our brief conversation. There is no surprise written on his face. He already knew. Lily and he must have communicated somehow. Has he mediated for me? Did she let him in just now?

He is holding a letter. 'This came in the post this morning, Dad. I thought you'd want to see it straight away.'

Not bad news? The thought flits through my brain as Luke passes it to me. The envelope bears a Buckingham Palace postmark. I slit it open with my butter-stained knife. The other three are quiet and still as I try to grasp the contents of the letter. I shake my head in wonder and pass it to Freya.

Lily can contain herself no longer, demanding, 'What?'

Freya lifts her gaze from the letter towards her. 'Miles is going to be awarded a C.B.E.'

'What's that?'

'A Commander of the British Empire,' Freya explains.

I'm not sure there's much of an empire left to command any more. 'I hope they're doing the same for Alan. Otherwise, I'm not accepting it.'

'Don't be awkward,' Freya reprimands me. 'I'm sure they will. It's the least you deserve. I think you should have been awarded a knighthood.'

I laugh. 'That's because you're hopelessly biased.'

'Sir Miles', she suggests teasingly. 'I think it has a certain ring to it.'

It's time, perhaps overdue, and maybe it is better that Luke and Lily are witnesses.

'Lady Freya. That certainly would require a ring.' I rise from my chair and kneel before her.

Luke is grinning. Lily grabs his hand and begins to bounce up and down.

- UNDER CONTROL -

'Freya, I love you very much. Will you marry me?'
Her eyes are moist and she looks too choked to reply.
Lily exclaims, 'Say please! Say please!'

ACKNOWLEDGEMENTS

I thank the excellent team at Spiffing Publishers for helping me bring my novel to fruition, in particular, Stefan Proudfoot for his imaginative cover design and Jessie Chapman for her expert copy editing. I am also grateful to Anna South, Jodie Archer, Alex Hammond and Edward Cadman for their advice on my manuscript.

Jill, my wife for over forty years, gave me her unwavering support, and helped me keep my life happy and under control.

Learn more about the author:

www.johnthorntonauthor.com